THE SHIP THAT
DIED OF SHAME

And Other Stories

The son of a distinguished surgeon, Nicholas Monsarrat was born in Liverpool in 1910 and was educated at Winchester and Trinity College, Cambridge. His first book to attract attention was the largely autobiographical *This Is the Schoolroom*, published in 1939. On the outbreak of war he joined the RNVR, serving mainly with corvettes: his wartime experiences are vividly descrived in *The Three Corvettes* and *Depends What You Mean by Love*. In 1946 he became a director of the UK Information Service in Johannesburg and subsequently in Ottawa. His most famous book, *The Cruel Sea*, published in 1951, is one of the most successful stories of all time and was made into a film starring Jack Hawkins. Other famous novels include: *The Tribe that Lost its Head* and its sequel, *Richer than All his Tribe*, *The Story of Esther Costello*, *The White Rajah* and *The Pillow Fight*. Monsarrat lives with his wife, Anne, in Malta.

THE SHIP THAT DIED OF SHAME

And Other Stories

NICHOLAS MONSARRAT

PAN BOOKS LTD : LONDON

This collection of stories
first published under this title 1959 by
Cassell & Co. Ltd.
This edition published 1961 by Pan Books Ltd.,
33 Tothill Street, London, S.W.1.

ISBN 0 330 10499 3

2nd Printing 1962
3rd Printing 1963
4th Printing 1964
5th Printing 1966
6th Printing 1966
7th Printing 1967
8th Printing 1969
9th Printing 1972
10th Printing 1972

FOR MAX WITH LOVE

Printed in Great Britain by
Hunt Barnard Printing Ltd., Aylesbury,
Buckinghamshire.

CONTENTS

The Ship that Died of Shame

THERE ARE a lot of things about this story that I still don't understand. I've had a good deal to do with ships—too much, maybe—and if there's one thing I know about them, it is that they are *not* alive. They are made of wood and metal, and nothing else: they don't have souls, they don't have wills of their own, they don't talk back. In fact, they're not like women at all. Writers of nautical romances may pretend— but I'd better start at the beginning.

The beginning, like almost everything in my life, goes back to the war.

My name is Bill Randall, and, if you used to read the naval communiqués with any sort of attention during the recent contest, you might remember it. I spent nearly all the war in Coastal Forces, which meant, for me, mucking about in motor gunboats and having hell's own fun in the process. The Beat-up Boys, they used to call us—and the name tells you just about all you need to know. We had been hired, it seemed, for the specific purpose of nipping across to the French, Dutch, and (later) German coasts, shooting up everything in sight, and nipping back again, cheating the dawn each morning by a few short minutes.

Our targets might be anything. It depended on our own luck. Sometimes it was a coastal convoy making for the Scheldt, sometimes German E-boats, sometimes minelayers off Calais, sometimes fishing craft, German-chaperoned, trying their luck east of the Dogger Bank. (If you even *fished* for the Germans, as far as I was concerned, you were a legitimate target.) Once it was a lighthouse, once it was a camouflaged gasometer, once (glorious moment) it was a train coming out of a tunnel north of Boulogne. We were sent over the other side to make trouble, any trouble, and we did just that, using (in their Lordships' convenient phrase) 'the widest possible discretion' in the process.

In between times we escorted our own East Coast convoys, and picked up clumsy RAF types who had come down

7

into the sea, and touched off drifting mines, and acted as target-towing ships. Motor gunboats could do anything—and that was especially true of mine, MGB 1087. Which brings us to the ship in this story.

MGB 1087 was a special honey. All gunboats are hit-and-run weapons, of course, and mine could do both to perfection. She was a hundred feet long, with four Packard engines of 5000 brake-horsepower, able to shove her along at nearly thirty-five knots. She was armed with a few depth-charges in case we got on the track of a submarine (we never did), six Oerlikons and eight smaller machine-guns, and two six-pounders—a gun that makes a hole approximately a foot wide in any metal, and more in a man. We had plenty of examples of both in those wonderful years.

MGB 1087. . . . I raised that boat practically from a toy yacht, and there wasn't a better one in any flotilla operating from any base; we must have finished the war with as good a record as you could find anywhere. On the shield of the forward six-pounder—the obvious place for scoring up 'trophies'—we painted the following tally:

Mines	.	.	.	126
Gasometers	.	.		2
E-boats	.	.	.	7
Steam Locomotives	.	.		1
Aircraft	.	.	.	8
Trawlers	.	.	.	3

Those were definite kills, the fruit of hundreds of nights of watching and waiting, hundreds of hours of cutting spray and pinching cold. There seemed no harm in being proud of them.

We were also well decorated. Hoskins (my First Lieutenant—I'll tell you about him in a minute) once suggested that we enlarge the trophy list to read:

DSO	.	.	1, *and bar*
DSC	.	.	1
DSM	.	.	3

That didn't seem a very good idea either then or now. . . . But we *did* get those aircraft, and we did get those seven E-boats and all the rest, and I suppose the medals were, in a way, the same sort of trophies. It seemed to me, though, that

8

it needed a special kind of outlook, unusual in our job, to paint them up in black and white for all the world to see.

The ship carried a crew of twenty-two mostly gunnery-ratings, and two officers. I was the Captain of MGB 1087; the other officer for nearly three years was my First Lieutenant, George Hoskins.

It's extraordinary how close you can be to a man and how many times you can owe him your life (and vice versa), and still know nothing about him. I liked Hoskins for his good qualities, exhibited on many occasions—his guts, cunning, and ruthlessness, all essential 'beat-up' attributes—and I shut my mind to the rest. He ran the ship efficiently—the guns were always clean, the engines smooth as machine-oil, the ship's company well organized and well looked after. But there was always something else, something I didn't know about and didn't want to know.

Perhaps it was in his eyes. Hoskins was a small man, neat, an RNVR Lieutenant who had been some sort of salesman before the war. We were together during all those three years and he never let me down on any of the dozens of occasions when that might have happened. He won his DSC, the one he wanted to chalk up as an advertisement on the six-pounder gun-shield; and he deserved to win it. But somehow his eyes said that the thing was *all* advertisement: that the point of the war was not really sinking E-boats and downing aircraft and killing Germans, but selling MGB 1087, and Lieut.-Commander Randall, DSO, and Lieutenant Hoskins, DSC, to the Admiralty and, through them, to the public, as the ace outfit of Coastal Forces.

In a way he had plenty of facts to support him. She *was* a wonderful ship, with a wonderful record. We *did* make the headlines on a lot of occasions. The basic virtue of that, however, was not in the headlines but in what we did to earn them: the actual sunk ships, the actual dead Germans, the actual few steps nearer to winning. I don't think Hoskins ever saw it like that. . . .

Whenever we came back into harbour with the dawn breaking behind us, and the ship perhaps scarred by machine-gun fire, and an entry in the deck-log such as '0125: sunk one E-boat' to tell the story of a wild, nerve-testing night, something in his eyes seemed to say: 'This ought to get us into the newspapers again. We ought to get another

9

medal. I ought to get my half-stripe with more money. We might even make it *two* E-boats. . . .'

Hoskins had a recurrent joke (if you can call it a joke). Whenever I remarked on the way he boosted the ship's reputation he used to answer: 'In this war you've got to look after number one.' Number One, as you probably know, is the Navy slang for the First Lieutenant. He was the First Lieutenant.

Perhaps it wasn't a joke after all.

My doubt of his 'genuineness' was often there, but I had only one concrete example to go on.

It was a very small matter when you look back on it: the question as to whether or not we had shot down an aircraft, and whether we should claim it as a 'certainty'. We had been caught one morning at first light still on the wrong side of the Channel, and still searching for the crew of a Lancaster bomber which had come down into the sea off Dunkirk.

We never picked them up, but we were picked up ourselves—by a patrolling Ju88 which nipped in from seawards and tried to dive-bomb us. On his way down he was squarely hit by our Oerlikons—we were *very* ready on the trigger that morning; you could see the bits flying and scattering behind him, and then he levelled off overhead without letting his bombs go. With a thin plume of black smoke streaming out of his tail assembly he disappeared inshore and out of our lives.

I never thought for a moment that we could claim that Junkers as shot down since he was still going strong, and it was obvious that he would at least reach his own coastline. But Hoskins, writing up the deck-log as we set course for Dover, entered the incident, without batting an eyelid as *'One enemy aircraft destroyed'*.

I said: "Oi!" and then: "We can't put that, Number One. He was still flying for home, happy as a lark."

Hoskins eyed me, smiling. "A lark with a pretty sore tail. . . . He'll never make it I'm damn' sure." We both had to shout above the sea noises and the roar of the Packards going full out. "You saw the bits and pieces. He was on his way down."

I shook my head. "He was losing height very slowly. You can't call it a confirmed kill."

"As good as." Hoskins was still smiling, in a vaguely

encouraging way as if I only needed a bit of jollying-along to see it from his angle. "I wouldn't give much for his chances." But then he added: "What's the harm, anyway?"

I stared at him—the small man, bright as a button even at five o'clock in the morning, looking up at me with those encouraging eyes. I wanted no part of any of this.

"People rely on our reports," I said shortly. I didn't want to touch on anything more definite, like honesty or truth; though I was still keyed up after the action, and felt the thing very simply and clearly myself. "There's a man at the Air Ministry adding these things up, and we don't want to muck up his figures." I pointed down at the deck-log. "Call it 'damaged'."

He shrugged, looking away from me "We're missing a good chance."

I didn't like that, either. "A good chance of what?"

"I mean," he said elaborately, "we *did* hit it and it *was* going down, and we want to keep our *own* record straight, just as much as some chairborne clot at the Air Ministry."

Listening to the careful phrases, watching him, I could almost see the headlines in his eyes, the headlines he wanted so much: '*Randall and Hoskins Again : Ju88 Destroyed in Dawn Action.*' I could almost see his private dream of the Admiral shaking hands with him, and the 'Mentioned in Despatches' citation coming by the first post in the morning. ... Without a word I scored out his entry in the deck-log, wrote in my own, and said: "That straightens *our* record."

Then I walked to the front of the bridge, glad as never before to feel the ship bucking under my sea boots and the fresh air coming inboard over the dodger.

But no piece of near-crookery by Hoskins could spoil those years, nor diminish the weight of tough achievement that MGB 1087 piled up. Let me just tell you one thing we did in that ship at that time, to give you the measure of it.

It happened some months after the invasion, when our job was to look after the 'shuttle-service' of Allied shipping that went to-and-fro, to-and-fro between England and Normandy, twenty-four hours of every day of every week: keeping the men alive and the weapons served, away eastwards at the tip of the spear-head now approaching the Rhine, the place where it really mattered.

No convoys were ever so important as those cross-Channel

ones—I know the Battle of the Atlantic boys will argue the toss about that, but if the flow of materials to France and Germany had ever been checked, even for half a day, we might have been driven back into the sea, and so lost the war in a prolonged and bloody stalemate. You've got to remember that there were things called V-Ones and V-Twos, robot-weapons aimed at London and tearing the heart out of it every hour on the hour, until we got a grip on the Calais coastline. . . . That invasion just had to stick.

I should explain also that it took place shortly after my wife had been killed in an air raid, when I didn't mind what went on so long as I could hit back and draw blood. That feeling came in very useful.

We were on independent night patrol when it happened, near the opposite coast and drifting with our engines stopped about six miles north of Mulberry Beach. We lay a little to the side of the 'fairway'—the buoyed channel that marked the way into the landing-beaches. It was a calm night, dark, with an edge of moon still showing above the horizon.

On our hydrophones there had been, for hours on end, nothing save water noises, and the occasional boiling sound made by a nearby shoal of fish. No shipping moved within miles of us, though there was a south-bound convoy—including troopers—due to pass through our sector some time after five in the morning. Waiting and listening for hour after hour, we did our best to believe that, in spite of the tight coastal blockade, there might still be something for us that night.

Then, a little after one o'clock, with the moon nearly down, we suddenly picked up the sound of engines coming towards us from the south—the French coast. It was a whisper at first, then a steady purring, then the loud beat that meant fast-moving diesels.

The Leading Seaman on the hydrophones pressed the earphones closer to his head for a moment, frowning. Then he said: "Uneven beat, sir. Must be two of them. Approaching one-nine-o degrees."

We trained our glasses and watched the bearing. One-nine-o degrees was up-moon, which gave us an initial advantage: it meant that we lay hid in an outer ring of darkness, looking towards the footlights. . . . Presently something came into view—two somethings, two vague blurs in the darkness, with two slivers of light gradually widening beneath them, the creaming of their bow waves. They were two ships, chugging towards us down the fairway as if they were driving along the Brighton Road.

They were small. They looked like us—or like E-boats.

I began to think quickly. It was far too early for our own mine-sweepers; they couldn't be other British gunboats because it was *our* sector; and the Yanks, however far they strayed from Omaha Beach, could hardly stray as far as this. In fact, it couldn't be *anything* belonging to our side: there was nothing due and there had been no emergency signal to alter the schedule. They *couldn't* be ours—or, if they were (for this was how I felt, after Lucille died), it was going to be just too bad for all concerned.

Hoskins, crouching by my elbow at the front of the bridge, said suddenly: "I think they're laying mines."

That of course was the obvious, the only answer, the sort of thing Hoskins always worked out seconds ahead of me. I did not mind. Mine-laying E-boats in the approach channel, with a convoy on the way. . . . They must have come in fast down the Dutch and French coasts, lying hid for one night on the way (though how they had got past our destroyer patrols wanted a lot of explaining), then slowed down, turned north up the marked channel, and set to work.

I called softly: "Signalman . . ." and dictated a warning signal for the incoming convoy. They would have to send mine-sweepers on ahead, or perhaps divert it altogether. But that was someone else's worry. Ours was here, and nearly within our range.

The blurred shapes were clearer now, resolving themselves into two small ships of our own size, fifty yards apart. If they were E-boats they would be armed like ourselves: the odds were thus two to one against us. But we had the moon and the surprise, and, above all, we had MGB 1087.

I said: "We'll go in, Number One. The starboard ship first. Then circle inshore and come back for the other one."

Hoskins said: "If we went between them, going very fast and firing to port and starboard at the same time, and then ducked out, they might start hammering at each other."

That, again, was Hoskins at his best: cunning, resourceful, ready to take a chance. It *was* a chance, because if the E-boats

13

were wide-awake, we might be caught in their crossfire—but then again they might hold their hand for fear of hitting each other. If only we could confuse them a bit. . . .

The thing suddenly clicked into place, and I said: "As we go through, we'll drop a depth-charge between them. The spray will hang for a bit. We'll turn quickly, and fire at one of them through it. They'll both answer back—and with any luck there'll be a riot and they'll start beating each other up."

Hoskins said: "Genius."

I pressed the button.

The roar with which our engines burst into life always startled me: it startled me now. 1087 jumped, then began to rip forward, the bows lifting, the spray whipping upwards and outwards. We started to weave towards the gap between the two E-boats, going our full thirty-five knots, the engines rising to a thick, solid howl as the screws took hold, and the whole ship bumping and shuddering as we drove onwards. Hoskins shouted his fire orders through the inter-com.; presently I pressed the firing bell, and all our guns opened up, half on one side and half on the other as we'd arranged, the red tracer-bullets fanning outwards in the darkness like the last, most decorative moment of a firework display. Other tracers—theirs—now began to come towards us, but sluggishly and wide of the mark: clearly the E-boats had been caught with their trousers way below their ankles, and we were scoring hits on both targets.

Just before we were level with them, our depth-charge went down, and then up! up! in a colossal cloud of spume and dirty water hanging livid in the moonlight, obscuring the battlefield.

We came hard-a-port, turning behind them in a tight circle and a fifty-degree heel, and began to fire *over* one E-boat, *through* the spray cloud, *towards* the second ship. Presently the latter, confused and hurt, started to blaze away at her best friend.

We slowed and came to a stop, our guns silent. I began to laugh, standing there on the bridge watching one set of Krauts lacing into another. One could only hope that it would be a very level battle, with both sides selling their lives most dearly. . . . We could see that hits were being scored by both E-boats, but the battle was *not* running level:

soon the nearest E-boat, which was engaging us as well as its chum in a bemused sort of way, lost heart, and the other closed in, intent on the kill.

The kill could not be denied. There was a rumbling explosion, and the losing E-boat glowed red as though in sudden anger. Her foredeck flickered as the flames took hold and she began to settle in the water. The victor ceased her fire, and edged nearer, hungry for prisoners. She was probably trying to signal us all the time to get us to pick up prisoners with her.

There was something of an uproar as she found what sort of prisoners she was picking up. Shouts of wrath and pain, guttural cries of reproach reached us across the water, sweeter than any music. While they were still sorting it all out we started up our engines, closed in to fifty yards, and turned to starboard so that all guns were bearing. Then I pressed the firing bell again, and we opened up with everything we had.

Two six-pounders, six 20-mm Oerlikons, eight machine-guns—it's a hell of a lot of metal in one place at one time, and it was far too much for this target. It seemed to hit that E-boat in one solid thunderclap; there was a small pause, and then she disintegrated with a quick, short-lived growl like an animal falling into a pit. Her main magazine bore the remnants skywards. . . . There were splashes as bits of everything fell back into the sea, and then complete silence— the silence of victory.

The score was two E-boats, two complete crews, and our only casualty a seaman who, catching his finger in the depth-charge release gear, lost a nail for King and Country.

I'd never felt so good before—or since.

Six years later I sat in the bar of the Coastal Forces Club tankard in hand, and wondered why I was unemployable.

It was a familiar train of thought, and entirely suitable to my surroundings. . . . I had always found the Coastal Forces Club depressing, not only because it was shabby and run-down, but because it was full of chaps like me—good at war, not much good at anything else, and so returning again and again, in thought and conversation, to the successful past, the only thing that was real for them.

Of course it *was* depressing, physically, with its cheap-looking bar, its indifferent servants who were always being replaced, and its members—mostly ex-RNVR types like myself—gathering there every night and getting noisy or morose over their watery beer. But though I knew all this I never stayed away from it for more than a few days. 'Keeping up the old wartime comradeship,' we called it, slapping each other on the back and using carefully preserved slang. (The bar was the 'wardroom', the wretched rooms upstairs 'cabins', the inaccurate telephone messages 'signals'.) 'Whistling in the dark' might have been a more accurate description, for that was what we were doing: keeping close together, going through a dead ceremonial like a court in exile, because the past was our whole life, and it was now too tough outside.

But why *was* it too tough, I wondered, not for the first but for the hundredth time? What sort of men were we, that the war had been so good to us and the peace so rotten? Why was it, for example, that in 1944 I could be trusted with a ship worth ninety thousand pounds and the lives of twenty-two men, and yet, in 1950, no one would trust me with a suitcase full of samples? Why had I been able to do such skilful and accurate things six years ago, while now I could hardly put a fresh ribbon in a typewriter? Why had it all dried up so soon? Why was I, in peacetime, such a dead loss?

I was trying not to be sorry for myself, but I *was* puzzled.

I sipped my beer, not looking at the hearty types round the bar who were showing signs of wanting to sing. Life had been fine at first, when we were newly demobilized: we all had a bit of money saved up, we all had our war gratuities, we all had a future as bright as the past we had been able to conquer so royally. I 'looked around' for a bit, loafing unashamedly, and then took a job in a firm of travel agents; it was all right to begin with, except that everyone seemed to know a lot more about it than I did. And then suddenly I got sick of it, and it didn't seem worth doing any longer, and I walked out. That was the first of many such walk outs.

I couldn't settle down anywhere. The succession of shoddy jobs multiplied, grew, faded, and disappeared behind me: I was salesman, clerk, courier, tutor, salesman, yacht broker, club secretary, and salesman again. The level drifted a little lower each time: the deterioration, though never too marked, was always there, always progressive.

Pretty soon I stopped being choosy about jobs, and started to wheedle and to agree with everybody who might have work to offer, and to call them 'sir' again. But by then it seemed to be too late, or else I had lost the trick, or I just *looked* no good. Whatever it was, the shutters were coming down, and even the foot in the door was being squeezed out into the cold again.

Only in the Coastal Forces bar, 'keeping up the old spirit' with a lot of other dead-beats, was life anything like a living thing at all.

If Lucille had been by my side it would all have been different; she would have taken me in hand, and organized things, and seen that I climbed instead of slipped. But she wasn't by my side; she had been dead these seven years, and I *had* slipped, nearly all the way down.

Now, on this summer evening in London, I was shabby, and out of work, and broke; and I knew it all.

The man next to me, a beefy boozer who tried to sell you insurance unless you shut him up straightaway, said:

"Do you remember that show at Walcheren, when old Jack Phillips bought it?"

He droned on while I said 'Yes' at intervals. We both knew it all by heart, and it hadn't been nearly as well-handled or as successful as we now made out. Then there was a stir at the door, and someone said: 'Of *course* I'm a member,' and a man walked in. It was George Hoskins.

We saw each other immediately. I rose, and he came across the room towards me. I said: "Hallo, George," and he said: "I thought I'd find you here."

We looked at each other. I knew well what he saw—a tall, thin man in an old grey suit, scuffed rubber-soled suède shoes, and a frayed RNVR tie. What *I* saw was very different: different from myself, and different from what the picture had been in the past.

Hoskins had blossomed. He looked enterprising, slick, confident—all the things I was not. He was well dressed, in a neat dark suit and a grey tie; he carried himself with assurance, and glanced about him with a wonderfully good-humoured air, as though to demonstrate that there was no shame in being a small man if you were a successful one also.

I knew, from the past, that there must be something snide about him—that, whatever he was doing, it was not quite straightforward. But it seemed to pay all right.

I felt him taking me in swiftly, as we faced each other in the centre of the room. His eyes, I noticed, were still encouraging, but now they were slightly ironic as well, as if we must both realize that much of the ground between us had altered. We hadn't met for five years, not since I was the Captain and he the First Lieutenant of MGB 1087. Things, he seemed to be saying, had moved on, hadn't they?

He looked round the bar, taking *that* all in, too. Then he said: "Chaps still fighting the war?"

It was what I had often thought myself, but it nettled me to hear it from him. I said, shortly: "Something like that," and asked him what he would drink.

"A large pink gin, please."

I ordered it and beer for myself rather glumly, while the other people at the bar eyed us in morose speculation. No one drank gin in the Coastal Forces Club any more. Gin was six-and-sixpence.

Hoskins faced me easily, legs crossed, one elbow on the bar—a negligent man at ease with all the world.

"Nice to see you again, Bill." He had never called me Bill. "What are you doing these days?"

I said: "Nothing much."

He nodded, as if recognizing one of his own thoughts in my answer. But he said: "That must be nice. Wish I could afford it."

I looked at him without saying anything; the suit I was wearing, and the shoes, and the tie, had all proclaimed the answer to his remark before it was made, putting it in a special category of insult. But it might be worth sweating this sort of thing out. . . . We talked idly, reminiscing in the best tradition of the Coastal Forces Club.

Presently I said: "What are *you* doing?"

"Oh, this and that." He waved his hand vaguely. "You've got to scratch a living where you can these days. It's not so easy either with all these bloody restrictions."

"I suppose not." The comment meant nothing to me, but from long experience I could tell that something was coming; and I wasn't prepared to baulk him in any way, however much of a spiv he sounded.

Hoskins bent towards me. "If you're not fixed up permanently," he said, "I've got an idea for a sideline that might be interesting. It needs someone like you."

I grunted non-committally. It was nice to hear that one was needed anywhere. I imagine that Hoskins knew that.

"It would take a boat, a first-class boat, and someone to run it. Two people, in fact—you and me." Round us, conversation had broken out again, and his voice was now masked by others. "A fast motorboat to make trips across the Channel and back." He smiled engagingly. "We've made enough of those in our time, God knows."

"What sort of trips?" I asked, though I knew the answer already. "Passengers? Freight?"

He nodded. "You could call it that. Fast freight.'

"But what about the boat? Who'll put up the money?"

He gestured again, his eyes meeting mine with particular directness. "I've got some friends. There are a lot of *other* people around here who don't like restrictions. . . . Are you interested?"

"Yes."

"Good show." He smiled as if he too knew the answers before they were given. Then he looked round the bar. "The house should now go into secret session. Isn't there anywhere else we can talk?"

"There's a writing-room upstairs. It's usually empty."

"OK. Let's take our glasses up."

As I felt in my pocket to pay for the drinks, he put a pound note down on the bar and said: "That's all right, old boy—expenses."

On the way upstairs I said: "I suppose you mean smuggling," and he said: "Yes."

I didn't make much objection when it came down to it: I was broke, and past caring much what I did as long as I could pay the long list of debts I owed, and organize myself a bit of elbow-room. Hoskins, expanding his ideas in the down-at-heel writing-room, painted a very rosy picture of our joint future: what fun we would have, how much we could clear each trip, how enormous a demand for our services there would be from those vague people who 'didn't care for restrictions.'

So far life in the Welfare State had given me nothing; but all that was now to be changed. Shortages, rules, regulations, import control—these, apparently, could combine to give us a very generous living.

I thought fleetingly of England, struggling with her screwed-up economics for year after year, trying to butt her way through the post-war mess, relying on people to go fair shares and not swindle on the rations. Then I thought of myself, struggling with *my* economics, and the shabby, shoddy life which was all I had won for myself in the process.

There was no doubt which was the more compelling picture.

It would be wrong to say that I hesitated for very long; or even at all.

Sometime during the evening I said:

"I wonder if we could possibly get hold of the old ship. She'd be ideal."

Hoskins nodded as if once more recognizing his own thoughts. "Funny you should say that," he answered. "I happen to know where she's lying. And she's for sale. . . ."

It was wonderful to see MGB 1087 again; though there was no doubt that she looked like hell.

She was lying in the yacht basin on the Lymington River in Hampshire. When Hoskins and I crossed the plank that served as a gangway and stepped aboard her it was like stepping into the decayed past. She wore an air of old-womanish neglect: unwanted, uncared-for, unloved. The paint was blistered and flaking off, all the metalwork rusty or green with verdigris; at the water-level a filthy fringe of weed killed the clean sweep of her lines. She had nothing left to show for the proud years. If it had not been for the deep scored furrow made by a two-pounder shell in her fore-deck I would not have recognized her, would not have claimed her as my own.

"Plenty to do," said Hoskins, looking round him with a faint—a very faint—return of professionalism. "But the builders swear the hull's still sound."

"We won't need four engines," I said. "Too expensive to run."

Hoskins grinned. "And we can use the space, too."

Down in the tiny wardroom, long closed and musty, we sat at the table where we'd both sat on hundreds of occasions in the past—sometimes safe in harbour, sometimes within gun-shot of an enemy coast—and listened to the water lapping against her bows, and planned a future for her. It wasn't going to be as worthwhile as the past, but we owed it to her to make a success of it.

I worked for nearly three months down at Lymington—and that was wonderful too. Hoskins remained in London, organizing our affairs and, I suppose, drumming up custom for the future; it was my job to dish up MGB 1087 so that she could face her curious assignment. Sometimes I caught myself thinking: all this is the First Lieutenant's job, really. ... But it was clear that the wartime roles were now reversed, and that when Hoskins had said, looking at the ship, "There's plenty to do", he had meant that there was plenty for *me* to do, and I'd better get on with it because that was what I was going to be paid for—by him.

It would have been irksome, a few years back, but now it was not—the intervening time had been too unsuccessful, too defeating, for me to cling even to the shreds of hierarchy. And, anyway, I soon found that I didn't really mind what label I wore, because I was working again, and close to the sea, and back home in MGB 1087.

The first things to be fixed up were the engines, which, having been grease-packed and sprayed, were still in good shape. We took two of them out; the remaining two, I calculated, would still give us a speed of between twenty-five and thirty knots—enough for most emergencies. But a more important thing was to simplify the controls since there would only be two of us aboard to work the ship. In the end we led everything up to the bridge: the steering-wheel, the engine controls, the lighting system—they were all there under the hand of one man, leaving the other half of the crew free to sleep, or work round the ship, or (when we came into harbour) to see to the mooring-wires or the anchor.

A general clean-up followed this reorganization. The ship was hauled out of the water, and scraped and repainted; the woodwork was sand-papered smooth, and all the metal cleaned and polished. With a spring-cleaning down below, and some extra lockers fitted in place of the two engines, that completed a refit which turned MGB 1087 from a hulk into a ship again. She wasn't a ship of war, of course: she couldn't hit her thirty-five knots, or punch holes in E-boats and aircraft, or scare the hell out of the fish with her depth-charges; but she was shipshape once more, and clean inside and out, and workmanlike, and I knew she would not let us down.

As soon as she was ready I telephoned Hoskins in London, and when he came down at the weekend we took her for a trial run, down river and out into the Solent.

It was grand to be at sea again, and we were lucky in our weather, which was clear, sunny, and calm. We crossed to the Isle of Wight, and then turned westwards down-Channel; the ship handled easily in spite of the loss of power, and she remained as dry as a bone inside. We spent nearly the whole day at sea, alternately speeding and idling, testing her engines, her steering, her electrics, her general seaworthiness. At the end, in spite of the long lay-off, there was nowhere we could fault her.

"She's still good," I said at last when we had seen enough and were setting course for Lymington River once more. "She'll take us anywhere."

Hoskins, who had been checking the small radio we carried, joined me at the front of the bridge, where I was steering by the remote-control wheel. The spokes of this, I could not help remembering, were hollowed out—'for small jobs', as Hoskins had put it. There were a lot of such hiding-places all over the ship, covertly installed by our own carpenter ('one of the boys,' Hoskins explained), tucked inside the navigation lights, and disguised as spare petrol tanks, and hidden in a false beam down in the ward-room, and masquerading as a cold-storage space. Even the pint-sized lavatory forward had a cistern that was something quite different. MGB 1087 had now become a high-class conjuring apparatus as well as a working ship.

Hoskins looked at me and grinned suddenly. I think he had enjoyed the day, too, and our re-encounter with the past. He gestured round MGB 1087, and then at the wide horizon.

"Randall and Hoskins again, eh?" he said cheerfully.

I supposed we could call it that, in a way. In spite of the details.

From the start, Hoskins handled the business side. I was employed on a salary basis, plus a commission on 'results', which the future would determine. Hoskins did all the accounting, as well as fixing up the various jobs; and I never had any sort of complaint in that line since, from the very beginning, we made a lot of trips, and a lot of money very fast.

"What do people need most?" Hoskins had once asked when we were working out our plans. "That's what we want to find out—then we'll give it them."

Put like that, our operations were practically a moral crusade since our only aim in life was to see that people were happy. Why, we were almost on the side of the Government. . . . I must say that 'what people wanted most' covered some damned queer things, particularly later on when we started to extend a bit; but to start with, it was in a way true that we were, as smugglers, quite respectable characters.

Brandy was our principal cargo on the first few trips: that, and French wines, and nylon stockings, and tinned ham, and cigars; all the little things, you see, that make the difference between life and the 'gracious living' that one sees in the ads. I used to think what a great deal of pleasure, and how little pain, we were giving; and, at the same time, what a lot of money we were making in this innocent fashion. . . . Sometimes we made it in one quick trip—from near Dover, across the thirty-odd miles to France, and back again in one night; sometimes we took it more easily, cruising along the northern French coast or as far south as St Malo, in the guise of English yachtsmen who could hardly bear to tear themselves away from so hospitable a playground. But as soon as we were loaded, we tore.

Hoskins had plenty of contacts in England and plenty in France: that much I could tell, though I never asked him about the details, preferring to be just the dull sailor who ran the boat. That part did not prove difficult. We never had any trouble with MGB 1087 in those days: she handled perfectly, my coastal navigation was still adequate, and Hoskins, who could tinker effectively with most engines, kept ours running smoothly.

We had our share of excitement in other ways. Let me tell you one thing we did in that ship at that time, to give you the measure of it.

It was about four o'clock one morning, when we'd just got back from a Cherbourg trip, and were feeling our way up the Lymington River to our anchorage. There were no shore lights, and we showed none ourselves. MGB 1087 inched her way upstream against the gently falling tide, creeping past the stakes that marked the channel, and the mud-flats that smelt richly of the sea, and the other boats at their moorings, and the beginning of the sheds and houses grouped round the anchorage. It was our own front drive and we knew it well, even in the pitch darkness which shrouded the hour before the dawn.

It reminded me of other nights in this same ship, when we crept our way along the Dutch coast or up the little estuaries, probing the defences, not looking for trouble, hoping for a quiet run in—and out again. Then, the enemy had been the Germans. But now. . . .

We were just rounding the last bend and shaping up for the ferryboat slipway when a searchlight was switched on, dead ahead, and a voice shouted:

"Motor-boat ahoy! Stop your engines!"

Instinctively I swung the wheel and took the ship across to starboard. I knew we were near the right-hand river-bank, but I didn't want to risk a collision—nor another boat taking too close a look at us. But the searchlight followed our sheer to starboard. At my elbow Hoskins said softly: "Keep her going—this looks official." The hail was repeated, this time on a peremptory note; and knowing what was bound to happen I eased back the throttle and threw the engine out of gear.

We grounded gently on the mud and came to rest, the stern swinging, the bows caught fast in the sucking clay.

Hoskins, not at a loss for a moment, faced the blinding searchlight and shouted: "You stupid clots! Where the hell do you think you're going?"

A stolid voice, unimpressed, answered: "Take our line. We're coming aboard."

There were two men, one small, one big. They brought their fast open launch alongside, and clambered aboard with an air of competence and authority which I did not relish. But we still had a part to act.

"What's this all about?" I asked peevishly as soon as they were on deck. "I thought we'd collide—and now we're aground."

"You'll float off all right at the next tide," said the small man.

"That's not the point. . . . What was the searchlight for, anyway?"

"Customs," said the small man briefly.

Hoskins said, surprised: "In Lymington?"

"We're not from Lymington," said the big man. "Let's see your log."

A prickling silence fell while the two of them peered at the deck-log on the chart table. Luckily it was written up every hour—a habit from the respectable past which now paid a dividend; and there was nothing wrong with our clearance papers. But I wondered, as we waited, if Hoskins felt as tight about the throat as I did. This could be total disaster.

"Cherbourg," said the small man presently. "Why so late getting in?"

"We were held up," said Hoskins. "We could have anchored down river, but I didn't want to hang about."

"And why no navigation lights?"

"They're fused," answered Hoskins promptly. "I'm sorry —I know *that* was wrong." And then: "Look, let's get this sorted out in comfort. Come along down to the cabin, out of the cold."

I must say that, during the next hour, Hoskins was superb. We sat round the table and talked and smoked. Presently Hoskins produced a bottle of brandy, winking, and said: "This hasn't paid any duty—yet," and poured out some generous drinks. We found out where they had both been during the war, and reminisced about that, and about smuggling generally, and some of the wartime Navy scandals in connection with duty-free cigarettes. . . .

The two men were suspicious—you could see that a mile off—and they were also good at their jobs and, of course, incorruptible. But to listen to Hoskins, we might have been safe in a pub ashore, with a couple of chance acquaintances who had turned out to be good company.

In spite of the ease which began to prevail, however, I found myself starting to sweat. The Customs men were certain to 'take a look round', if only as a matter of form; and on this trip we couldn't stand even the most cursory look. Perhaps we had become careless, but this time the ship had been loaded on the supposition that we *wouldn't* run into trouble. As well as a lot of Dutch cigars and some lengths of cloth in the lockers aft, we had thirty-six dozen bottles of wine—claret and burgundy—hidden under the floor-boards and in the fake buoyancy chambers and under the seats at the back of the bridge. We were crammed with the stuff: to all intents and purposes, MGB 1087 had red wine running out of her ears.

I began to sweat some more.

The hour passed; the convivial party must soon draw to a close. Presently, I knew, the small man would point to the brandy bottle and the cigars, and ask: 'Have you got many more of these?' and the big man would rise, and stretch, and say: 'I'll just take a look round. . . .' And we would listen to him walking about, and lifting things, and then after a pause he would call out: 'Joe—just come here. . . .' The party was convivial, but not convivial enough: duty lurked round the corner, and the big man and the small man were not the sort of people to forget it. No British Customs men ever were.

Hoskins said: "Excuse me, chaps—nature calls"; and I heard him walk forward to the lavatory. There was silence round the cabin table while he was away—in spite of the brandy, my tongue was dry as bleached sand—and then he came back, and stood in the doorway, not looking at me, and said:

"It's up forward, if anyone else wants it."

The small man nodded, and said: "That's for me," and disappeared. When *he* came back, the big man rose, and stretched, and said:

"I'll just take a look round before we go."

Hoskins said: "Sure—help yourself," and then he suddenly looked down at his feet, and called out: "For Heaven's sake—we're half full of water!"

It was true, like a nightmare that suddenly takes an incomprehensible turn. Water was seeping across the cabin floor-boards and starting to gurgle round our feet. Even as I looked, the boat gave a lurch, and more water sprayed in, in a solid cascade from forward. MGB 1087 was awash, fore and aft.

The ensuing chaos, ably promoted by Hoskins, was our salvation.

"We must have holed ourselves when we went aground!" he shouted, and immediately, for no very clear reason, he darted up on deck as though he could find the answer there. Then, inexplicably, all the lights went out. I could hear Hoskins blundering round above our heads, and then jumping down again through the forward hatch. He shouted: "It's coming in fast—you'd better get on deck!" and the Customs men, groping in the dark, stumbled up the ladder to the bridge. The ship was settling down, though it was clear that she would not settle very far. Ahead of us, the moon gleamed on the uncovered part of the mud-bank that held our bows, and there could not have been more than three feet of water round our hull.

Hoskins shouted again: "The pumps—get the pumps going!" and helped by the Customs men I started the small auxiliary pump in the after-part of the ship. There was still a lot of noise, and movement, and fluent cursing from Hoskins as he searched for the leak. Then I heard his voice once more, above the putt-putt of the motor pump, calling out: "She doesn't seem to be holed—I wonder if it's that damned valve in the lavatory," and then, with a loud shout like a man lighting on a burglar in the basement: "That's it —it's been left open!"

There was another long pause, and then Hoskins joined us on deck, his sea boots clumping like thunder. "Just got to it in time!" he gasped, as though he had run five miles to tell us the news. And turning to the small Customs man, reproachfully: "You have to close the inlet valve after you've used the lavatory. Otherwise it floods in—it's below the water line."

"Oh," said the Customs man, crestfallen. And then: "I'm very sorry—I didn't know."

"I should have told you," said Hoskins magnanimously. He looked round at the rest of us. "There's not much harm done, anyway. She's flooded about eighteen inches all round, but I've shut the inlet valve and we can pump her out quite easily by the morning."

"I'm very sorry," said the Customs man again. "I should have thought of it."

"We'll send you a bill for a new carpet," said Hoskins jovially. He peered down the ladder into the wardroom, where the water gently lapped and swirled. "Looks like the party's over," he went on. "We'll have to doss down in the wheelhouse tonight."

"Are you sure you're OK?" asked the big Customs man solicitously. He had not spoken for some time, and I had been afraid that he must be brooding, not without suspicion, on the turn of events; but apparently his silence was due to embarrassment only. "We can give you a shakedown ashore, easy enough."

"We'd better stay aboard," said Hoskins. "Thanks all the same, but I'd like to watch that pump. We want to get her dried out before the tide comes up again."

We waited in reflective silence. Perhaps it was only my conscience which made me think: they *can't* have been put off from what they were going to do—they must still want to search the ship. But it was not so. Noise, movement, crisis, and their own sense of social guilt had altered the picture altogether. When the small Customs man shifted his feet and said: "Well, in that case . . ." I knew that we had won the round, after all.

The two of them climbed into their launch very shortly afterwards, still apologizing, still offering hospitality, still wishing us the best of luck, and cast off. Then their boat chugged away up-river, while MGB 1087 settled comfortably on the mud, and the tide slackened, and away to the east the dawn came up to cheer us as we stood safe on our own deck.

I ran my hand over my face—grey, bristly, at least ninety years old.

"That was a stroke of luck."

I could just make out Hoskins in the cold half-light, bending over the motor pump aft. He straightened up.

"You've got to keep your head, that's all."

I was still puzzled. "But surely that valve in the lavatory is automatic. You don't have to close it yourself."

"It *was* automatic." I could see him grinning as he walked towards me. "And it is now. . . . There was just a short time this evening when it kind of got stuck. Anyone who used the lavatory after me was bound to start it flooding." And he said again, as if to a child: "You've just got to keep your head."

Hoskins handled the business side. Judging from the size of the cheques that went into my bank account he was doing it very well: in one period of four months I banked nearly three thousand pounds, and the average throughout that year was over four hundred pounds a month. I could not help being aware that we were branching out, extending markedly the basis of the brandy-and-nylon run with which we had started operations. I could not help being aware, also, that we were handling some very questionable cargo in the process.

That much was obvious, simply from the look of the people who came down to see us whenever we berthed, whether it was in England or in France. Glorified barrow-boys, I would have called them if it had not been clear that they would never do anything as straightforward as push a barrow; smart, slick young men in black overcoats and curly-brimmed hats, who manhandled their cigars and paid us out in great greasy bunches of fivers. It was not pleasant to see them aboard MGB 1087. . . . I can't claim that I gave a great deal of attention to the details of these transactions, because, basically speaking, I just didn't want to know. But I *did* know that during that time we carried, among other items, some crates labelled 'Scrap Metal' which actually held Thompson sub-machine-guns: and an innocent-looking trunk crammed with faked ration-cards printed in Bordeaux; and case upon case of bottles which, though hailing from a second-rate wine merchant in Paris, yet bore the ornate practically genuine label: 'JOHN HAIG'S VERY OLD SCOTCH WHISKY'. . . .

When I protested, not very strongly because I was getting too deep in and too aware of that mounting bank balance, Hoskins simply said:

"We're in the cash-and-carry business—and there's plenty of both. You just leave it to me."

I left it to him. There had been a time when I seemed to have a choice in the matter; but that time, along with a lot of other things, was vanishing.

It was during this period that I became aware of something else: that MGB 1087 was not behaving as well as she ought to.

It showed itself in little things: things that ought to have gone right and actually went wrong. Once we suffered from oiled-up plugs, which kept the engines coughing and spluttering all the way back from Calais. Once we had a steering breakdown which very nearly put us ashore between St Malo and Dinard. On another occasion we spent six precious hours of darkness when we had hoped to clear harbour

29

unobtrusively, trying without success to start the engines; thus losing the tide, the cover of night, and (very nearly) our clean record. Once, water in the switchboard put every moving thing out of action, and cost us five hundred pounds for an unfulfilled contract.

There was absolutely no reason why MGB 1087 should start behaving like this. She was as good as the day we bought her. Both Hoskins and I lavished hours on her maintenance, and each breakdown won her a thorough overhaul. But it was certainly true that she was giving us a lot of trouble; and even when there was no ascertainable mechanical fault, she seemed to act in a curiously sluggish way, as if she were beginning to lose heart. . . . I knew it was silly to endow a ship with a heart, of course. Perhaps my nerves were getting a bit out of hand with the continual risks we were running. But that was how she seemed sometimes—human, unreliable, inexplicably disinclined to try.

One of the worst times was when the engines failed in bad weather when we were off the entrance to the Lymington River. Something in Hoskin's manner when we left the other side had told me that this was a special trip—which must mean either a very ticklish or a very expensive cargo. But as usual I had paid little attention to what we were carrying, and I only discovered what it was at the very end. Before I found out we had almost run aground. MGB 1087 could not have chosen a worse moment to pack up, and if it had not been for a change of tide, which carried us away from the point again and gave us some sea room to play with, we would have gone ashore, and probably broken up. As it was, we drifted for nearly three hours before we got going again.

As soon as we got in, Hoskins said: "I'm taking the steering-wheel ashore for repairs. It may have to go up to London."

I stared at him. "The steering-wheel? There's nothing wrong with that. It's those blasted engines that keep playing us up."

"The steering-wheel," he repeated, with a sort of false impatience, as if he couldn't be bothered to argue.

Then I remembered the hollowed-out spokes, the hiding-place that we had never used. Light broke in.

"Why didn't you tell me?" I asked. "What's inside?"

Hoskins said: "Very small mink coats."

30

I grinned. "Don't be a sap. What have we brought over this time?"

Hoskins said: "Dope."

I thought he was still fooling. I said: "It's you that's the dope . . ." and then the bell rang again. "Good God! Do you mean drugs?"

Hoskins nodded. I could see that he was already gauging my mood, knowing that I was bound to kick up a fuss, not knowing how seriously I would take it. Just before I started to speak, he said: "It's *very* remunerative. I can assure you of that."

We did have a blazing row; but I remember it chiefly because it was the last time I objected to anything we did. I was damned angry—because I now realized without any doubt that Hoskins did not care how far he carried this game. At one point, when I said I wanted to get out there and then, he came back very toughly indeed:

"You can't get out—you're in this, boots and all, and don't you forget it!"

"But drugs," I repeated, still appalled. "It's so—rotten."

He swore vividly, and then: "Don't be so ruddy moral," he said. "It gets you nowhere. . . . By God, I remember when I wanted to claim that Ju88 and you bawled me out like a blasted clergyman. I thought you'd got wise to things these last few months."

I said: "Perhaps I have."

"Well, you'd better stay that way." He came close to me, a small man no longer unsure of himself and violently determined to keep me in his grip. "You haven't done so badly this last year, have you? You'd have a hard time talking yourself out of this if it ever came to a showdown." His eyes were holding mine with extraordinary menace. "Don't get any funny ideas, will you? We're both in this, up to the eyebrows, and we both stay in. . . . Now get that steering-wheel unshipped."

It was, as I said, the last time I made any sort of protest.

After that things went from bad to worse. It was as if Hoskins, given virtually a free hand, was determined to go to the very limit in order to demonstrate that he was master of a dangerous trade—and of me. I can hardly tell you the sort of jobs we did during those horrible months.

Narcotics became nothing special in our cargo lists, and

31

adulterated liquor a pleasing variation on an evil theme. Once there was a tough-looking woman with two terrified girls who cried the whole way across and were taken ashore in a drugged stupor. When I asked Hoskins who they were, he said: "Meat. . . ." Once there was a coffin, a lead coffin, which we lashed to the back of the bridge—and dumped into deep water off St Catherine's Point. Once we gave passage to some wretched stateless Jews, without papers of any sort, who went ashore at Southampton and walked straight into the arms of the police at the end of the jetty. Hoskins, when he saw this, only remarked: "What a waste of money—their money." I wondered if he had organized *that* as well.

Such were the outlines of this infamous period, such the sort of exploit we had worked our way up to.

Perhaps it was just a coincidence that MGB 1087 seemed to be deteriorating at the same pace during all this time; but it was certainly true that she was not the ship we had known in the old days. I found that I couldn't trust her any longer; she was like a sulky, ill-bred child whom one remembered, only a few years back, as having been a positive angel, exhibited proudly even at grown-up events. . . . Now she broke down on dozens of occasions, sometimes when it did not matter, sometimes when it mattered a great deal. She was sluggish, she wallowed heavily in any sort of a sea, she broached-to and shipped water no matter how carefully she was handled. Life aboard her had become a chancy and uncomfortable affair; and occasionally, as on one of the last trips we made in her, it was highly dangerous as well.

I remember that trip very well; except for our final one, it marked the worst thing we did in MGB 1087.

The ship had been under repair for a fortnight down at Portsmouth when Hoskins telephoned me from London.

"How's our little friend?" he asked, as soon as I reached the hotel call box.

"She's OK now," I said.

"She'd better be. . . . We have a trip to make two days from now. It's got to go like clockwork."

"All right," I said.

"Now, listen. . . . About ten miles west of Hythe"—and he gave more particular directions—"there's a creek running right up into the marshes. It has plenty of water at high tide.

32

There's a side lane off the main Folkestone road that goes right down to the water's edge."

I said I could find it from the chart.

"I want our friend in there at eleven o'clock at night the day after tomorrow. Can you bring her round by yourself?"

"Yes."

"That's fine, then." And he repeated: "But it's got to go like clockwork."

"What is it this time?" I asked after a pause. I didn't really care.

"Something special." Hoskins sounded nervous and jubilant at the same time. "The biggest thing we've ever done." Then I heard him laugh, unpleasantly. "You could almost retire after this one. Does that tempt you?"

I said: "I'll be there," and rang off. There were no jokes between us now—and that hadn't been a joke, anyway.

Waiting with MGB 1087 among the briny, low-lying marshes, with the moon glistening on the wet fields and the seabirds crying like anguished ghosts all round me, I found myself hoping that this time something would go wrong, and that Hoskins would not show up—or that the police would do so in his place. But punctually at eleven o'clock I saw the dimmed headlights of a car turning off the main road towards me, and the purr of a heavy engine growing louder as it approached. I waited. Presently a dark shape came into view, bumping unevenly down the rough farm lane. It was a small truck; it stopped and turned, and backed towards the ship's side, as if the whole thing had been rehearsed.

A man jumped down from the tailboard, and another—Hoskins—ran round from the driving cabin. Without a word the two of them started to unload something from the back of the truck—small oblong boxes, eight of them. Still silent, breathing deeply with the effort, they manhandled the consignment aboard, and then down into the cabin. I did my share of the work, levering the heavy shapes over the edge of the combing, and down the steep ladder.

In the faint glow from the shaded cabin-light I saw that the boxes, wooden but securely bound with steel, were all identically marked with two intertwined letters—the Royal cypher that the Post Office used.

Not till the last one was aboard did anyone speak. Then the unidentified man said gruffly: "Eight of them. OK?"

33

and Hoskins answered: "Eight. Yes." That was all. The man walked back to the truck; the engine started; and it bumped away again towards the main road.

Hoskins, beside me on the bridge, said: "Let's get going. I want to be in mid-Channel by daylight."

That was a hell of a trip, the worst we had had so far. We were headed for a beach some miles to the south of Le Touquet, a safe 'outlet' which we had used many times before. We should have completed the crossing at easy speed in time to close the French coast at dusk and keep our rendezvous at midnight. As it was, we were a full twenty-four hours late on the assignment, and only with great good luck were we able to make delivery on the other side.

I learned afterwards that the French 'contacts' were convinced we had made a break for a Spanish port, and that a reception committee had been warned to stand by at San Sebastian. Such were our friends and such our reputation. But our failure to turn up the first night was certainly none of our own choosing.

Once again, MGB 1087 just would not play. Within ten minutes of starting out we were brought to a dead stop by weed wrapped round the screws. It took me two hours of alternate diving, hacking away for a few seconds with a knife, and then coming up for air before I could clear it.

It had to be me that did the work, because Hoskins said he could not stay underwater at all. But perhaps it was better to have something definite to do, even something as cold, wet, and miserable as this, rather than to wait inactive for the ship to get moving again. Hoskins was in a remarkable state of nerves during all this period. We were still land-bound near the mouth of the creek, and every time a car's lights travelled along the coast road he watched them as if they were a gun pointed at his stomach.

I wondered what on earth we could be carrying for him to have so obvious a dose of jitters. . . . But when I asked him, all he would say was: "Don't you worry about what it is. I can tell you this, though; if we're caught with it we'll each have about ten years to worry in—if not rather more."

I remembered those Post Office cyphers, and the weight of the steel-bound boxes. For the first time I really felt like a criminal on the run.

Presently we got the ship going again, and headed out into

34

the Channel on our course for Le Touquet. Though we had lost two hours, it shouldn't have been difficult to make them up. MGB 1087 had plenty of speed in hand for an occasion like this. But now, it was clear, she had other ideas. . . . Everything happened to us on that trip: an oil leak, a short circuit, dirty petrol, horrible weather, and a loose rudder-pin. The compass went completely haywire. The first shore light we saw was Dieppe—at least seventy miles off our course. We were stopped, at one point, for nearly nine hours while I tried to trace an electrical fault. Hoskins was seasick (that, I didn't mind). The Primus stove wouldn't work at all. The least pressure on the steering-wheel threatened to tear the rudder loose altogether.

MGB 1087, in fact, behaved all the time as though she could hardly bear to be touched.

Perhaps it sounds odd to say that I found out the reason for all this when we reached the other side. But that was how it seemed.

We made our delivery just as Hoskins must have planned, even though we were twenty-four hours late. I took MGB 1087 limping into the little bay south of Le Touquet, and ran her aground on a gently shelving beach from which we could retreat quickly if necessary. Four dark figures rose to meet us, four men who first flashed torches in our faces as though they could hardly believe we had turned up, and then set to work unloading the boxes in total silence. When this was completed, still without a word spoken, we backed off again, and then turned quickly southwards for St Valery.

We reached harbour at first light, nearly out of fuel and dead tired. Neither of us had shut our eyes for two and a half days.

I slept late in the little cabin under the shadow of the tall quay wall. I was roused by Hoskins clambering down the ladder with his arms loaded. He seemed in good spirits; he carried loaves, cheese, fruit, and a copy of the *Continental Daily Mail*.

There was something in the careful way he put the paper down on the cabin table that caught my attention immediately. It was as if he were saying: 'Now you're going to find out what this is all about. . . .' The paper lay between us like the dividing line of a frontier: I knew that if I picked it up and read it, I would be in Hoskins's country for ever.

"Hallo," I said blinking. "What's the news?"

He grinned amiably. He said: "You're famous. But they don't know your name yet."

At that I flipped the newspaper open without lifting it, and bent towards it.

There was little room for anything on the front page, save the story of the daring daylight hold-up of a Post Office van in London three days before. It made tough reading. The van had been forced into a side street by a car full of masked gunmen while on its way from the Bank of England, and the contents, a shipment of bar gold, transferred immediately to a second waiting car. The thieves had got clean away, though not without a brief and bloody struggle. Two men had been killed, shot down in cold blood—a bank messenger, and a Post Office driver who bravely tried to tackle his assailants.

The escaping car, in an eighty-mile-an-hour chase, had knocked down a child outside Edgware Road Station, a girl of five, who was critically injured and was not expected to live. The trail had been lost somewhere in South London. It was thought that the gold might already have reached the Continent.

> The thieves [concluded the newspaper] have thus brought off the biggest haul of its kind for many years. Bank officials now disclose that the consignment of gold was on its way to Heathrow Airport, en route for America. Its value is estimated at £400,000. It was contained in eight wooden boxes, marked as usual with the Royal cypher.

We lay low for a long time after that. With the spectacular hue-and-cry which the gold robbery set in train, it was a bad moment to attract any sort of attention; and we could certainly afford to take a rest. . . . We were paid, I learned from Hoskins, four thousand pounds for that trip to France —only one per cent. of the total haul, but a lot of money anyway. With all the rest of what we had banked it was enough for me to suggest to Hoskins once more that we get out and stay out.

"It can't last for ever," I said. "We've had hell's own luck all the time, and we've done very well out of it. I want to call it a day."

"You can't," he said, not for the first time. We were sitting in the Berkeley Buttery in Piccadilly, spending, elegantly, some of our winnings. "And, anyway, what's the point? We're on to a wonderful racket. Why not make a career out of it?"

"Because we're bound to be caught in the end."

"Why? If we do just one good job a month in future—and, with the contacts I've got now, that shouldn't be hard—we can still make all the money we need. One job a month, carefully planned, isn't likely to land us in trouble."

"They'll get wise to us in the end," I insisted. "In fact, I don't know why they haven't done so already. It *must* attract attention, the amount of travelling we do in the ship."

"Don't you believe it." Hoskins tossed back his drink and beckoned a waiter for another. "They're not as smart as that, not by a hundred miles. As long as we keep on looking like amateur yachtsmen who can't resist the call of the sea, we're quids in."

The call of the sea. . . . The way Hoskins said it excited my special loathing. The sea did have a call for me; it had always done so; and to hear the phrase drip thus smugly from his tongue seemed to cheapen intolerably one whole side of my life.

"Well, I'm not staying in for ever," I said shortly. "You can do what you like. I'm getting out pretty soon."

"That," said Hoskins after a pause, "would be very unwise."

We were staring at each other across the bar table, in such naked mutual dislike that it seemed absurd that we could be committed to any joint enterprise. I found myself wondering if other criminals found that they were tied to each other in the same disgusting way. . . . I knew, in the back of my mind, that what he said was true: that he held the whip hand, and that, having made me his accomplice, he would never let me go. If I did walk out, now or at any time in the future, he would find some way of seeing that the police got on to my track. How he would do it without involving himself at the same time I didn't know. But I knew he *would* do it. I was in that sort of position, and he was that sort of man.

I said, feebly: "We'll see."

I knew then that relief must come from somewhere else:

37

not from my own efforts, and not from Hoskins's good offices. There was no such thing as the latter. In some way, I must be rescued—by fate or by accident. Or by something.

The revolting series of crimes which came to be known as the 'Raines Murders' filled the front pages of all the English newspapers, and of many others, for several weeks. From the newspaper point of view the story had everything: blood, sex, mystery, a quaking public, and a resounding official scandal—in that Raines had been committed to an asylum some years before, and had then been pronounced sane and set at liberty by a panel of Home Office doctors.

But sane or not—and it was always fun to confound the experts—the facts were that Raines had recently, within the space of ten days, criminally assaulted and then strangled four children, none of them over eight years of age, and had then disappeared completely.

He was, of course, reported from scores of places, being identified from the 'Wanted for Murder' photograph in the newspapers, which showed a pudgy, bald, egg-shaped man looking for all the world like a stage bishop. He was 'an obvious gentleman', the papers always said, with carefully manicured hands; a man, as one bereaved mother described him, who talked like kindness itself.

Kind he may have been—he was certainly free enough with bags of sweets and offers of a nice ride in his car. But 'gentleman' was a trifle off the beam. Four children was Raines's current score: four children all killed in the same unprintable way, followed by a month of nation-wide man-hunting, a torrent of clues, evidence, near-arrest, and public outcry, and then—silence.

Though it was dusk, I recognized Raines as soon as he came aboard.

Hoskins brought him down, of course, ushering him on board as if he were the rich owner's favourite son. Standing on the bridge, watching the back of Raines's head as he minced down the ladder, I found myself thinking: no, this is too much—and then I followed them below in order to be introduced. . . . I remember that handshake across the table of the half-lit cabin, as something specially degrading. His hand—plump, smooth, slightly moist—closed round mine with an embracing warmth, as though he were sure that this small contact would make us friends. I thought of what had lain within that hand only a few weeks before, and my throat and tongue were dry as I withdrew my own hand from his grasp. The police doctor's phrase, I remembered, had been 'manual strangulation'. Now it wasn't a phrase any more.

Raines did not speak—indeed, I never found out what sort of a voice he had. After half-rising for our greeting, he sat hunched in one corner of the wardroom, with the look of a doomed man about him—a man living in an ultimate kind of hell which, after showing him briefly the bright lights of conquest, had left him alone in a pit of fear. You're on the run, I thought, with *that* on your conscience and the police of many countries searching for you; and we are helping you because our help has been bought, and we may be the last and best friends you make on this earth.

I took one more look at the smooth bald head and the drooping, egg-shaped face below it, and then I broke for the open air.

When Hoskins joined me on the bridge:

"How could you?" I asked him in a frenzy of disgust. "You must be crazy!"

"It's a job." His voice was off hand, but I knew that he did not really feel like that about it; he realized that this was very near the last margin of evil, even for him, and the only way to endure it was to turn aside from its implications. "He's a piece of cargo, just like anything else."

"He's not like anything else! He's wanted for rape and murder, and he did them both—four times, with kids of seven and eight—only a few weeks back." I swallowed. "This is the most horrible thing we've ever done."

"Look," said Hoskins. He came closer to me, dropping his voice. "We both know he hasn't a hope in hell of getting away. The police in France will pick him up the same day as he lands. And in the meantime——" He made a curious fluttering movement of his right hand as though he were handling bank-notes. "In the meantime, we cash in."

"No matter what he pays——" I began.

"Raines was a rich man," said Hoskins, interrupting. We were both whispering now, mindful of the obscene figure sitting within a few feet of us at the bottom of the ladder. "Look here, that man had twenty-five thousand pounds

39

tucked away. Twenty-five thousand pounds. Now it's going to be ours—all but five thousand."

He was watching me closely, his eyes gleaming in the darkness. Probably he was trying to persuade himself as well. . . . I knew suddenly that nothing he was saying was making any difference to me, *because it didn't have to*. I was still sick with disgust, but in the back of my mind I knew that we would make the trip as planned. It wasn't the money, it was the whole horrible machine that I was caught up in. We were in the cargo business, and Raines was cargo, and we would carry him as we had carried liquor and drugs and dead bodies and stolen gold and illegal immigrants in the past. I knew, once more in deep disgust, that I was simply going through the motions of dissent; and that I would stay in this business, with Hoskins by my side, until the sea or the law caught us and dealt with us.

When I had said: "This is the most horrible thing we've ever done," I had already known that we would do it.

Something made me walk a few steps forward and peer down the ladder into the cabin again. Raines was still sitting where we had left him, his body hunched, his hands hanging slack between his thighs. He noticed my movement and his eyes rose to meet mine. There was no expression in them. I might have been exchanging glances with a slug. Yes, I am Raines, he seemed to be saying: you may not like me— nobody does—but you are taking twenty thousand pounds of my money to get me out of this. When do we start?

I drew back again and moved across to the controls. Poor old MGB 1087. . . . Just before I started the engines, I said: "I don't think she'll stand for this."

It began to blow as soon as we left the shelter of Lymington River, a tough, blustering south-easterly wind that was clearly going to give us a lot of trouble.

We had a long way to go—across the Solent, westward of the Isle of Wight, over to the French coast near the Cherbourg peninsula, and then south towards St Malo. That was where Raines said he wanted to be put ashore, Hoskins told me—in a country district that would give him a better chance of slipping past the police than anywhere north of Paris. So, St Malo it was to be. But before that we had to cross about a hundred miles of the most open part of the Channel in the teeth of a rising wind and a short, steep sea that was already seamed and flecked with white foam.

There was nowhere round the whole coast of Britain where the weather could so swiftly deteriorate.

We sailed at about ten o'clock that night, and by dawn we had crossed the Solent and were rounding the Needles, the westerly tip of the Isle of Wight. But now we started to meet the full force of the wind and the main anger of the sea. MGB 1087 began to labour as the waves tossed her about blindly, throwing her many degrees off her course. Sometimes she buried her bows deep in the trough of the sea, sometimes she rose high on the crest of a wave, and her screws, shuddering and racing wildly in the free air, shook the whole ship. Ahead of us, a lowering sky and a torn sea was now our only horizon.

We wrestled with these enemies for over three hours before I began to have doubts about the outcome. Raines remained below, 'sick as a dog' as Hoskins told me spitefully. Hoskins himself was beside me on the bridge, tending the engine-controls and occasionally taking a spell at the wheel.

We were both very tired already, and drenched to the skin; though even now we had hardly left the English coast, and there were hours of this battle and of worsening weather ahead.

"I don't think we can do it!" I had to shout to make myself heard, bending towards Hoskins under the lee of the bridge-rail. "We're not making more than two or three knots headway, and the sea's getting worse. If anything goes wrong with the engines, we're sunk."

Hoskins looked round him at the flurry of foam and dark water that contained and threatened us. "Sunk is a good word!" he shouted back, and grinned. I almost liked him at that moment. He sounded something more like the old Hoskins, at his best when we were in a rough corner with things going wrong.

But we *were* in a rough corner. MGB 1087 was now taking huge punishment with every wave, and labouring exhaustedly under it. Everything above decks ran with water, and we had shipped a lot of it below in the cabin and the engine-space.

The wind had begun to howl at us; under the livid sky the waves seemed to race and roar against the ship, throwing themselves against her with the full shock of malice. Even if we turned round now, we would have a wild time getting back to shelter; and if we didn't turn, there would come a moment when we would bury our bows beneath tons of water for the thousandth time, and not come up again.

Tough as she was, she was not built for this sort of thing, and we knew it, and so did she.

MGB 1087 settled the question for us. Towards midday the engines began imperceptibly to fail.

It was sea-water, I suppose; or the harm done whenever the screws raced free; or the oil-level, which was erratic; or the terrific weight of the sea surging perpetually against us. Or perhaps she was just ashamed of us all. . . . Whatever it was, she started to miss successive beats, and the revolutions dropped steadily.

Hoskins and I looked at each other. In that horrible sea, the inexorable falling of the engine-speed drained the heart of its courage.

"We'll have to turn back!" I shouted. The wind was plucking the words from my mouth as I spoke them, and again I bent towards him behind the shelter of the bridge. "Maybe she'll pick up again if she's running with the wind."

Hoskins stared at me, his face taut. I could tell that he was starting to be afraid, as I was. We were then twenty miles south of the Needles, twenty miles from any sort of shelter; and to reach it we would have to bring MGB 1087 round, beam on to this villainous sea, with the engines failing, and then struggle for home, with all the fury of the storm on our trail. Even if she came round without mishap we would be taking a frightful chance, running before such a gale with the cockpit being swamped by every second wave.

But the turn had to be made. If we didn't make it and make it soon, it would be too late, and we would simply keep on until we headed for the bottom.

Whether or not MGB 1087 could in the future complete the journey, she had now been beaten back in surrender, and we had to face the fact that we were in her hands.

I had a wicked time working to bring her round. It took nearly an hour of successive attempts, with never enough power to complete the full turn. Time and again she came halfway round, until she was lying in the trough of the waves; time and again she stuck there, with the screws thrashing ineffectually, and the sea dealing her blow after blow as she lay broadside on. She would reach that certain point, with the rudder hard over and the engines feebly pulsing, but she always lacked the power to complete the half-circle and turn her stern to the wind. Time and again we would abandon the effort and bring her bows up to the wind again, preparatory to another try, another wild stab at it.

All the while the ship suffered fearfully: pounding, shuddering, shipping solid black cataracts of water, unloosing below decks a frightful clatter as spare gear and crockery and oil drums broke adrift and thrashed about.

Finally she made it. There must have been a lull, or else the engines summoned a few extra revs. She did come round after a terrible moment of indecision, and turned her back to the storming sea. Then the worst part of the voyage began.

I had a feeling that she would never live. There was something in the touch of her, in the way the wheel spun loosely in my hands, in the sound of the dying engines, that told me that MGB 1087 was not going to make harbour. Our progress grew slower and slower. Far away ahead of us I could see the vague outlines of the land, but it was like a promise that would never be fulfilled—it came no nearer, grew no clearer to the eye.

More and more often the solid seas crashed down upon our stern, driving it deep under water, and then roaring along the upper deck with the sound of unloosed thunder. Hoskins and I clung helplessly to the bridge-rail. I found that my hands, clawing at the wheel, were without feeling, and my whole body cold to the bone. The engine-beat dropped further as the whole ship was invaded and swamped. Already she seemed to have grown smaller under the triumphant attack of the sea, and shrunken in defeat.

She was lying down under it all; as if now, at last, she had had enough of us and the things we had done to her. She was not trying any more.

There was a sudden confused noise from below, above the groaning and the clatter, and the door at the head of the cabin-ladder burst open. Raines appeared. He was a fearful sight—grey-green with seasickness, glistening with terror. He had upon his face an extraordinary luminous pallor as if he were already dead. He reminded me of the children he had killed. . . . He tottered towards us, looking round about him fearfully, and gestured at the roaring sea as though he could not believe what he saw.

The engines spluttered and died.

Now we lay there helpless, taking every blow that fell, settling lower beneath the scudding spray. MGB 1087 had become a waterlogged wreck, drifting down wind uselessly as the gale screamed round her rigging and the sea slugged and slugged at her hull. Hoskins touched Raines on the shoulder, and pointed to the land, still a long way away, vaguely glimpsed through clouds of flying spray.

It was doubtful whether he meant anything special by this pointing, but Raines took it as a definite directive. He nodded, and seemed to be gathering himself together. Then, as yet another sea swept unchecked along the deck and drenched us all, he jumped.

It was perhaps the best thing to do, though not for him. He had not the build for swimming, nor the strength, and we could only watch him drown. I had never before seen a bald head sinking lower and lower in the water, surrounded by thrashing arms. There was a moment when he seemed to be bubbling fantastically at surface-level, like a suspect, simmering egg. . . . I found that I still hated him, even as he disappeared.

I hated Hoskins, too—the man who had brought us all here, who had done this to me and to the ship. MGB 1087 was heading for the sea bed now—full of water, all her buoyancy lost, the great weight of the keel and the engines starting to drag her down. Thus we were all dead or dying: Raines, Hoskins, the ship, and I; dying in hatred and shame and anger, amid the raging sea.

Hoskins clutched my shoulder. When I turned, his face was close to mine, and enormous—the face I had grown to loathe, constricted now with cold and fear. Honour had caught up with him—with both of us. The ship trembled under our feet, and slid lower.

Hoskins cried out: "I can't swim."

I wanted to laugh, but much more I wanted to save my breath. I said:

"That's all right with me," and as the ship foundered I struck out for the shore. I never saw him again.

Well, that's the story, and probably you see what I meant

when I said, at the beginning: there are things about it that I don't understand. I've got plenty of time to work it out—ten years, as Hoskins once forecast. (They traced the payment for the gold robbery to my bank account. Perhaps I was lucky—three of the principal characters were hanged.)

What made MGB 1087 lie down and die? For that was what did happen, after all—not suddenly but progressively. In spite of all the care we spent on her she did grow less and less dependable, and in the end she just gave up without fighting. It was as if the last trip, the worst thing we ever asked her to do, decided the matter for her.

But that's surely a fanciful idea. There was no *real* reason for her giving up, even on that final voyage. The weather was terrible, but we'd had terrible weather on lots of occasions, particularly during the war, and she had always survived it—and even seemed to thrive on it.

Of course, during the war we had to fight the weather for different reasons. There was usually a stake that the MGB 1087 could be proud of then—in fact, many such stakes, for years on end.

Perhaps it was I, and not the ship, that was at fault. Perhaps I handled her badly, or forgot things, or just lost the knack; perhaps I was ashamed of the frightful things we did, and the shame became translated into action—or lack of action.

It may have been my fault we were wrecked. I don't think so. I was always trying my very best, I'm afraid.

Oh to be in England!

As the huge and stately *Queen Anne*, pride of the trans-Atlantic fleet, edged away from New York's Pier 90 and set her course for the Statue of Liberty and the open sea, I scanned the passenger list in the main lobby. No matter how many times I begin a crossing—and this was probably my thirtieth—there is always an intriguing interest in seeing who one's fellow passengers are. They can make or break a voyage, even in so vast a ship as the *Queen Anne*.

My eye ran rapidly down the list. There was a film actress whose première had been a resounding success, another whose last film had fallen flat on its face in the middle of Broadway. It would be interesting to watch them being saccharine-sweet to each other. There was a returning ambassador, and a famous novelist who breakfasted on martinis and always insulted everyone within earshot (he was a well-known trap for the hospitable). There was a financier who should have been in gaol, and a deported British gangster who was on his way there.

There was, in fact, nothing much out of the ordinary in the *Queen Anne*'s passenger list. I knew about half a dozen of the people. It was likely to be an average voyage, quiet, pleasant, and luxurious.

A hand fell heavily on my shoulder, and a manly voice said: "If you're looking for me, I'm not on the list!"

I turned, startled, to find that it was Sebastian Sibling.

I don't need to tell you who Sebastian Sibling is; there are probably not less than six of his films, new and old, playing in different parts of the world at this very moment. I had known him before the war, when he was a bit-player in minor English films. But since then he had graduated to higher spheres.

Nowadays he was, inevitably, the top-billed star in those intensely patriotic dramas in which the hero does everything single-handed. It was Sebastian Sibling who had purged the U-boats from the Atlantic, rolled back the Germans in the Battle of the Bulge, conquered Burma, subdued North

Korea, solved everything in Kenya, and defeated the entire Russian spy-system in West Berlin. However black things might be you knew that, as soon as Sebastian Sibling came galloping to the rescue, our side was going to win.

We shook hands. He was looking swaggeringly handsome, dashing, sure of himself. A couple of passing women, who were certainly old enough to know better, stared at him in adoration. He threw them a glance, and then a courtly bow. I felt like a farmhand in the presence of royalty.

"Sebastian!" I exclaimed. "How nice to see you! But your name's not on the passenger list. Are you travelling incognito?"

I had meant it as a joke, but he took it quite seriously. "No, no—not this time," he answered. "I just made up my mind to come at the last moment, that's all. We're going to make a film in France."

"What about?"

"Dunkirk."

In spite of myself, I gave a sigh of relief. The evacuation, I knew, would be in safe hands. Indeed, it might not even be necessary.

Since the *Queen Anne* was dropping most of her passengers at Southampton on her way to Cherbourg, I asked him:

"Are you staying in England at all?"

He gave a ferocious frown and a gesture which, in a lesser man, might have been a shudder.

"Good heavens, no!" he answered. "I haven't set foot in England for over a year. It would cost me far too much."

"Compared with New York? Surely not!"

"British income tax, old boy!" he explained. "I tell you they're all ready to *murder* me! I reckon it would cost me £75,000 if I stepped ashore at Southampton!"

"But why so much?"

"Oh—back taxes," he said airily. "And it would establish my residence again; I still own a house in London, you know." He paused, long enough to give an award-winning smile at a trio of teenage girls who hurried off utterly overcome. "I'm an American resident, for tax purposes," he explained, "and I'm going to keep it that way. England's really quite impossible!"

I thought this an odd and rather unpleasant remark from a man who had made enormous sums of money out of portraying heroic, do-or-die, my-country-right-or-wrong Englishmen on the screen. Apparently, in spite of his swash-buckling air, there were some things that Sebastian Sibling was still scared of. . . . But I said nothing. Perhaps, when you reached the top (as he undeniably had), the perspective altered. We arranged to meet later in the bar, and I left him to his ecstatic public.

I saw a good deal of Sebastian Sibling during the next four days. The *Queen Anne* is about the size of a moderate block of flats, but people are apt to congregate in the same places—the Old English Bar, the ornate Look-Out Grill high up in the stern, the smoking room with its club chairs and oak-panelled walls. Sebastian Sibling held continuous court in all these places, and I watched and listened to him doing it. It was not a pleasant experience.

He seemed to be morbidly fascinated by his tax problems and their devious solution, and he gave us the benefit of his views for hours at a time. If he used the phrase 'It would cost me £75,000 to land in England' once, he used it twenty times. Though he was still 'technically' an Englishman, England was absolutely finished, he assured us. The tax structure was sheer robbery. A gentleman simply couldn't live there any more. They robbed the rich, and gave it to heaven-knows-whom. He was well out of it living in the States, and he advised us all to do the same.

There was a dogged English journalist on board who took exception to this odious monologue, and said so. He tried to needle Sebastian Sibling about his patriotic films and gestures on behalf of England compared with his unique bashfulness when it came to paying income tax for the privilege of citizenship. But he got nowhere. The man's self-assurance was unpuncturable.

"Do you remember that film you made about the Battle of Britain?" asked the journalist at one point. "*The Threatening Sky*, wasn't it?"

"You bet I remember it!" answered Sebastian Sibling smugly. "It grossed three million dollars, and I had a percentage deal!"

"It ended, as I recall, with you standing on the white cliffs of Dover reciting that thing from Shakespeare."

"*This sceptred isle!*" declaimed Sebastian Sibling suddenly, in a sonorous, carrying voice. *"This other Eden, demi-Paradise! This happy breed of men, this little world! This precious stone set in the silver sea! This blessed plot, this earth, this realm, this England!"*

Several people in the bar, deeply affected, turned aside to wipe away a furtive tear. Not so the journalist.

"Don't you believe that any more?" he asked bluntly.

"Of course, I believe it," said Sebastian Sibling. "Historically, that is."

"But not strongly enough to make you want to go ashore at Southampton, and pay your share?"

"Not if it costs me £75,000," smirked Sebastian Sibling. "There *is* a limit, you know. . . . Catch me making that mistake!"

We anchored in Southampton Road to transfer our passengers to the waiting tender (among them the journalist with a foreboding gleam in his eye), and then we upped anchor again and set off for Cherbourg. It was a blustery day, with poor visibility. The *Queen Anne* moved very slowly indeed, but the crunching shudder that went through her when she ran aground on Calshot Spit could be felt all over the ship.

There was no panic. Tugs arrived and pulled us off again without much difficulty; the anchor was dropped, and divers went down to assess the damage, while the passengers crowded the rails or went inside to keep up their courage with Scotch highballs, martinis, old brandy, gin-and-tonic, and loud talk about the perils of the deep. Sebastian Sibling was foremost in the latter area. The whole episode, he said, recalled his wonderful film about the Spanish Armada, in which he had played Sir Francis Drake (the winner), and saved England from frightful maritime disaster.

There was a stir in the Old English Bar as the *Queen Anne*'s third officer came in, mounted the platform and held up his hand for silence.

"Here's the latest news, ladies and gentlemen," he announced as soon as we were quiet. "The damage is very slight—just a few rivets, really—but we'll have to put back into Southampton. The company will of course arrange alternative transportation by air for all passengers going to Cherbourg."

I became aware that Sebastian Sibling was listening with unusual intentness and that, though the evening was cool, he seemed to be finding it unduly hot.

He stood up when the third officer finished speaking. "Won't the ship be going to Cherbourg, then?" he asked uncertainly.

"A little later," answered the third officer. "But we have to go into dry dock first. Just to fix things up."

"Dry dock?" stuttered Sebastian Sibling, shorn of his swagger at last.

"Yes," said the third officer, reassuringly. "The King George the Fifth dry dock, the second largest in the world. Luckily, it can just take us."

It was really quite a moment—for me, for a lot of my fellow-passengers, and possibly for the two watchful men in bowler hats who were waiting on the quayside—when, early next morning, the *Queen Anne*, all eighty thousand tons of her (and with her, Sebastian Sibling), moved twelve hundred feet inland, to plant herself bodily and firmly on English soil.

The Reconciliation

"I WILL never divorce you, James," declared Marjorie Howgill.

It was somehow symptomatic of their entire marriage, thought James Howgill morosely, that even this sentence of hers, which should have been full of flashing fire and determination, only sounded flat and dull. Marjorie, he believed, could have made a list of the Seven Deadly Sins sound like a gardening catalogue.

They sat opposite each other in the comfortable, rather prim, wholly domestic London house. The radio played innocuous dance music on a waltz-time theme, the cat purred by the hearth; outside, a slight drizzle fell on the tidy pavements of a tidy Chelsea square. It had been like this for a full ten years, he recalled: their 'ideal marriage' had turned into a Darby-and-Joan affair at least a quarter of a century before its time.

Now, as he had told her, he wanted to be free of it; not for any special reason (there was no other woman in any serious sense) but simply because his excess of boredom had made that freedom essential.

If he were not married to Marjorie, he thought—Marjorie, who had changed from demure bride to sober matron in the course of a few months, and had stayed like that ever since—if he were not married to Marjorie he might be able to take a second chance with someone else before it was too late. After all, he was only thirty-five. But if he didn't make the break soon. . . .

Her voice interrupted him. "Are you really telling me the truth, James?" she asked. "Is there another woman?"

He hitched his shoulders irritably. "No. I've told you."

"Why all this nonsense, then?"

Nonsense, he thought. What a word, for his seething discontent. . . . "I just want to be free, that's all. It's so desperately dull, like this. We don't mean anything to each other any more."

"Oh, I wouldn't say that," said his wife.

"Well, *I* say it!" he snapped, with increased irritation. He looked across at her. Even at a moment like this she was so damned *reposed*. . . . Pretty, of course, but dull, dull, dull. . . . They hadn't exchanged a word beyond the ordinary civilities for years; and as for *romance*. . . . "There's nothing left of our marriage, and you know it," he went on.

"What you really need is a good holiday," she said sensibly.

"I don't need a good holiday, or any other kind of holiday," he almost shouted. He was especially annoyed because Marjorie was not the only person who had said this to him lately: his doctor, called in to treat a recurrent asthma attack, had produced the same idea; so had one of the old fools at the office. Just like a lot of blasted parrots. . . . "I need to be *free*, that's all!" he said, with absurd emphasis. "And I'm going to be!"

"I will never divorce you," she repeated. "I don't believe in it."

"We'll see about that. . . . I'm leaving you, anyway."

"Leaving?" she echoed in dismay. "But where will you go?" With perverse pleasure, he noted that it was her first sign of excitement for as long as he could remember.

"A hotel—anywhere!" He was standing up now, the very picture of a man driven to desperate determination. "I just can't stand this sort of life any longer. Both of us are just mouldering away to nothing! I'm not going to have it like this for the rest of my life."

"But you can't simply take off into the blue."

"Just watch me!"

"James," she said solemnly. "I meant what I said. Whatever you do, I won't divorce you. As far as I'm concerned, we're married, and that's that."

"We'll see. . . . I'm going now."

But Marjorie Howgill had the last word—the most annoying last word any wife could have devised.

"Then I'll pack for you," she said.

James Howgill took his holiday; it seemed the simplest way of initiating the break. He went for three weeks to a small hotel on one of the Italian lakes where the food was wonderful, the sun a blessing, and his sense of freedom positively rapturous. He had never felt so young nor been so happy in ten long years. . . . He enjoyed a brief 'romance' with a French girl who approached the whole thing on such a matter-of-fact yet generous basis that only a boor or a fool could have remained aloof. There was nothing to it of course; they were simply ships passing, not too hurriedly, in the night. But it was an augury for the future which he cherished. Life, for James Howgill, was not yet over.

When he returned to London he settled down in a small service flat near Jermyn Street. There was no word from Marjorie, and he did not attempt to make contact, even indirectly: he was seeking to show her that his determination was as strong as ever, that he proposed to live alone for as long as he cared to, and that their marriage (divorce or no divorce) was over.

But presently, as the months went by, the situation began to irk him. Their friends had accepted the break with twentieth-century tolerance, and it seemed to have been established, without undue embarrassment, that the Howgills had decided to separate. But it was still less than satisfactory. This was not the sort of freedom he wanted. He was married, and yet he was not married. If any 'chances' came his way he was still not free to make the most of them. The wonderful sense of liberation which he had experienced in Italy had degenerated into a drab, somewhat dubious, marital twilight.

By and by, grown impatient, he went to call on the firm of solicitors who had handled his affairs for fifteen years. They were not exactly go-ahead, but they might have some ideas.

Mr Johnstone, senior partner of Seymour, Johnstone, Cripps & Knatchbull, received him with the deference due to a medium-rich stockbroker, and the reserve natural in a man-of-law whose speciality was property management. Though he knew James Howgill's situation from hearsay, he had been hoping that it would not be necessary for his firm to take a hand in it. Seymour, Johnstone, Cripps & Knatchbull did not greatly care for divorce; indeed, in the time of Seymour the word itself had scarcely been permissible.

When James Howgill had told him what he had in mind:

"My dear Howgill," said Mr Johnstone, "you astonish me!" He did not look astonished, merely attentive in a portly sort of way; but it was enough. "You say there is no possibility of a reconciliation?"

"None whatever," replied James Howgill firmly.

"Perhaps you have—ah—other personal plans?" inquired Mr Johnstone delicately.

"Not at the moment," said James Howgill. "But of course I might have later on. Just now I simply want to be free. That's all."

"Ah, freedom," intoned Mr Johnstone, looking as though he would like to make a rather long speech about it. But he collected himself in time. "And Mrs Howgill—you say she will not take any action herself? In any circumstances?"

"So she said. And I believe her."

Fingertips together, lips pursed, Mr Johnstone considered the matter. "Then, if you are so determined, you must initiate divorce proceedings yourself," he said finally. "Let us review the possible grounds of such an action. Mental or physical cruelty?"

James Howgill shook his head. "No. She's not like that."

"Desertion?"

"I don't see how we could make it stick."

Mr Johnstone frowned at the slang phrase. "Make it stick?—ah—quite so. Let us agree that the desertion, if any, is on your side. There remains——" and here he gathered himself together, impelled to face crude reality "——the possibility of another man."

James Howgill shook his head again. "No. She's not like that, either."

"You are certain?"

"As certain as anyone could be."

"Women unaccustomed to living alone sometimes——" began Mr Johnstone, and then coughed. "We must take steps to find out," he concluded finally.

"How do you mean?"

Mr Johnstone leant forward. If it were possible for so benign a man to look conspiratorial, he did so now. "We must have her watched," he declared finally.

"Detectives?" asked James Howgill, slightly appalled.

Mr Johnstone raised an admonitory hand. "Private inquiry agents. Of the most discreet kind. It happens that I know the very firm. I will see that they get in touch with you."

The 'private inquiry agents, of the most discreet kind', resolved themselves, three days later, into a man with the especially discreet name of Bates. Bates did not look like a detective; indeed, he did not look like anything. He was small, grey, invincibly ordinary; he did not even wear a bowler hat. One could not have picked him out in a crowd, thought James Howgill, looking at him with curiosity; in fact one could scarcely have picked him out in an empty room.

For some reason, Howgill found this anonymity comforting: he had been feeling slightly guilty at the idea of employing detectives to watch his wife, but this man somehow excused the whole idea. Hoping for limited liability, he had got it in Bates, most limited liability of all.

The two of them settled, with reasonable briskness, the necessary details which Bates must have in order to begin his vigil: Marjorie's address, her appearance (James Howgill produced a year-old snapshot), her known habits (very few), her principal friends. Then Bates folded away the slip of paper on which he had taken his notes and stood up.

"Leave it to us, Mr Howgill," he said. "If she's playing you up, we'll find it out."

James Howgill did not care for the phrase at all. "It's very unlikely——" he began stiffly.

"Human nature," said Bates, not hearing him. "You think you've seen it all, and then you suddenly get a thumb right in the eye. . . . What coverage do you want?"

"I beg your pardon?" said James Howgill, taken aback.

"One man can't work all the way round the clock," said Bates. Somehow, discussing terms and (presumably) money, he had taken on a certain measure of authority. "That's human nature of another sort. . . . Over the years, we've worked out the best way. It takes three men, in three watches: 8 am to 4 pm, 4 pm to midnight, midnight to 8 am."

"Like the Navy," said James Howgill.

"No doubt. . . . Do you want them all?"

"I hardly think that will be necessary."

"Two out of the three, then?"

"Well—yes."

"Which do you want to leave out?"

James Howgill felt uncomfortable. "The night-time one," he said at length. "I don't think——"

Bates appeared surprised. "Very promising watch, the midnight to 8 am," he said. "If there's any real funny business——"

James Howgill felt a sudden need to end the conversation. "To start with, I'd prefer to leave out the night-time watch," he said firmly. "The other two will be quite enough."

Bates shrugged. "Suit yourself." He prepared to take his final leave. "You won't see me again," he said, surprisingly. "After this, only written reports. Once a day, delivered by hand. In case of emergency, one of my associates will telephone. In case of special emergency, I will telephone myself."

"Very well," said James Howgill.

"Terms," said Bates, his authority now coming to a sharp head. "Five pounds per watch per day. Payable in advance."

"Very well," said James Howgill.

"Expenses extra."

"Very well."

"Photographs by arrangement."

For two days, during which James Howgill endeavoured to suppress his guilty feeling that what he was doing was not cricket, nor indeed any other game he would care to be caught playing, the reports from Bates were dull—as dull, indeed, as Howgill had expected them to be. 'Made visual contact with Subject, established residence, etc.' said the first; and the second: 'Subject shopped Regent Street, Bond Street, Piccadilly: all female wearing apparel.' Even apart from the atrocious phraseology it was not a particularly good twenty pounds' worth, save from the moral aspect; and James Howgill, given a few more such innocuous days, might well have called the whole thing off, there and then. But only those first two reports were innocuous.

The third report was narrative in style, and longer. 'Subject was called for at own residence by an Unidentified Male Escort at 6.20 pm,' it began. 'They emerged at 7 pm. They seemed on good terms with each other. Subject was laughing frequently. Followed taxi to Savoy Hotel, where Subject and Escort partook three martinis each, plus sandwiches. They then went to Haymarket Theatre, sitting in stalls, fourth row. They emerged at 11.10 pm, and took taxi to Cascade (superior supper-and-dance club in Clarges Street). Watch ceased at midnight in accordance with your instructions, by which time Subject had not reappeared.'

James Howgill read this through a second time very carefully, with an odd feeling of depression. All sorts of phrases in it started promising trends of thought; and yet his prime feeling was one of disappointment. How very unlike Marjorie it was! 'Male Escort'—'On good terms with each other'—'Three martinis'—'Supper-and-dance club in Clarges Street'—it could be construed as the road to ruin itself. And she had actually stayed out after midnight. . . . That was something which hadn't happened for a very long time.

Apparently it was something he would have to get used to; for Report No 4 gave him a great deal more to think about. 'Subject emerged from residence at 12.10 pm,' it began. 'Took taxi to Brown's Hotel, and lunched with Male Escort of previous night. Subsequently visited Odeon Theatre, Leicester Square. Sat back row of balcony. Could be observed holding hands. Subject returned home 5.45 pm, reappeared at 7.30 pm in evening attire. Took taxi to Barchester Hotel. Met in foyer by Male Escort (not same as previous) whom she greeted as "Darling". They proceeded to suite 807 on eighth floor. Dinner for two served at 9.00 pm (lobster, champagne, other courses). Discontinued watch at midnight, as arranged.

'Note: Escorts will henceforth be identified as Nos 1 and 2. No 1 is medium build, conservative dress, military bearing. No 2 identified from hotel register as Jack Carpenter, American citizen, New York.'

While James Howgill was reading this with feelings so mixed that he could not have classified any of them, his office phone rang. It was a man's voice, low-pitched, authoritative.

"Mr Howgill?"

"Yes."

"I have a message for you from Mr Bates."

"Who?" asked James Howgill, confused by the conspiratorial tone.

"Mr Bates."

"Oh yes! The——"

"Quite so," interrupted the voice swiftly. "The message is as follows. Bearing in mind the reports on the matter we have in hand, do you wish to increase coverage?"

"Well, I don't know," answered James Howgill. And in truth he did not. The last report was astonishing: he was once again sorry that he had put the thing in hand, but his reasons were now very different. His wife? Holding hands in cinemas? Champagne suppers with Americans lasting half the night? She must be out of her mind! . . . Wishing to gain time, he said: "Are you—er—one of the——" (how did one say it?) "——the people involved?"

"That is so," answered the voice, extremely cagily.

"Which one?"

"You mean, the time of day?"

"Yes."

"I cease operations at midnight," said the voice.

"And you really think——"

"It is Mr Bates's view that we will not bring this matter to a satisfactory conclusion unless we cover the remainder of the twenty-four hour period."

"Very well," said James Howgill, after a pause, unhappily. "Let's do that."

"I may say that Mr Bates is extremely optimistic," concluded the voice, and rang off.

If Mr Bates was optimistic, James Howgill was not. He was, in fact, vilely depressed. It was really too bad of Marjorie to behave like this. . . . She had never done so with him; indeed, the most defeating aspect of their marriage had been that she never wanted to go anywhere, and was content to sit placidly at home from one end of the year to another. But now, without him, she seemed to have gone off the rails completely.

Twinges of jealousy, unknown for ten years, assailed him. How dare Escort No 1, 'of military bearing', hold her hand in a darkened cinema? How dare Jack Carpenter, American citizen, ply her with lobsters and champagne up till midnight and beyond? Dash it all, she was a respectable married woman!

But there was worse to come.

First it was Report No 5. 'Flowers were delivered to Subject's residence at 10 am,' it began forthrightly. 'They appeared to be roses. Subject partook of lunch with Male

Escort No 1 at Zoological Gardens restaurant. Escort appeared in bad temper, subsequently quarrelled outside Reptile House and walked away. Subject returned home, later emerged and drove to Barchester Hotel, where she dined in grill room with Male Escort No 2 (Carpenter).

'Subject partook of wine and was overheard to say: "I am bored," to which Carpenter replied : "Lucio —'s (name not clear) plane is due at one o'clock. Let us meet it." Subject said: "My goodness, do you know him?" and Carpenter replied: "We have been buddies since Hoover was a boy." '

'At twelve midnight they summoned taxi and told driver to go to Heathrow airport. I reported this to my relief, who followed them thereto and will doubtless give details later. As they drove off, Subject inquired: "Is he really as devastating as they say?" Reply was inaudible.'

James Howgill was digesting this with increasing dismay, when his telephone rang. This time it was Mr Bates himself, his voice positively charged with excitement.

"Mr Howgill," he said, "I think we're on to something big."

"What do you mean?" asked James Howgill.

"I can't communicate the details over the telephone," said Bates curtly. "But I'm sending a report by special messenger. It should be there any minute."

"Special messenger?" repeated Howgill, in agony. "What *is* it?"

"You saw the last report?"

"Of course."

"Then you know that Subject met a certain party at Heathrow."

"What party?" The ridiculous word seemed to touch a raw nerve.

"I can't say over the phone," repeated Bates. "But I'll tell you this, Mr Howgill. That extra coverage was cheap at the price!"

James Howgill tore open the envelope. The first sentence and the name it contained hit him like a monstrous wave.

'Passenger arriving at Heathrow was Lucio Ambrosini,' it began. 'Name will be familiar. Subject, Escort, and Ambrosini drove off in Rolls-Royce (hired) after animated greeting, press interviews, etc. Prior to departure, Ambrosini embraced Subject and remarked: "I like you, baby. Let us get this show on the road." Party drove to Barchester Hotel, where Ambrosini has so-called Presidential Suite (14th floor). At 3 am party emerged, drove to Cascade Club, subsequently to Milroy (Park Lane), Giotti's (Conduit Street), and the Ring of Belles (off Grosvenor Square). On returning to Barchester Hotel (6 am), Escort No 2 (Carpenter) said goodbye in foyer, remarking: "I know when I am licked." Subject and Ambrosini proceeded to Presidential Suite, Ambrosini inquiring: "Are you licked yet, baby?" and Subject replying: "I have only just started. What is for breakfast?" Ambrosini answered: "Fried Ambrosini." Both laughed. Subject had not emerged from Presidential Suite at 8 am.'

Lucio Ambrosini. . . . The name itself was enough for a divorce action thought James Howgill in a fury: Ambrosini had been cited in at least five of them to the accompaniment of uproarious scandal and maximum headlines on both sides of the Atlantic. He was rich, elegant, much travelled; a household word in far too many households. He was a true 'international playboy', though he held some marginal diplomatic post which could not have occupied his time for more than a week in any one year. He drove racing cars into trees, horses into water-jumps, women into transports of delight and floods of tears. He was Lucio Ambrosini, married three times, the bane of husbands from Capri to Cape Cod. It was said that he only had to look at a woman——

James Howgill crumpled up the report, and hurled it into the fireplace. Then he reached for his hat. This ridiculous thing had gone far enough.

James Howgill faced his wife, across the sitting-room—his own sitting-room.

"But where have you *been*?" he asked again. "I've been ringing the doorbell here for nearly a week." He tried to make his tone a commanding one, but it came out as a sort of pleading complaint—the way, in fact, that he felt at this moment. Marjorie was really looking quite beautiful. . . . There had been all those men. . . . And Lucio Ambrosini to top them off. . . . She must have something, after all, and he had never been able to find it until now. . . . His thoughts were confused, while she, he observed with deep misgiving, was composed and cool.

"I was away, James," she answered. "It was lonely here. I took a little holiday."

"A holiday? Where?"

"I stayed with some friends in Scotland."

"What friends?"

"You don't know them, darling." She smiled. It was difficult to say what sort of a smile it was. It might have been secretive. It might have been shy. It was certainly new—or perhaps he hadn't noticed it before. "You've been gone such a long time," she went on. "I'm bound to have made a few new friends."

"How long were you away?"

"About six weeks."

He stared at her, full of jealousy, full of suspicion, yet powerless to make anything of it. He knew she was not telling the truth, yet he could not charge her with it. That would mean confessing about the detectives, and he was ashamed of them and of a lot of other things. And if he told her about the detectives she might be angry, and turn him out again. He couldn't stand that. Not now.

"I hope you haven't been too lonely," he said awkwardly.

"Not too lonely. Of course I've missed you."

Marjorie smiled again, the same smile. It annoyed him, plagued him, and intrigued him. He felt a wave of pure astonishment sweep over him. After all these years she suddenly intrigued him. . . . Once again, he thought: She must have something, in spite of everything.

Looking at her, he knew it was something he had to have, this time for good. She was not the old Marjorie at all. She was tantalizing, feminine, new. Above all she was his, to be defended against all comers. If other men were attracted they'd just have to keep their distance.

On an impulse he walked over and kissed her. Even her lips felt different now. He found himself swearing that they must belong to him, and to no one else.

"It's nice to be home," he said, unsteadily.

Touching his hand, she said: "It *is* a nice house, isn't it?"

For a moment she wanted to tell him that while she had been away, the house—their house—had been let; and to a film actress, of all people. But she decided not to. James was odd about things like that. And strait-laced too. He might not understand. And she could not bear to spoil this moment. James was positively ardent. Life had really been very dull without him.

"It's lovely to have you back," she said. "Please stay."

"For ever," he answered determinedly. "Among other reasons, I don't believe you're safe to leave alone."

"Why, James! What *do* you mean?"

"*You* know," he said, with possessive warmth. "But let's never mention it again."

The List

THE DISTRICT Commissioner's office rose like a bastion in the centre of the dusty, sunbaked Basuto village. It stood for authority and sometimes for punishment; but it could stand also for protection, and even hope.

In the eyes of Daniel Mfutu, the slim young Basuto now trudging up the steep path towards it, it stood for hope—the greatest hope of all his life.

In his yellow blanket and woven 'beehive' hat, Mfutu was like a hundred others, old and young, who gossiped in the shade of their mud huts or went soberly about their business. But soon—if all turned out well, if the hope of his life came true—he would discard the tribal blanket which he despised, and take on the white man's clothes: trousers, a shirt, perhaps even a shiny grey jacket. Then he would indeed be a man.

When Mfutu came near to the District Commissioner's office, under the eyes of a khaki-clad sentry half asleep on the *stoep*, he slowed his steps, peering towards the thing he was looking for, the green baize noticeboard which ruled much of the life of the tribe. On it were many things he knew by heart: orders about cattle and goats, orders about caring for the water in the dam, orders to assemble here, not to assemble there.

But it was a new notice he was looking for; and presently, with a leap of his heart, he saw that the new notice was there.

His own name caught his eye first: 'No 7. MFUTU, Daniel.' He had passed! Then he read it carefully.

'The following are declared successful candidates in the November examination for Clerks, Grade VII (Filing and General Duties).'

There was a list of ten names only. He counted carefully. His own name was indeed seventh.

After the leap of the heart, there came the stab of terror he had known so many times in the last few weeks. The examination had been hard enough—the examination which

63

was going to transform his whole life, make him into a great man instead of a Basuto boy; but he had managed to conquer it with not too many foolish mistakes, not too much bad spelling. The waiting had been worse; alone in his small hut, by night and by day, while the white man read his answers and passed judgment, he had known all the terrors of defeat.

But now was the worst thing of all. On the list his name was seventh. There had been strong rumours that, when the time came to take on the new helpers in the District Commissioner's office, there would be room for only five. His seventh place, after all his hopes and tortures, would not be high enough.

In urgent need of help, he turned towards the sentry, nodding over his rifle. He said: "Can I speak, please?"

The sentry, a fat man in a great heat, came to with a jerk. "What's that? What do you want, boy?"

"It is this list." Mfutu pointed. "My name is on it. I have succeeded."

"All praise to you," said the sentry ironically. "Great things will now happen in Basutoland."

"I am seventh," said Mfutu patiently.

"Wonder of wonders," said the sentry.

"Is it yet known how many are needed?"

The sentry stared at him irritably, scratching. "If it is *yet known*," he answered, mimicking, "it is not yet known to me."

"How can I find out?"

"You wait and see," said the sentry.

"But I must know," said Mfutu in agony.

"You wait," repeated the sentry.

A voice called suddenly from within, a white man's voice, fruity, irritable, bored. "What is it, corporal?"

"Nothing, sir," said the sentry.

"Then don't make such a hell of a noise."

"Sir!" said the sentry, as he had been taught.

"Ask him!" whispered Mfutu urgently.

"Go away," said the sentry. "You disturb the peace. It is an offence."

"But how can I find out?"

"Ask some wise man. But do not bother me."

Like his father before him, Mfutu trudged up the hill to see Peremboli, Peremboli the ancient one. He had never

64

done so before, and he feared and loathed the encounter, but it was a time for courage and hard things.

"Greetings," he said, at the door of the darkened hut.

Peremboli, an old veined man in a filthy skin adorned with monkey tails, stared at him, saying nothing.

"I need help, my chief," said Mfutu.

"You come to me?" said Peremboli, still staring with angry eyes. "I thought you were studying to be a white man! White men do not come to Peremboli. They go to other white men, or"—he spat—"to policemen."

"I need help," said Mfutu, in miserable fear. He would do anything, bear any insult, if he could only be one of the chosen five, and escape his dull life and poor fate.

"Yes, you need help," said Peremboli, cackling suddenly. "You are on the list. Mfutu, Daniel. Number seven."

"How many will be chosen?" Mfutu did not pause to wonder how Peremboli already knew so much. Peremboli knew all.

"They say, five."

Mfutu swallowed. "I *must* be chosen!"

"Must?" repeated Peremboli. "You want so much to be the white man's little dog?"

"It is my chance, my only chance. If I am not chosen I will be nothing, nothing at all, for evermore. Can you help me, Peremboli?"

Peremboli stared at him a long time, an old evil man with the wisdom and cunning of nearly a hundred years.

"We will see," he said presently. "It is a difficult matter. . . . He suddenly darted out a skinny hand. "You will bring me three things. First, a copy of the list, the list of names."

"Very well," said Mfutu.

"Then, twenty shillings."

"Very well," said Mfutu, though his heart quaked.

"Then, a written piece of paper, signed by you."

"What paper?" asked Mfutu, confused.

"A promise," said Peremboli. "A promise that if you are chosen you will give me half what the white man pays you. For ever. Until one of us dies."

Mfutu returned next day, sick at heart, but knowing that now he could not turn back. He was committed to the way of Peremboli, which, in spite of all things, he secretly believed. He had copied out the list of names. From the village usurer he had borrowed the twenty shillings at wicked interest. He had written out his promise, the promise which would steal half his earning-money away for ever. But he must be chosen! He must! He must!

Peremboli tucked the letter of promise deep within the folds of his loin-skin. Then he looked at the list of names for a long time, while within the twilight hut the flies buzzed and Mfutu stood trembling and sweating.

At last Peremboli spoke.

"The way is clear," he said. "There are two bad names here. Two men who are weak. . . . If their names disappear for ever, your name will be number five."

"How can they disappear?" asked Mfutu fearfully.

"One is Korale," said Peremboli, not hearing him. "He is a cripple, a limping man. The other is Thomas Bira, whose wife hates him."

Mfutu waited.

"Limping men like Korale find death often. Indeed, I can already see death for him."

"What manner of death?"

"Death by water." It came like the sound of an incantation. "He is a limping man, living alone. He fetches his own water from the dam, secretly, at nightfall, since he is ashamed of such a task, and fears to be seen by the women. . . ." Peremboli's voice sank to a whisper. "A limping man, with a heavy water pot, at the edge of the dam in the darkness. . . . Is it any wonder I see death for Korale?"

After a long silence Mfutu asked, scarcely able to mouth the words:

"What about Thomas Bira?"

"Korale first," answered Peremboli. "His death is the nearer."

Two days later, Mfutu went to Peremboli's hut again, but covertly, and at night. He was afraid, but fear and hope still drove him on. One day he would be a great clerk in the white man's office; before that could come to pass he must follow the old ways of Peremboli.

Standing in the darkness, Mfutu said: "Korale is dead."

"Yes," said Peremboli. "Alas. . . ."

"What now?"

Unseen in the darkness, Peremboli stirred. The smell of the forbidden smoke-weed drifted between them, heavy, acrid. Then he spoke, and once again it had the sound of an evil incantation.

"The wife of Thomas Bira," he said, "has stood where you stand, many times. But think no shame of that! I am old, and she is ill-favoured. . . . First it was to have a child. But she could not. She hates Thomas Bira as he hates her: no union such as that could be fruitful. Then it was to see if she might be rich—some matter of an uncle, in the village up the hill. But when he did die, it seemed he was poor, after all. . . . Then lastly, it was to find out if Thomas Bira, her husband, might himself die."

"Well?" asked Mfutu, steeling his spirit.

"Her courage failed her at the last. She is resigned. She will live with him till the end."

"Well?" asked Mfutu again.

"She is resigned, as I have said, because she is ill-favoured. But if there were to come a lover—a young man, let us say, who would marry her when she is free—her courage might return again."

"I have looked on this wife of Bira," said Mfutu, sick at heart. "She is ugly indeed. And old."

"Some thirty summers."

"I have seen only seventeen," said Mfutu.

"Yet a clerk in the white man's government," answered Peremboli, overriding him, "finds favour with many women. Marriage is no great matter. If his wife is beautiful, well. If she is old and ugly, well also. He will not starve for love."

Mfutu turned and stumbled out into the moonlight. But though his heart quaked, he knew once more what he had to do.

In the darkness, under the trees by the further end of the dam, her ugliness was hidden, and she was warm and urgent. Her face, pock-marked by the sickness, could not be seen. But Mfutu saw it with his closed eyes, none the less. He was appalled. Her loving seemed to him like antique lust. He was appalled—but the time for flinching was past.

"I must go," she said, towards morning. "My husband sleeps pig-like, but he might wake, and find me gone. . . ." She touched his shoulder. "You promise?"

"I promise," said Mfutu.

"Say: 'I love Reneira Mira, and will marry her.' "

"I love Reneira Mira, and will marry her."

"When did you first love me?"

"I saw you at the dam with the other women," he said, almost choking on his lies. "You were very fair. I knew then."

She sighed. "Soon we will be together for always."

"You promise *me*?"

"I promise."

"When?"

"Tonight, if all goes well. I have the herbs kept hidden. It will be sleep first, and then death."

"Be careful," he said fearfully.

"I will be careful," she promised, "because of our great love."

A week later Mfutu, standing in the shadows at the edge of the *stoep*, read the new notice on the green baize board.

"Amended List of Examination Candidates," it read; and then further down: "No 5 Mfutu, Daniel."

His heart glowed with pride, almost burst with pleasure. Though he had done fearful things, they were now safely past; though he must pay half his wages to Peremboli, and must marry an ugly woman whom he hated, yet he was already marked for greatness. He could escape the past; he would be an honoured man, a great man, a filing clerk.

Then his eye was caught by a new paragraph at the foot of the notice.

"To assist those who may be looking for immediate employment," it said, "it may be stated that present intake requirements indicate not more than three vacancies in Grade VII during the next two years. At the end of that time, fresh examinations will be held."

He read and reread this many times, with a slowly sinking heart. The language was difficult, but presently he conquered it. It seemed that, after all his desperate climbing, it was not enough to be number five on the list; he must be number three.

With the grasping of this, he grasped all the fresh terrors of the future as well. But, near to great promotion, he was a stronger young man already. Without a word he turned, and trudged off again towards the hut of Peremboli.

The Thousand Islands Snatch

On the broad waters of the St Lawrence, near Montreal, where the river widened yet further to become Lac St Louis, a small trim motor-launch was at anchor, and in the motor-launch three men of a wonderfully diverse type sat waiting. They were indeed so diverse that perhaps only a major crime could have brought them together.

One of them, a small bald man by the name of Curly Bates, was pretending to fish. The second, who had the look of an Italian about him (but a big Italian, fleshy, sensual, gross) was enjoying the sun, and day-dreaming as usual of women and violence. The third man, who was called Paxton (his surname? his given name? no one knew for certain, and no one would ever ask him)—the third man was a grim, lean man with an air of command. Of the three, only Paxton was doing any work: and the work he was doing at that moment was to stare up river through his 10 × 50 Zeiss binoculars, with a look of such concentrated watchfulness that it was enough to threaten the peace of the whole lake.

Away from the watching boat it was a lazy June afternoon; the American bank of the river was almost lost in the heat-haze; on the Canadian side there was only the activity at the Royal St Lawrence Yacht Club—sails hoisted and lowered, power cruisers sliding in and out, yachts moving like drifting paper boats in the still air. All else was embalmed in tranquillity. The water, running against the bows of their launch, spoke musically of small things—wavelets, little fish, fronded green weed waving like women's hair. Even the huge airliner taking off from near-by Dorval seemed to float in the sky overhead, idle and thrustless.

Presently Curly Bates—he who was pretending to fish—looked up from his task, jerking his trailing line irritably.

"Hey, Pax!" he called out over his shoulder. He had a flat nasal Cockney voice, product of a childhood spent, forty years earlier, in a London slum. "Hey, Pax! Tell us something."

Dino, the big Italian, turned over from his contemplation of the sky. "What's eating you, Curly? Not the fish, I'll bet." He laughed, a big throaty chuckle. "What's on your mind, Curly?"

Paxton, their lean leader, said nothing. He was in the bows of the boat, his back towards them, his big binoculars still trained on the head of the lake.

"Hey, Pax!" repeated Curly Bates. He did not like Dino, he did not trust him, he did not want to talk to him. His loyalty was towards Paxton, and his only job was to run the motor-launch—their floating get-away car.

Paxton, still intent, threw over his shoulder: "What is it?"

"What happens if they change their minds, go somewhere else?"

"You nuts?" interrupted Dino crudely. "This job set up six months ago! What you mean, change their minds?"

"People change their minds," said Curly Bates sulkily. "And I'm not talking to you, Dino, any road."

Paxton dropped his binoculars and turned to face them. His pale face was grim. "Quit scrapping," he said curtly. "You're like a couple of women. . . ." He addressed Curly Bates. "Don't worry your head, Curly. Men like John Harper Harrison don't change their minds. If you've got that amount of dough you plan ahead, see? If he says he'll spend fifteen days in June on the Canadian side of the St Lawrence, he'll do just that. If he says his boat will berth at the yacht club here on June 12th, that's the day it will berth. If his daughter's going to be with him, then his daughter's going to be with him."

"That daughter," interjected Dino. He kissed his fat brown fingers. "I seen photographs. It'll be a pleasure."

"Besides, if there's a change of plan," continued Paxton, ignoring him, "Joe would tell us. What do you think we've got a man on board for? If something does go wrong, or if Harrison's got to rush back to New York to make another million dollars, Joe will get word to us."

"That Joe!" said Dino, this time with contempt. "That Mex!"

"Cut it out!" said Paxton coldly. "He's a Mex, you're a Wop. What's the difference?"

"And I'm a Limey," cackled Curly Bates. "What are you, Pax?"

"I'm the boss," said Paxton. "Now get back to work, for the love of mike."

He raised his binoculars again; Curly Bates let out a few more feet of line; Dino subsided against the back of the motor-boat's rear seat. Silence returned to the launch. At the faint sound of a gun a line of big racing yachts started out from the Royal St Lawrence Club, creeping against the tide, scarcely moving. All else was summer and warm peace.

It was half an hour later that Paxton, after hard staring towards one particular point of the south-west channel, said suddenly:

"There she is now!"

They watched the big white motor-cruiser coming down the river, changing from a bright pinpoint to a definite shape and size, emerging at last as a tough craft with a creamy bow wave; passing successive channel markers, passing Pointe Claire, making for the red buoy near which they were anchored, turning at last towards the yacht club and her appointed berth. She was gleaming white, with spotless deck planking and two long mahogany cabin-tops; she passed near enough for them to read her name and port of registry on the stern: "*Shearwater*. RYC Rochester, NY."

When she was close by Paxton dropped his binoculars. To Dino he said: "Look the other way, you damn' fool!" and to Curly Bates: "Fish, you! Reel in your line, and let it out again." A moment later, when the cruiser was stern on to them, making for the Canadian shore, he said softly: 'That's Joe, peeking out of the galley. . . . Harrison's got the wheel. . . . There's the girl in the cockpit. . . . Looks like we're in business."

They knew a great deal about the *Shearwater*, these three, and they knew more still about John Harper Harrison, her owner, and his daughter Ellen; this boat and her complement, indeed, had been their exclusive preoccupation for the last six months. They knew that Harrison (a widower, steel and airline interests, taxable income about $280,000 a year) was on his annual month's cruise in the *Shearwater*, and that this year it was the St Lawrence River, between Lake Ontario and Quebec (last year it had been the Florida Keys, the year before that, Bermuda).

They knew that the daughter (eighteen, good-looking,

always in and out of the gossip columns) was with him, and that she liked going out alone in the small launch (sixteen feet, twenty-two knots) which *Shearwater* carried with her, slung in davits amidships. They knew that *Shearwater* herself was sixty-two feet long, with twin diesels (fourteen knots), and carried five people in all—Harrison, his daughter, a professional skipper, a mechanic-deckhand, and Joe the steward (*their* steward). They had known that she was due at the Royal St Lawrence today, and that she would stay there a maximum of five days.

They knew the police set-up at the nearest township, Dorval; they knew in what circumstances the Royal Canadian Mounted Police might be called in; they knew the details and limitations of local liaison with the FBI. They knew the extent of the river patrols in the Thousand Islands area, one hundred and fifty miles up river. Finally, they knew that the maximum penalty for kidnapping in Canada was life imprisonment, as against an almost certain death sentence in forty-two of the forty-eight United States.

"All right," said Paxton, when they had watched *Shearwater* safely berthed, and John Harper Harrison had strolled ashore like a visiting royalty. "We'll go ahead as planned." His voice was taut and controlled, reeling off his orders as a matter of cold logic. "Curly, start her up, and go up river to Pointe Claire. . . . Dino, you'll go ashore there, pick up the car, go down to the yacht club, make contact with Joe. We'll all meet at nine o'clock tonight at the Drion motel."

"Suppose Joe can't make it ashore?" queried Dino, as Curly wound in his line and prepared to start the motor.

"You'll have to wait," Paxton told him curtly. "Joe will find a way somehow—stands to reason he's got to buy supplies, or fix up fresh milk, or collect the mail, or something. Just wait for him. *Don't* go near the cruiser yourself. *Don't* take the car into the yacht club grounds. Let Joe make the move." Their engine sputtered into life, and he began to haul in the anchor line, hand over hand. "There's only one more thing we want from Joe," said Paxton. "And that is, how long they're going to stay there. Then we can set the time for the snatch."

John Harper Harrison, who was a big man even when he was sitting down, glared across the lunch table at his daughter's empty chair. *Late again, by thunder ! There wasn't a man in New York who would dare do this to him. . . .* He was a man much given to glaring, an old-time starer-outer, a level-eye expert with a nation-wide reputation even among those best qualified to meet his glance; and now, as that glance left his daughter's empty place and travelled round the canopied deckhouse where their table was set, and across *Shearwater's* gleaming upper deck, and along the wooden quay to which they were moored, it finally came to rest on Joe the steward—and Joe, he decided, would do as an interim target.

"Joe!" he called out brusquely.

Joaquin Barzan, who had been staring out across the lake in a manner which might have been vacant, came to life. He was small, dark, and nervous; his spotless white ducks looked bigger and better than the man himself, and he seemed to be making an effort to grow into them—as if, having crashed the wrong party in the wrong size of costume, he hoped to get by with a brave show of nerve.

"Sir wants?" he asked, looking fixedly at John Harper Harrison's Palm Beach shirt.

"Did you tell my daughter lunch was ready?"

"Sir, yes."

"Where was she?"

Joaquin pointed ashore. "Over club house, sir."

John Harper Harrison grunted. It was not a reassuring sound. Playing around again, it indicated irritably; drinking with a lot of nincompoops. . . . What's the good of a boat like this if she never uses it? Then he realized the absurdity of his thoughts, and the glare subsided gently to a grin. Ellen was late because she was young and enjoying herself with a lot of other kids, and who but an old fool of a doting father could be jealous of that? Certainly not John Harper Harrison, who had more common sense in his little finger. . . .

Observing the grin and the general air of magnanimity, Joaquin Barzan plucked up the necessary fortitude.

"Sir," he said, "how long we stay here, please?"

John Harper Harrison, who had been contemplating with due pride of ownership the way in which *Shearwater's* upper deck curved gracefully towards the bows, said: "What's that, Joe?"

To a man with a conscience it sounded faintly menacing,

but Joaquin had an appointed task as well as a conscience. He summoned his courage afresh:

"How long we stay here, please sir?"

Harrison knit his brows. "Who wants to know? I'll tell the skipper when I'm ready to move."

Joaquin licked his lips, "Sir, must buy vegetables, milk, ice-cubes, club sodas, bread, meat——"

"All right, all right," said Harrison, prepared to be testy again. "I get the message. . . . You can plan on four or five days."

It was not enough for Joaquin, not enough by at least fifty per cent, but he did not dare to push the thing further. Instead, lifting his eyes towards the end of the dock, he said: "Sir, daughter come now."

"About time, too," growled John Harper Harrison. Then he surrendered to the pleasure of watching his daughter approach through surroundings which (he admitted grudgingly, as an American patriot) were not bad, not bad at all.

The lawns of the Royal St Lawrence—beautifully laid out, shaded by great trees, contained at their margin by boat docks, floating pontoons, and a huge assortment of craft—were a fit setting for a girl who was really very beautiful indeed. Of course (thought John Harper Harrison, who had made $12,000,000 by being a perfectionist) she still dressed in the absurd way that all the kids affected nowadays—blue jeans that any self-respecting labourer would have thrown away at the week's end, a 'top' which would scarcely have served her mother as a handkerchief—but the total effect was certainly there. . . . Ellen Harper Harrison stepped along the dock as if it and all the world belonged to her, shedding two young men on the way, waving good-bye to a third, cutting a broad swathe through a score of impressionable Canadian sailors. She had only been in the yacht club area twenty hours, but already the word had gone around. She was that kind of girl, and a great many enthusiastic young men would have confirmed that it was the only kind to be.

Now she stepped on board, tossed her beach bag aside, sat down at the table under the canopy, all in a graceful series of movements which deserved, perhaps, a wider audience.

"Hi, Daddy!"

"Hi Daddy nothing!" growled John Harper Harrison. "I'm hungry, you're late. . . . If you can't get up for breakfast, you might at least be in time for lunch."

"You wouldn't want to see me at breakfast time," said Ellen, with practised evasion. "I look perfectly horrible."

Harrison surveyed his daughter, as Joe served the iced consommé. She was beautiful, all right—beautiful, wilful, adored.

"You force me to tell you that you look wonderful at any time."

"Why, Dad! *Thank* you!"

"Your mother used to squeeze compliments out of me in much the same way. . . . Are you enjoying yourself, baby?"

"Oh, yes. I always do on these trips. I loved that run from Kingston. Those Thousand Islands are cute. And that Seaway Project!"

"It's a good construction job," said her father, who did not waste praise on other people's efforts. "Do you like it here, too?"

"Very much."

"Lots of boys?"

"Lots."

"What about Greg?"

Ellen tossed her head, in a very old-fashioned way. "Oh—him!"

"Oh—him!" mimicked John Harper Harrison. "A month ago, young lady, we heard nothing but Greg Perring this, Greg Perring that. He was going to co-ordinate the entire field of science and philosophy, and you were going to marry him. What's happened now?"

Ellen, giving most of her attention to the breast of duck which Joe had conjured from the galley hatch, shrugged her shoulders. "He's so feeble. . . . To begin with, he ought to be here. *I'm* here," she said, with a finality so devastating that it must have been unfair. "Why isn't he? Montreal is only a couple of miles away."

"Perhaps he's working," said John Harper Harrison in a tone meant to be mildly sarcastic. "You know—work. . . . Sake's alive, Ellen, give the boy a chance. He's a scientist, not one of those darned fly-by-night playboys. And if he said he'll meet you, he'll meet you."

Curly Bates sniffed, an eloquent sniff, the sniff of a Cockney, however small, for an Italian, however big.

"You got cold?" asked Dino belligerently.

"I'm not cold, and I'm not hot either," answered Curly Bates disdainfully. "I seen you, Dino, looking at the girl when she's sunbathing. If you're getting ideas like that we're better off without you."

"I am a man," declared Dino grandly.

"You're a——" began Curly Bates.

"Cut it out!" snapped Paxton without removing his gaze from the ceiling. "I'm thinking."

There was silence. Curly Bates adjusted a screw on one of his wire reels; Dino flexed his muscles. Then Paxton said:

"We've got to get hold of Joe again. Just to make sure. . . ." He rolled over. "Curly, you'd better go this time: Dino's been around the yacht club too much already." His face, intent on planning and commanding, took on a bleak concentration. "Go down in the car, make contact with Joe. He'll be hanging about near the boat if he's got any sense. But stay under the trees, where it's dark. If he can get time off, bring him back here. If not, ask him if he's got any more news, if he knows *for certain* when they're sailing."

"OK boss," said Curly Bates.

"And don't get picked up," said Paxton. "They've got watchmen, remember. Just stay out of sight."

"Better let me go, Pax," said Dino. "I look more like club member, yes?"

"You look more like a dog's dinner," said Curly Bates. He was putting on his coat. "Trust me, boss. I'll bring him back."

Joaquin Barzan was ill at ease. The garish lights of the motel room bothered his eyes; Paxton's gaze was too close, too probing; Dino's disdain too obvious. Only Curly Bates was prepared to be generous and companionable; but then, Curly Bates was a dog, just as he himself was a dog.

"Let's get it straight," said Paxton for the third time. "Do you know for sure when you're moving?"

"Day after tomorrow," answered Joaquin. "That is, I think so."

"Think?"

"I ask twice already," said Joaquin miserably. The air

round him seemed thick with suspicion and contempt, as if, whatever he said, these people would only take it at half its face value. "I'm afraid to ask again."

"What you afraid of?" asked Dino.

"Too many questions," said Joaquin. "Make suspicion."

Dino snorted. "Too many questions," he mimicked. "What you think you put on boat for? Serve cocktails? Make beds? You want easy money, hey, Joe?"

"I work hard," said Joaquin. "Find things out, come and make report."

"Big deal!"

"Cut it out," said Paxton. "How many times do I have to tell you, we all have a job to do." He gave each one of them in turn a hard stare. "Do you think I would have picked any of you meatheads if I could get along without you? It's like working with a bunch of performing fleas, all different breeds. Now, listen, all of you. Today's Monday. If they're likely to move off on Wednesday, we'll have to do the job tomorrow. We're quite far enough from the Thousand Islands base as it is—hundred and fifty miles—say, seven hours—and we can't risk letting them get any further away. Next stop might be Quebec City. . . . So that means to-morrow."

They were all looking at him—ready for the long-planned action and yet now, when they were on the brink of it, touched by doubts. Paxton, aware of this, swung his feet off the bed and sat up straight, assuming full control by this one simple action.

"Curly, take Joe back to the yacht club now. . . . Joe, settle down on board again, don't open your mouth, don't try to get in touch with us. Above all, don't quit the job. Stay with Harrison till he pays you off. When the police come, play it like I said—you know nothing, it's just a summer job, you haven't any friends, you haven't talked to anyone."

Joaquin nodded. "I do that."

"We won't be seeing you again," said Paxton. He was standing up now, hands on hips, giving orders. "Not for some time, anyway. You'll get your cut when it's safe to send it. But don't—*don't*—come anywhere near us even if you know where we are. If the police watch anyone on board it will be you. Just remember that."

"I remember."

"You better," said Dino ferociously. "If you do give them a lead, I cut your throat. Personally. That's for sure."

Joaquin hesitated, nervous, unhappy. He wanted to say that he wouldn't let them down, that he could be trusted, that he didn't have to be bullied and threatened like this, that he was an equal. . . . But no words came, and he turned awkwardly and went out, followed by Curly Bates.

"You don't have to pressure him, Dino," said Paxton when he was gone. "He'll do all right."

Dino expelled his cigarette smoke, derisively. "I know his sort," he said. "The police get after him he'll crumple up, start to talk."

"You forget something," said Paxton. "He's got nothing to talk about. We're going to disappear. On one of the Thousand Islands. *Thousand* Islands," he repeated, with special emphasis. "Joe doesn't know which one."

Ellen Harper Harrison was bored—or as bored as she ever permitted herself to be. It was true that the cruise from Rochester to Montreal had been fun, and the Royal St Lawrence club was a handsome and cheerful place to tie up to. It was true that an appropriate and even flattering number of young men were concentrating their attention upon *Shearwater*, and (though they were sailors) their attention was far from nautical. It was true, once more, that she liked Canadian young men—they seemed less brash, more civilized, than many of their American counterparts. (When she asked her father what was the explanation of this, John Harper Harrison had replied: "Parliamentary democracy", which seemed to her a very odd explanation indeed.)

But in spite of all these things, she was bored; and the reason, she realized, was that she missed Greg Perring, whom she had thought of until quite recently as her fiancé; and this reason, naturally, made her furious as well.

Her father, innocently reading his morning newspaper under *Shearwater's* awning, was startled to intercept, when he chanced to glance up, a look of such concentrated dissatisfaction upon his daughter's face that he came to the alert instantly.

"What's the matter, honey?" he inquired. "You look as though you wanted to sink the boat with your bare hands."

"Nothing like that, Daddy," she answered, relaxing

under his concerned look. "I was just thinking, that's all."

"Glad I'm out of the line of fire," he said. "If I *am* out of it."

"Oh, it's not you," she reassured him. "It's not *Shearwater* either. As if it could be!—oh, I suppose it's Greg."

"That *feeble* young man."

"Yes, that feeble young man." Newly aroused, she faced him squarely. "What's he playing at—just tell me that! He *lives* here. Why hasn't he called me?"

"Does he know you're here?"

"Of course. I told him."

"When?"

"When I last wrote." She saw a shadow of a smile on her father's face, and she could not help reacting to it. "Oh, all right—it was a month ago. But he knows! He's methodical! He must have put it down in his diary! So why isn't he here?"

"You couldn't call him, I suppose?"

"Why, Daddy—you must be out of your mind!"

John Harper Harrison grunted noncommittally. He was far from agreeing, but he was not at home either in these affairs or in this age-group. If Ellen were so certain that mid-twentieth-century *mores* did not permit her to call up a young man she was obviously dying to see, then Ellen was right and he, her father, was wrong, and that was all there was to it. There had been many such revelations the last few years, and he had learned to bow before all of them.

About to return to his newspaper, he asked, by way of a change of subject: "Are you taking the launch again this afternoon?"

"I suppose so," said Ellen dispiritedly. "Actually, I'm lazy. I may not go."

A sudden disturbance at their side resolved itself into Joe, juggling with an ashtray which finally dropped and splintered on the deck.

"Joe!" said John Harper Harrison in startled reproof. "For Heaven's sake. . . ."

"Sir, very sorry!" Joe retrieved the broken pieces so awkwardly that he dropped most of them again and had to do it a second time. When finally he had finished he straightened up and addressed Ellen: "You go in boat, please?"

"I don't know, Joe. It doesn't matter. I'll tell the engineer if I want it."

"Nice day, plenty sun," said Joe, oddly persuasive.

"I'll tell the engineer," said Ellen again.

"You know," said John Harper Harrison in a voice suddenly altered, "I think you *will* go."

"Why, Dad?"

Looking past her, smiling broadly, her father said: "Come aboard, Greg!"

They had strolled ashore arm in arm, watched with shadowed eyes by half a dozen young men who would have made fantastic sacrifices—even their hopes of winning the next sailing race—for the same privilege. But the air of close companionship was illusory. It did not take long for them to reach disagreement.

"But, honey," said Greg Perring, "I had to *work*! We were snowed under, right in the middle of something important. I just couldn't leave."

"You didn't want to."

"That's perfectly true—I didn't want to." Greg, a good-looking young man (but thin, thought Ellen) with a remote air of inner calculation (sometimes he just wasn't there at all, she objected) made the rash admission far too readily. "It really was important, like I said."

She took her arm away at that, and they stood at the end of the dock under the great plane trees. "What's more important than me?" she demanded.

"It depends what particular area we're discussing," answered Greg judiciously—much too judiciously. "In a way, there's nothing more important to me than you because I love you. In *another* way, this thing that we're working on is more important still because it's the very essence of my job——"

"I just don't want to hear," said Ellen with vehemence. And then: "What is it, exactly?"

He grinned suddenly, maddeningly, and answered: "It's a new kind of metal suitable for the trigger mechanism of a——"

"Greg Perring!" she burst out. "I believe you're just trying to make me mad. Trigger mechanism! Is *that* more important than meeting me?"

"We are hoping," he said, with that earnest concentration which concealed an even more annoying sense of the ridiculous, "that history will say 'Yes' to that."

"Well, I say 'No' to it." She looked at him with undisputed dislike. "Luckily, everyone hereabouts doesn't feel the same way as you."

"H'm."

"There are plenty of boys who put me right at the top of their list."

"H'm."

She glared at him. "What does that silly noise mean?"

"I suppose it means that I'm not the competitive type."

"And what does *that* mean?"

"Cut it out, Ellen!" he begged, by now slightly harassed. "You know what I mean. If you love me, that's wonderful. If you fall for someone else when I'm not there, there's not a thing I can do about it."

"You could make an effort."

"It's not a question of effort. It's simply a matter of *you* making up your mind what you want."

"I never heard anything more feeble in my whole life."

He shook his head. "Not feeble. Just common sense. I'm not a battler, sweetheart. You know that. I'm a man of reason—or I try to be."

"Sometimes I wonder," she answered exasperated, "if you're a man at all."

"You must make up your mind about that, too."

"Greg Perring, I believe you're doing all this on purpose!"

After lunch, during which John Harper Harrison observed them with the detached puzzlement common to a lot of parents in the same situation, Ellen announced that she was taking the launch out.

"Can I come along?" asked Greg.

"I usually go alone," answered Ellen coolly.

"That's when I'm not here."

"And it's my last day."

"That's another good reason."

"Oh—all right!"

Her father, looking up as the launch drew away, caught sight of Joaquin's face. It had on it a look of such anguished despair that he found himself staring. Then he relaxed. Must be toothache, he decided. No one could have worries as tough as that.

The look which had crossed Joaquin Barzan's face as *Shearwater's* launch drew away bearing Ellen Harper Harrison and that disastrous extra passenger, Greg Perring, was nothing compared with the spasm of rage and shock which contorted Paxton's whole being about five minutes later. From their usual anchorage in midstream he had watched the launch leave the yacht club, and set course upstream; only now, as it came within easy range, did he notice that behind Ellen, sitting competently at the wheel, was a second figure—a young man, lounging on the back seat, looking about him with an air of peaceful enjoyment.

Paxton drew in his breath sharply as his binoculars gave him the bad news; and then the other two with him in the launch noticed the second figure, and the shock spread to them swiftly.

"Hey, Pax!" said Curly Bates sharply. "Look—there's someone with her!"

"*Mamma mia!*" exclaimed Dino. "Pax, there's a man——"

"I've got eyes!" snarled Paxton. His eyes were glued to the binoculars while his mind raced over the turn of events. The second figure was a young man—just a kid by the look of him, but a second person none-the-less, a complication, a swift jolt to their plans. The girl had never taken anyone else along before, and their schedule had not allowed for anything of the sort. Of course, it had to happen today. . . .

The launch drew level with them, half a mile away, then continued on up the channel, leaving them hard-breathing and dismayed.

Dino's face was sweating, "What we do now?" he asked tensely. "She not by herself this time. . . . Just let me get my hands on that Joe—that stupid Mex——"

"It's not his fault," said Curly Bates.

"He could have told us," said Dino, on the verge of a wild rage.

"How?" asked Paxton, his voice like a lash.

Dino began to bluster. "How do I know 'how'? It's his job, isn't it? He was to tell us the plans. Now we've got two people instead of one. What we do? Tell me that!"

Curly said: "We'll have to put it off, that's what."

Paxton dropped his binoculars and rubbed his eyes. Then

he glared round at them. "I'll make the decisions, and I'll give the orders. . . . We can't put it off, that's for sure. This is the last day. They'll be gone tomorrow."

"But we can't take both of them."

"Why not?" snapped Paxton.

"We only want the girl. That's what the plan was. We can't change it now."

"Why not?" said Paxton again.

"Hey, that's right!" said Dino, beginning to recover his spirits. "We take them both. Not so difficult. What he look like, Pax?"

"Just a kid. Twenty-two or three, maybe."

"I take care of him," said Dino. "I take care both of them."

Their boat rocked gently in the tideway, the sun fell warmly on their backs. *Shearwater's* launch was a mile away now, diminishing rapidly. There were still the two figures in it, but somehow, now that they faced it, the fact seemed less important.

"Let's work it out," said Paxton. His cold eyes were coming alive again. "The job's got to be done today. Otherwise we lose out. And it's not Joe's fault—this guy probably came along at the last moment. There's still three of us, don't forget, and two of them. . . . It's a darned nuisance, but it's not the end of the world. Dino, when we land, you look after the boy."

"I look after him good," said Dino, grinning.

"Not too rough," warned Paxton. "Just rough enough. . . . Curly, you stick with the boat, have it ready to move. I'll see to the girl myself."

"I don't like it," Curly said nervously. "It's not what we planned."

"You don't have to like it," growled Dino. "Just keep boat going."

"But do you mean," Curly asked Paxton, "we take *both* of them up to Thousand Islands?"

"Why not? The place is big enough."

"But we don't want *him*."

"Might have rich father," said Dino. "Hey, Pax, how about that?"

"We'll see," said Paxton. "But anyway, he's got to come with us. We can't turn him loose now, and we can't leave him behind—not unless we bury him."

There was no change in his tone of voice as he said that, and there was none in Dino's as the latter answered, almost jovially:

"We could do that. . . . How you with a spade, Curly?"

"That's enough of that!" said Curly fearfully. "You both promised——"

"All right," said Paxton, cutting it short. "He goes with us. He needn't give us any trouble. It's just too bad he came along, that's all. Too bad for him." He raised his binoculars again, taking a last look at the launch, now a small white dot on the wide surface of the lake. "This isn't going to change anything. We'll give them half an hour, like we planned. Then we'll get going."

"But you can't really believe that!" said Ellen scornfully. "It's so—" she realized that she had been overworking the word "feeble" recently, and she changed the adjective at the last moment: "—it's so *useless*. Even if there's no more war there'll always be competition in the world. Especially in America. You've got to join in. Otherwise you'll be left behind."

"I don't mind being left behind," said Greg Perring.

"But you compete in your job, don't you?"

"On the contrary," he answered, annoyingly like a school-master, "scientific research is a matter of teamwork and nothing else. I don't want to get *ahead* of Martin and Sep Johannsen and the others. I just want to work with them."

"But you still want your team to be the best team."

"Certainly."

"There you are, then. That's competition."

"But it's not personal competition," he insisted. He saw a frown cross her face as she lay gracefully relaxed in the sunshine, and he added: "It's no good, Ellen. I just don't believe in fighting, kicking the ladder away, anything like that. That's what's wrong with the world nowadays. Too much scrapping and snarling, not enough sharing and helping. I can't change that feeling. It's part of me. It's the way I am."

She dribbled some sand between her slim fingers. "Wouldn't you fight for me?" she asked.

"There's no reason why that should ever be necessary. This isn't a jungle. Not unless we make it so."

86

"Well, just so long as I know."

Presently, to bridge a silence in danger of becoming awkward, he raised himself on one elbow and looked about him. A few feet away the water lapped against the stern of their boat; the small beach on which they were lying was peaceful and deserted, and the view of the lake was magical. But then he noticed that their peace was going to be threatened.

"Darn it!" he said suddenly. "There's another boat coming."

"Why does that matter?" she asked wilfully.

"I wanted you to myself."

"Why, Greg Perring! Isn't that competing? Don't you want to share me with everyone else in the whole wide world?"

"You know I don't."

He watched the intruding motor-launch nose its way inshore, grounding on the beach a few feet from their own boat. There were three men in it; when it reached the shallows two of them—the two tallest—got out, and waded the last few feet ashore. One was dark and fattish, the other lean; they were both curiously purposeful.

"They're coming to speak to us," said Greg, annoyed.

Without opening her eyes, Ellen said: "Don't forget that we are all brothers."

When he was still twenty yards away, the lean man called out: "Have you folks got any gas to spare?"

"Sorry," said Greg. "We've only——"

"It doesn't matter," said the lean man. Suddenly he and his companion were standing right over them, hands deep in their pockets. "We don't need any."

As in a dream, Greg watched the two guns come out. The lean man was staring down at them with wolfish eyes; the fat one was smiling, not pleasantly.

"Ellen!" Greg shouted out, in anguished warning.

"Stand up!" commanded Paxton. "Both of you. But nice and slow. My friend is impetuous, and I"—his gun-muzzle dropped, to point directly at Ellen's horrified face—"I am just a bundle of nerves."

Taken by surprise, they could do nothing; the fantastic dream continued, but swiftly it assumed an ugly air.

"Stand up!" repeated Paxton to the girl. The gun in his

hand did not waver; seen from the ground on which she lay, he looked enormous and coldly menacing. "Both of you. Get moving!"

"But this is ridiculous——" began Greg Perring, and then broke off with a cry of pain as Dino stepped forward and kicked him viciously on the knee-cap.

"Didn't you hear?" asked the Italian roughly. "He said to stand up. He meant it."

They both got to their feet. On Ellen's face amazement struggled with a growing fear. "My father," she began, and stopped, more fearful than ever. The buttressed world of John Harper Harrison seemed very far away at that moment. Instead she turned to Greg Perring. "Greg!" she called out. "Do something!"

"Don't do something, Greg," said Paxton with horrible familiarity. "It might be the wrong thing. Just start walking towards the water."

"You must be crazy," answered Greg bravely. "I'll do nothing of the kind. You can't get away with this, whatever it is." He looked out across the lake; there were no boats near, no help on hand; it was part of the hideous dream that they were isolated, trapped, naked to their enemies. "You must be crazy," he repeated. "What is it you want—money?"

Dino stepped up to him again. With one hand he grasped his shirt collar, with the other—fleshy, powerful—he gave him a brutal slap across the mouth. As Greg fell back holding a bleeding lip:

"Time you learnt take orders," said Dino.

Paxton, looking at the girl, said almost conversationally: "I'd hate to have to do that to you. But that wouldn't stop me."

Ellen stared back, torn between her fear and a fiery disgust.

"You brutes!" she said savagely. "You filthy low-down ——Greg! Hit him back! You're taller than he is! He's just a fat greasy——"

"He's got a gun," said Greg, mumbling between thickened lips.

"He wouldn't dare use it. You know what these cheap gangsters are. Hit him."

"Lady," said Dino, "I throw away my gun and still

murder your boy-friend. And then"—he leered—"I start on you."

"It's no good, Ellen," said Greg.

"Spoken like a man," said Paxton. "A sensible man, but a man at that."

"What is it you want?" asked Ellen.

"You," answered Paxton. "You and lover-boy. In that boat." He pointed to the launch. "Now let's cut out the conversation and start moving."

The launch had a small cabin, not much more than a box under the foredeck, and in this Ellen Harper Harrison and Greg Perring lay for more than seven weary, fearful hours, while the boat sped westwards, first into the afternoon sun, then through the long twilight, then stealthily in the darkness. Sometimes they moved swiftly, and the engine noise in the confined space beat mercilessly on their eardrums. Sometimes there were long silences as they went through the locks, broken by footsteps, shouts to and from the shore, and the thud of ropes falling on the deck overhead. They did not talk: fear and shame seemed to divide them; and they did not cry out, even when they had the chance. Dino had warned them of this, peering down into the cabin.

"You make noise, be the last noise you make," he said as they were approaching the first lock. With the point of his pistol he touched Ellen's shoulder; it was like some grotesque, horrible caress. "Just remember that."

"Leave her alone," said Greg, rising on one elbow. "We won't call out."

"Smart boy," said Dino.

The cramped cabin had a small porthole, and through it Greg watched their progress as long as the light lasted; past Ile Perrot at the head of the lake, up the long stretch to Cornwall and the giant Seaway operations, then more slowly as the river narrowed and the successive rapids forced them to take the canal-and-lock system. Greg knew it well; he had been born in a small St Lawrence River town; he loved it as one of the most beautiful parts of Canada. To see it now in these brutal circumstances was specially unnerving.

His knee had swollen and stiffened; his lip hurt abominably; he was ashamed of himself, and mortally afraid for Ellen. This was a kidnapping, obviously; it must have been planned weeks ahead, and two of the three men looked as though they would stop at nothing. (His mind registered automatically that the third man, whom they called Curly, was of a different metal; a weak point in the team, maybe— but the team was defeatingly strong anyway. . . .) He blamed himself for not doing more, not doing *anything*, when the thing first started; but how did you call for help when the nearest human being was five miles away, how did you make a move with a gun at your ribs, how did you argue with an armed man? Ellen had said: "Do something!" (he recalled the shameful moment). Perhaps another sort of man would have "done something". As for him, he was not that kind of man—perhaps, as she had said, he was not a man at all—and as a result the two of them were in mortal peril, and Ellen worst of all.

He turned over, sick at heart, and lay down again as the boat gathered speed and the noise of the engine mounted intolerably, thudding deep within his brain.

Towards ten o'clock their speed slowed down as if they were approaching another lock, or feeling their way along a difficult channel. Greg Perring peered through the port-hole again, but he could see nothing except distant shore lights. The engine slowed further, and then cut out; there was a gentle bump against the hull, and then the cabin door was pulled open, and Dino's voice said:

"Get moving!"

They crawled out awkwardly, cramped from long in-action, stiff and cold in their thin sports clothes. Greg looked round him cautiously, trying not to attract attention. The boat was alongside a small jetty: in the moonlight he had a glimpse of a house, a house which seemed to be surrounded by water, before Dino pushed him roughly in the ribs and said: "Out, you! And no tricks."

Paxton led the way: Ellen and Greg followed him: Dino and Curly Bates formed the rearguard. A rough stone path led to the front door of an unlighted house. Paxton unlocked it and they walked through, still in darkness.

Paxton said: "Draw the curtains, Curly," and when this had been done he clicked the light switch.

They might have been anywhere, thought Greg. It was a summertime sort of room—shabby cane furniture, rough-cast walls, a staircase leading to a wooden gallery above. It had the look of a hunting cabin or a summer cottage. The lights were dim, the windows thickly curtained.

"All right," said Paxton. He sat down heavily in an armchair and expelled a long breath. Then he looked at Ellen. "This is it, and you'd better make the best of it. We didn't expect the boy-friend, but there's lots of room. If you both behave yourselves there'll be no trouble. If you try to make a break it'll be just too bad."

"What's going to happen?" asked Ellen. In spite of herself she was trembling, her whole body desperately cold.

"You're on an island," Paxton went on as if he had not heard her. "A small island, just about the size of this house. The mainland is two or three miles away, whichever way you look. There's no telephone. The boat has been padlocked. Your windows are boarded up. There wouldn't be anybody to wave to, anyway."

"But what's going to happen?" asked Ellen again. "What do you want?"

"Half a million dollars," said Paxton.

"From my father?"

"Right."

"You'll never get away with it," said Greg.

"That'll be too bad for both of you. . . . I've written him a note. You're an educated guy," Paxton said ironically to Greg. "What do you think of this?" He drew a piece of paper from his pocket, and read: "*We have your girl. She is still alive. We will tell you what to do.*"

"Short and sweet," said Dino in the silence that followed. "When will you send it, Pax?"

"Two or three days. We'll let him sweat first."

"Well, now we know," said John Harper Harrison.

He faced the policeman across the broad table in *Shearwater*'s main cabin. He was not the man he had been a week earlier; he seemed to have shrunk—in stature, in confidence, and in strength. It had been, for him, a horrible week, the worst he could ever remember. The finding of the abandoned boat three miles up the lake had posed fearful questions, and a yet more fearful uncertainty. Anything might have happened, from a drowning to an elopement; the glare of publicity ('Ten Million Dollar Princess Vanishes') had been especially hard to endure, though the newspapers had been helpful, and the concern of strangers was kindly meant.

But now he had the answer, perhaps the worst answer of all the ones he had imagined. It lay on the table between himself and the local police-sergeant, the letter which said:

We have your girl. She is still alive. We will tell you what to do.

"Postmark Montreal," said the police-sergeant presently. He was a quiet man, a slow-talking French-Canadian who had spent a lot of time with John Harper Harrison during the past week. The latter, used to a more forceful, higher-pressure version of the arm of the law, had found him vaguely irritating. The guy needed a shot in the arm, or maybe a bomb under his desk.... "That doesn't help us very much."

"Well, it's a start," said Harrison. A week ago he would have been striding about, banging the table, telephoning, making the biggest possible scene. Now he sat still, unhappy and afraid. "What's the next move?"

"We examine this," answered the sergeant after a pause. He pointed to the letter. "I will submit it to the Bureau. Then we look for suspicious characters in the area."

"But she may be hundreds of miles away, probably in the States," objected Harrison. "This should go to the FBI straight away."

"A crime committed on Canadian soil——" began the sergeant.

"To hell with the protocol!" said Harrison in something like his old manner. "I want my girl back. I want this to be handled properly!" He caught the policeman's eye. "Look, I know you'll do your best. But this is a kidnapping! It's a federal offence, or whatever you'd call it here."

"A Criminal Code offence, applicable to all the provinces," said the policeman formally.

"Well then, what about it? Can't you call in the FBI? What's the set-up here?"

"We have the local police, here at Dorval. We have the Quebec Provincial Police, of whom I am one. And we have the RCMP."

"The Mounties?" inquired Harrison doubtfully. "Red Coats? Horses? We could use something a bit more up-to-date."

On the policeman's face provincial pride struggled with

national honour. "You will find," he said at length, "the RCMP are sufficiently modern."

"And they cover the whole country like the FBI?"

"Yes."

"OK. Call them in."

"The Provincial Police——"

"Look," said Harrison again, "I want all the help I can get, and I want proper advice—whether to tell the newspapers, whether to pay up when these gangsters ask for it, whether we want to set a trap for them. Most of all, I want my daughter back. If it costs a million dollars, it costs a million dollars."

"That is a huge sum."

"I haven't another daughter," said Harrison. "And I'm quite sure they know it."

The RCMP sergeant, a tough and trim figure in brown instead of the expected scarlet ("That's mostly ceremonial," he said in explanation) came straight to the point.

"Firstly, Mr Harrison," he said, "I suggest that you don't tell the newspapers about this letter right now. There may be a time for that later, but at this point we want to do our planning under cover. I take it that you'll co-operate."

"Sure, I'll co-operate."

"I mean," said the sergeant, giving him a close look, "you'll do what we suggest, and *no more*. If you've got any ideas about paying up without telling us, better let me know now. Then we don't get the wires crossed."

"I want my daughter back."

"Sure. *We* want her back just as much, but we want to catch these birds as well. If you try to handle it in a different way than us, without telling us, someone's liable to get hurt."

"You mean Ellen?"

"Yes sir."

"All right. I'll work with you."

"I'd like that to be a promise, sir."

John Harper Harrison looked at him, ready to flare up. But the sergeant was not an impressionable sort of man. "You have my word," he said at last.

"Thank you, Mr Harrison. . . . Now then, this young man she's with"—he looked at his notebook—"Greg Perring.

93

What do you know about him? Is it conceivable that he could be one of the gang?"

Harrison shook his head. "I hadn't thought of it, which is probably the best answer I could give you. No, he's a decent young chap. I'd trust him. He's a research scientist with Baker Steel."

"What sort of work?"

"I gather it's classified. Wouldn't that mean you'd have a security check on him somewhere?"

The sergeant nodded, and made a note. "That simplifies things. . . . Who else have you got on board here?"

"Skipper and engineer. They've both been with me more than five years. I'd trust them too. And Joe—he's the steward. Joaquin something, his real name is. He's new this year. He's my houseboy at home."

"What's he like? I'm asking this because these people obviously knew your daughter's movements, and the boat's movements as well. They couldn't do all that just by watching—a boat is too mobile. They're likely to have a contact on board, or in your office if you keep in touch all the time."

"I keep in touch," said Harrison ironically. "Well, he's just Joe. A Mexican. Good boy. A bit shifty—but maybe that's my prejudice." He frowned suddenly. "You know, you might have something there. He *has* asked a couple of times when we were due to sail—that sort of thing. Said he had to buy stores—which is true. But now I think of it——"

"Let's take a look at Joe," said the RCMP sergeant.

It was a model cross-examination: concise, subtle, not unduly prolonged, but with just enough menace in it to hammer Joaquin Barzan right into the ground. He was a terrified man to start with—that much was evident, and it gave the sergeant the start he needed. Within a few moments he had established—without any room for contradiction, any possibility of doubt—that Joaquin Barzan was in the biggest mess of his life. The rest was easy. Joe broke in just under an hour.

"Penalty for kidnapping, life imprisonment," said the RCMP sergeant, ice in his voice, towards the end. "Penalty for conspiracy to kidnap, or acting as an accessory before or after the fact, the same. . . . Come on, Joe—they've left you holding the baby, and you'll wind up in jail with the kid in your arms. Do you think they're going to send you your cut? You must be nuts! You'll never hear from them again. How much did they promise you, anyway?"

Joaquin Barzan stared ahead of him, miserable and afraid. It was true what the policeman said—Paxton and Dino and Curly (yes, even Curly) treated him like dirt, and now they were far away, and he would never get a penny from all this trouble. They had tricked him, and this policeman knew everything, and he would go to prison for ever. He swallowed, and in swallowing gulped down bitter defeat as well. But he could still show them.

"They promise fifty thousand dollar," he whispered.

John Harper Harrison jumped to his feet, his fist clenched. "You dirty double-crossing son of a——"

The sergeant held up a commanding hand. "Just a minute, sir. He's all that, and more, but in a thing like this time is important." He stood up, towering over a trembling Joe. "All right—let's have it. Where are they?"

Joe swallowed again. "You let me go?"

"Talk first," said the sergeant. "I'm making no promises at all."

"Thousand Islands," said Joe.

"Whereabouts in the Thousand Islands?"

"I don't know," said Joe—and he sounded truthful. "One of them, I guess. They didn't tell me which."

"But it's a house on one of the islands?"

"It's a house, yes."

John Harper Harrison said: "Well, that narrows it down a bit."

"It narrows it down," said the RCMP sergeant, "to the Thousand Islands. And that's not so hot as a label, either. At the last count there were over seventeen hundred of them."

Ten days in the shuttered, curtained house had taken toll of all the five people imprisoned there. Between captives and captors, indeed, the line of demarcation was as thin as a nerve-string. They were tied to each other by fear and hatred; not one of the five was free from the peril of making a false step, not one of them looked forward to a new morning with new hope.

Ellen was mutinous, but she dared not go too far. She

vented her discontent only upon Greg Perring, charging him
with cowardice, indecision, ineptitude—all the sins in the
North American calendar. He made allowances, for he
knew both her fear and his own hesitation. To all her com-
plaints he would answer: "Wait, honey—something is bound
to happen." Himself he reassured by saying: "I am thinking
and watching all the time." It was true enough but it did not
pay him much of a dividend, even in the realm of self-
respect.

Paxton, who had planned this thing meticulously and
warily, had not realized how difficult it would be to keep his
team together. Curly Bates was dependable, but he was
getting jittery. Tinkering with the motor-boat engine, he
did the same small job time and time again, and still returned within a few hours to do it all afresh. Moreover, he
was discontented with his role; he felt himself to be the chore-
boy of the team; he did all the cooking, with singular ill-
grace; he had driven three hundred miles, to Montreal and
back, to pick up their car and to post the ransom note, and
he knew he must repeat the journey before long.

He quarrelled incessantly over his division of labour with
Dino—Dino the indolent and complacent, who felt himself
above such routine work but who, seeking an outlet for his
energies, began to give them trouble of a special sort.

It was a point which Greg made to Ellen late one night
when they were reviewing their situation. Their moods,
dictated by her, varied from day to day. Sometimes the two
of them were divided by silence, sitting mute and apart in
their locked room. Sometimes they clung to each other in a
loving, simple hunger for comfort.

"Those three are all so different," said Greg on this
occasion. "Paxton is a real lone wolf, cunning and stone-cold.
Dino is just the opposite—a gorilla, a coarse sensual animal.
Poor old Curly is a sort of old-maid office boy around the
place. I don't know how he got into this act, but I'll bet he's
sorry now. He's the weak point in the trio."

Ellen tossed back her hair irritably. "All right—so they're
all different. Where does that get us?"

Greg grinned ruefully. "Sorry, honey. This is just the
egghead approach. But since they're so different, they're
bound to disagree. Perhaps they might quarrel seriously.
It's really our only hope."

"But is that all we're going to do—just wait and see what happens?"

"We haven't much choice."

"Well, I hope my father is a bit more enterprising."

Greg said, almost to himself: "Of course, we might help it along a bit."

The next time Curly Bates brought up their food, Greg told him: "I want to see Paxton."

"Oh, do you?" Curly sniffed. "What about?"

"I don't like the way Dino's always hanging about this room, unlocking the door and looking in all the time."

"What do you mean?"

"You know what I mean," answered Greg. "Let me speak to Paxton."

"You won't get much change out of him."

But Curly must have spoken to Paxton, perhaps with some spirit, because he came upstairs within half an hour.

"What's this about Dino?" he demanded. He stood framed in the doorway, a tall figure, remote, dangerous. "What are you beefing about?"

"The idea is kidnapping, isn't it?" said Greg. He spoke in very measured tones, as if reviewing a friend's problem in a helpful spirit. "Miss Harrison's father will pay up, and she'll be able to go home?"

"That's the general idea."

"Is it Dino's idea too?"

"What do you mean? I'm dealing this hand."

"We see a lot of Dino," said Greg. "Too much. He's always in and out of here. He seems to take a special interest in Miss Harrison."

"So what?"

"How does that fit in with your plans? Or don't you care what happens to her?"

"What the hell are you talking about?"

Greg looked at him. "If that Italian Peeping Tom has his way, he's going to complicate things. Or was it your idea? Was that to be part of his cut?"

Paxton stared back at him, ice-cold, halfway to anger. "I don't operate that way. No one here operates that way. We had to rough you up a little—it was a pleasure, as Dino would say—I don't like snotty kids any more than he does—but as far as the girl is concerned——"

His voice tailed off, and Greg said very quietly: "It would bear watching."

Dino played into their hands; perhaps he was ordained by fate to do so. Twice during the next day he unlocked the door of their room, and stood talking, or staring at Ellen. Each time Greg waited a few moments, and then called out in an urgent voice to Paxton or Curly, and Paxton shouted an order from the room below, and Dino shuffled out, angry and humiliated. Then it happened the third time, and the third time was the last time.

This time he was drunk (there was liquor in the house and not much else to do but drink it). He came in as usual, and stood lolling in the doorway. Ellen was lying on her bed, ignoring him, reading an old newspaper. Presently Dino said:

"You very pretty girl."

"Cut it out, Dino," said Greg, rather more loudly than necessary.

"Shut your trap!" returned Dino angrily. "You get in my hair, I cut you up good."

"Leave the girl alone," said Greg, again raising his voice.

"I no touch the girl," said Dino. He sidled forward, his feet slurring on the rough boards. "But I like to. . . . What you say, Ellen? Pretty girl, nothing to do? You like talk to Dino?"

He was standing over the bed, rocking slightly. Ellen, not looking at him, only half attending, was startled to hear Greg say, in a low violent whisper:

"Scream!"

She dropped the newspaper. "What?"

He said again, in a taut voice she had never heard before: "Do as I say! Scream! Top of your lungs!"

It was a very creditable scream; it rang through the old house, stirring the rafters. Dino fell back, foolish and astonished. Swift footsteps sounded on the stairs, and Paxton appeared at the doorway, shouldering his way past Dino.

"What goes on?" he demanded.

Greg was on his feet, pointing at Dino, simulating an extreme horrified anger.

"It's this man," he said, his voice trembling. "This filthy gorilla! He tried to—my God, don't you know what's going on round here? Get him out of here!"

Paxton swung round. "What's going on, Dino? Didn't I tell you——"

"I no do nothing," said Dino stupidly. He backed away out of the doorway, on to the wooden balcony. "I speak to her, she scream." Then he seemed to pull himself together, and he stepped forward again, facing Paxton, his face sulky and determined. "I talk to her if I want."

"You leave her alone," said Paxton in a quick furious temper. "I've told you, you'll spoil everything, you dirty——"

Instead of finishing the sentence, he raised both his hands, and pushed Dino in the chest. It was meant to propel Dino out of the room again, but Paxton was tense and on edge, and Dino was tottering drunk, and the push was decisive. Dino staggered back, hit the low balcony rail, and toppled over. He fell ten feet in a curving arc, and landed with a horrible cracking crunch on the tiled hallway below. The angle at which his head took the floor could only have meant a death sentence.

From the cellar below them came the rhythmical sound of digging—the scrape of metal on hard-packed earth, the noise of soil loosely thrown aside, the sound of a foot keeping up a regular, forceful beat. Curly Bates, whom Dino had once asked: "Are you any good with a spade?" was now giving him a sardonic, workmanlike answer.

"I could listen to that for ever," said Greg Perring.

Alone of the three in the untidy sitting-room, he seemed at ease. He sat on a sofa beside Ellen. Paxton faced them in an armchair, a gun resting in his lap. Paxton was still tense, though he made an effort to disguise it. An observant student of behaviour might have deduced a good deal from the crossing and uncrossing of his legs, the slight twitch at the mouth, the restless eyes. From the complete picture of a strong man in full command, something had been stolen, and more still was leaking away below the surface of self-control.

Ellen was badly shaken. Things had moved too fast for her during the past few hours; it was as if the prolonged nervous strain of their confinement had suddenly flowered into a distraught confusion. At times it seemed as if Dino had actually been threatening her, and that Paxton, and not her natural guardian Greg Perring, had come to the rescue. She could not forget the way Dino had suddenly disappeared off the balcony, as though wiped out with a sponge, and the horrible sound of his fall. . . . Greg's easy confidence seemed, in the circumstances, a purely provocative piece of acting.

Now she spoke her mind, though her mind was far from clear.

"I know you can listen, all right, Greg," she said sullenly. "But that isn't much of a contribution, is it? You needn't sound so pleased with yourself."

"Oh, I'm not pleased with myself," answered Greg. His voice was careless and light. "Not yet. But we *are* making progress."

"Is that so?" growled Paxton.

"I should think it's obvious."

"It's not obvious to me," said Ellen. She suddenly burst out, nervous and strident. "Oh, don't be such a—a *brain*! You weren't so quick on the ball when that horrible man tried to attack me. No, that took guts!"

Paxton inclined his head. "Thank you, ma'am. Luckily, I have brains as well."

"Oh, I wouldn't say that," said Greg Perring, as if they were discussing a third person whose feelings need not be spared. "After all, it did happen, didn't it?"

"All right, big shot," said Paxton. "Tell us about it." His eyes blinked, and he shifted his gun from one thigh to the other. "Tell us how the All-Canadian boy wonder saved the day."

Greg gestured expansively. "If I had interfered," he said, "Dino would probably have killed me. So I got you to do the work instead. That made your team one short—one out of three. The odds are levelling out."

"Tell me more," said Paxton. If he had looked more sure of himself, the irony would have been successful; but the three words came out almost as a plea for information. "What happens next?"

"I'll tell you," said Greg Perring. Out of sight his hand was lightly pressing Ellen's wrist, asking for patience, asking for control. "This thing is a problem, almost a scientific problem. You have to state it, and then you have to find the answer." His voice, measured and detached, was well calculated to induce the utmost irritation. "Your team is starting to fall apart already. Originally there was Dino, Curly, and you. You killed Dino for us—and don't think I'm not grateful. Curly is next. Curly scares easily. You've noticed it? So I'll try to scare him. You'll probably scare him yourself, accidentally, because you can't help doing it. But either way, he'll be scared. If you let him loose he'll certainly break. If you keep him here, you're isolated—you can't buy as much as a pack of cigarettes unless you go yourself. And there's much more than a pack of cigarettes to be bought, isn't there?—There's another ransom note to be delivered or mailed. You can't go yourself, because Curly can be trusted here even less than outside. Therefore Curly will have to go. That will be the last you'll see of him. That will leave you."

Paxton was staring at him, held by the calm voice, wanting above everything to shout him down, aware of the futility of doing so. "Let's hear what you're going to do to me."

"I'll think of something," said Greg coolly. "There's a weapon to be used against every kind of animal."

Paxton swore at him crudely and coarsely, and then pulled himself together and said in a level voice: "You annoy me, lover-boy."

"Be careful," said Greg Perring. "That might be the weapon."

Back in their room, Ellen clung to him. "Greg, you're being wonderful! I've suddenly realized. I think I'm falling in love with you all over again."

He smoothed her hair. "I'm bound to say I hadn't noticed it."

"I'm sorry. . . . I'm all mixed up. I feel so tired all of a sudden. But I do love you. What can I do to help?"

"Keep your nerve," answered Greg. "This is just a chess game, a needling match. We're going to win it."

"How can you be so sure?"

"Brains," said Greg, touching her forehead, and then his own. "Brains. Man's answer to the ape." He cocked his head towards a footstep on the stair. "That's Curly now. Time to go to work again."

"What shall I do?"

"Look sorry for him."

Curly Bates came in carrying a tray. A revolver protruded awkwardly from his belt; it gave him an inappropriately raffish air, like a bad stage pirate who should really have been playing the comic ship's cook. He put down the tray without his usual greeting, and turned to go.

"Well, Curly," said Greg softly. "Been doing a little digging?"

Curly Bates said nothing.

"What's the matter, Curly? Aren't we friends any more? You could use a friend, you know—the spot you're in."

Curly Bates turned, a hunted expression on his face. Then he kicked the door shut furtively, as if concealing the action even from himself, and spoke almost in a whisper:

"Pax said I wasn't to talk. . . . What do you mean, I could use a friend?"

"You've been doing a little grave-digging?" repeated Greg.

"You know dam' well I have."

"How many for? One or two?"

Curly stared at him, uncomprehending. "One, of course. Poor old Dino. What are you getting at?"

"So far, one grave is enough. But that still leaves two of you."

"All the bigger share," said Curly jauntily.

"Sure. But who gets the biggest share of all?"

"It's Pax and me now. Equal shares."

"The one that gets the biggest share," said Greg, "is the one that's left."

"Poor Curly," said Ellen.

Curly Bates started. He looked from one to the other, his eyes flickering. "Pax wouldn't do that," he whispered hoarsely. "That thing that happened to Dino was an accident. You saw it."

"I saw it happen," said Greg. "It might be that Paxton is what they call accident-prone. Accidents to other people."

"He wouldn't do that to me," said Curly again.

With perfect timing the door burst open, and Paxton stormed in. He was shaking with anger, and with something else.

"Curly!" he shouted. "You disobey orders again and I'll finish you off for good!"

"I was only——" began Curly.

"Cut it out!" said Paxton, nearly screaming. "There's a boat coming—a big launch. Get these two down in the cellar. Tie them up. Gag them. Do it good, or I'll sink an axe in your head! Then come up and help me out. It may be just strangers snooping about. But we can't take chances. Now get going!"

As Ellen and Greg came out on to the landing—covered by two guns, closely shepherded by their gaolers—they heard for the first time the approaching, steady snarl of a big engine.

The RCMP corporal in charge of the forty-nine-foot patrol boat prided himself on his ship-handling. He had served five years in the war-time Navy, and while he subscribed to the biblical canon that the RCMP could do anything on God's green earth, he retained a private conviction that a bit of sea-time never hurt anyone, whether he were a policeman or not. He brought the powerful cruiser round in a broad swirling sweep against the swift St Lawrence current, edging as near as the depth of water allowed to the island they were making for; and then, at the word of command, the smaller power-boat was launched from a ramp at the stern, and sped off towards its target.

The whole manœuvre, conducted while the parent ship was still moving at twenty knots, was the corporal's pride and joy. As usual, it went like clockwork—RCMP clockwork, with just that touch of naval know-how which distinguished sailors from people.

In the smaller boat, an outboard-launch now making a beeline for the island ahead, sat the RCMP sergeant who had first interviewed John Harper Harrison, down at Dorval. He had been seconded for this systematic search duty, and he had been on it now for ten weary days. The island ahead was simply the next island on the list—a list compiled with the help of real-estate agents, scores of interviews with residents, and local gossip, and comprising every single property in the Thousand Islands area which had been rented to anyone during the last twelve months. The total was one hundred and thirty. The house he was now approaching was the eighty-fourth.

As a CIB sergeant, he had learned in a hard school that the work was not glamorous, nor did it involve the steel-sharp application of brilliant deductive powers. It was for the most part simply eliminative leg-work. This present case was a good example, and already he had had enough of it. He had interviewed scores of people, ranging from writers who had rented island properties in order to get away from it all (and who didn't in the least appreciate official interruption), to daydreaming honeymoon couples who appreciated it even less. The result so far had been a complete blank. None of the eighty-odd island houses looked anything like a criminal hide-out; and none of the people, whether normal or not, had betrayed guilt or embarrassment of the sort he was looking for.

He was beginning to suspect that Joaquin Barzan might be wrong. The rest of his gang might have lied to him, or the hide-out might be on one of the river banks, not on an island. Or it might not be rented at all, but belong to a long-term resident who had taken to crime. Or to a long-term resident who was himself being held captive. Or it might be abandoned and empty (there were quite a lot like that), in which case he would have to compile a whole new list.

There were a lot of angles; and meantime the case was nearly a fortnight old, the newspapers and the public were getting restive, and the Commissioner, reacting in an entirely human way to John Harper Harrison's platinum-edged prestige, was beginning to send lengthy mimeographed messages starting: 'It is not understood . . .'

The sergeant sighed. To the constable at the helm he said: "There's a wooden dock there, round at the side. Must be someone at home. There's a motor-boat alongside."

As the launch slowed the sergeant looked up at the house. There was nothing to distinguish it from the other eighty-three houses, except that all the curtains were drawn.

Through a slim gap in the sitting-room curtains, Paxton watched the police boat approach. The sight of the two uniformed figures disturbed him, just as the launching manœuvre—the big boat dropping the small one with such neat dispatch—had started a train of uneasy thoughts. It was a good deal too efficient for his comfort. . . . The last twenty-four hours had been very bad ones. Dino's death, Greg Perring's expert needling, Curly's wavering support, all had made their mark on his confidence. He recalled Greg's crack about the team falling apart. And now here were the police on his own front doorstep, at a crucial moment of an operation which he had meant to keep far under cover.

As he watched, the pencil-thin shaft of sunlight coming through the curtains fell on a face deeply lined, set in a harsh mask of tension. He was ready to fight, but the battleground seemed suddenly to have shifted under his feet.

He turned as Curly came up behind him. "Well?" he asked brusquely.

"All done, Pax," said Curly. "They can't move. I used that insulating tape for the gags."

"OK."

Curly peered through the curtains. "Who is it, anyway?"

"The police."

"Cripes!" Curly was visibly shaken. "What do we do?"

"Nothing. We let them do it. We haven't anything to worry about."

"But why are they here?"

"Guesswork," said Paxton. "They'll go away again. Just give the right answers." He stared hard at Curly. "And don't try anything funny."

"You know me, Pax."

"That's what I'm afraid of."

The knock on the front door sounded very loud in the stillness.

Curly said, nervously: "Why don't we just not answer?"

"The boat, stupid," said Paxton. "He knows there's someone here."

At the opened door, Paxton nodded to the sergeant and said:

"Yeah?"

"Good morning, sir," said the sergeant, for the eighty-fourth time. "I'm making a routine check on some of the houses hereabouts."

"What's the trouble?"

"No trouble," said the sergeant. "Just routine. Can I come in?"

"I guess so," answered Paxton with an ill grace. He led the way into the curtained sitting-room.

"You must like it dark," observed the sergeant.

"We overslept."

The sergeant glanced at his watch. It was half-past two. "You sure did."

Curly stepped forward from the shadows. "Hallo," he said awkwardly. "I'll let a bit of light in."

Dust fell thickly from the curtains as he drew them back. It hung inexorably in the sunlight, making the unkempt room shabbier still.

"That's better," said the sergeant. He turned to face them. "Can I have the names, for a start?"

"I'm Barber," said Paxton. It was the name in which he had rented the house. "This is Phillips."

"Been here long?"

"Couple of months."

"Canadian citizens?"

"American."

"Where did you cross the border?"

"Thousand Islands Bridge. . . . What is this, anyway?"

"We're checking the area," said the sergeant curtly. "Are you here on holiday?"

Paxton simply nodded, but Curly volunteered: "Doing a bit of fishing."

"Is that so?" asked the sergeant. "How are they running?"

"Pretty good."

"Any goldeye?"

"A few," said Curly.

"You're lucky," said the sergeant. He glanced round the room. On the table was a litter of cups and dishes, and on one side of it a tray set for two people. "Anyone else in the house?"

"No," said Paxton.

"You're a bit behind with the washing-up," said the sergeant.

"You know how it is on holiday," said Curly ingratiatingly. "Things pile up."

"I guess so. . . . How long are you staying?"

"Month, maybe," answered Paxton.

"That's a good long holiday."

"We like it here."

"We're glad to have you," said the sergeant. He looked round the room again listening to the absolute stillness all over the house. He had the impression that the other two were listening to it also. A board creaked somewhere, and Curly Bates began to whistle loudly and tunelessly.

"Well," said the sergeant. "That's about it. I'll get going."

"Good luck with it," said Curly.

"Thanks," answered the sergeant. Now he was almost affable; for some reason it was much less reassuring than his earlier curtness. "Same to you with the fishing. *And* the washing-up."

"You crazy fool!" stormed Paxton furiously. "What did you open the curtains for? Didn't you see the dust come off them? He must have known they hadn't been touched for days."

"It looked so funny," said Curly, "the lights on when it was daylight outside."

"It looked funnier still the way you played it." He stared viciously at Curly Bates. "And what was that about fishing? Why did you have to make such a production out of it?"

"I was just talking."

"I told you *not* to talk. . . . What was that fish he mentioned?"

"Search me! Gold something or other."

"But you said you caught it!" shouted Paxton in renewed fury. "It's probably something that stays a thousand miles from here! Haven't you any sense at all? He was just testing you out."

"Seems I can't do a thing right," said Curly sullenly.

"Dam' right you can't. . . . And all that about the dishes." He mimicked, savagely: " 'You know how it is. They *do* pile up. . . .' What do you think you are? An old woman gabbing over the back fence?"

"Why don't you leave me alone?" said Curly between a whine and an angry retort. "Always picking on me. . . . What's it matter about the dishes, anyway?"

"It matters because——" Paxton's eyes had gone round involuntarily to the table, and on the instant he stopped, drawing in his breath with a sharp hiss. "It matters more than a pinhead like you could ever guess!" he said, with sudden startling venom. *"Did you put that tray there?"*

"Of course I put it there. I brought it down when we——"

"That's what the cop saw," said Paxton almost to himself. "A separate tray, set for two people. . . .'

"Gee, Pax," said Curly, alarmed at his tone, "I didn't realize—I didn't think——"

Paxton's eyes came round to Curly again. There was evil

hatred in them. "I could just pull a gun and plug you, here and now."

"Leave me alone!" said Curly shrilly, backing away. "The kid said this would happen."

Paxton advanced on him. "What do you mean by that, you dope?"

"You got rid of Dino, didn't you? And now you're fixing to get rid of me."

With an enormous effort of self-control, the sweat suddenly standing out on his forehead, Paxton pulled himself up. Greg Perring had been right—the team *was* falling apart, and he could not afford to let the process go a single inch further. It appalled him to think that, in blind rage, he had been about to hit Curly Bates, whip him till he was senseless, even shoot him as he had threatened. If that had happened he would truly have been alone, and the game would have been over and the whole project lying in ruins.

He sat down, and momentarily covered his face with his hands. It had come down to this: Curly Bates was a hopeless fool, but Curly Bates was all he had.

After a moment, he said: "Sorry, Curly—forget it."

"Well——" said Curly uncertainly, still injured and uneasy.

"Forget it," repeated Paxton. "We've got to work this out."

"Do you really think," Curly ventured presently, "that the copper noticed anything?"

"Maybe not." Paxton wanted to believe that with all his heart. "That tray could have been for you and me, I suppose. . . . We've got to go ahead, anyway. No sense in just sitting here. You'd better deliver the second note, like we planned."

"When?"

"Tonight."

"Well——" said Curly again.

"What's the sense in waiting? If the police are on to us we'll find out soon enough. If we're still clear, the quicker we get this over with the better. Longer we stay here, the more attention we attract."

"Reckon that's true."

"You better pull out tonight, as soon as it's dark. Pick up the car again, drive west to Kingston, mail the note there." He went into more details, while Curly listened. At the end he said: "It's just you and me now, Curly. I blew my top a while back. Forget it, like I said. We can pull this off if we try hard enough."

"Sure thing, Pax. . . . You think it's all right about the police?"

"Don't give it a thought." It was essential to build Curly up again. "That cop didn't look so smart. . . . Just you wait— another fortnight, and we'll be living it up in South America."

"*Olé !*" said Curly Bates, absurdly.

"That's the stuff, Curly."

It was night. The curtains were drawn again, shutting out the world, though the wash and suck of the river round the foundations of the old house still sounded faintly. Once more the three of them sat in the sitting-room; Greg and Ellen on the sofa, Paxton watching them from the armchair opposite. But already there was a subtle difference which he tried and failed to ignore: he was now outnumbered— they were still a team, and he was not. He was one man alone, a long way out on a long limb.

It might have been this sense of isolation which had prompted him to untie the other two and bring them up from the cellar. Though still a gaoler, he was imprisoned also, and he needed someone—even his prisoners—to salve the dire moment.

Greg, by contrast, was in high spirits; it was as though he knew exactly what to say on all occasions, and this was one of the easiest.

"How were the police?" he asked. "Observant? Hot on the scent?"

"I wouldn't say that," answered Paxton.

"Very deceptive, the police. . . . I'm sure they noticed lots of things, and they've gone away for reinforcements. I bet poor old Curly made plenty of mistakes."

"He did not," said Paxton.

"Where is he, anyway? I miss that razor-sharp conversation."

"He's gone ashore."

Greg raised his eyebrows. "So soon? Isn't that rather unwise?"

"Why?" Paxton did not want to know the answer—he even feared it—but for some reason he had to talk and to listen.

"He's in such bad shape." Greg turned to Ellen. "Wouldn't you agree?"

"Terrible shape," answered Ellen in her best social manner. "I was *so* sorry for him."

"He's all right," said Paxton.

"Oh no he's not," countered Greg. "I scared him, like I said I would. It wasn't very difficult. All I did was point out that the ranks—your ranks—were thinning out rather quickly, and he was probably next on the list. He didn't appreciate the idea at all."

Paxton smiled, without humour. "I know. He told me. He doesn't believe it now."

"I wonder. . . . I suppose you scared him too?"

"I scared him, and then I unscared him."

"I wonder which operation he'll remember when he's picked up."

"He won't be picked up," said Paxton curtly.

"Of course he will. That policeman probably recognized him. Or he'll go through a bunch of photographs and pick him out. With Curly's record——"

"Curly hasn't got a record."

Greg looked at him unwinkingly for a full half-minute. Then he said: "He really should have told you."

"Told me what?"

"He's got a record as long as your arm. Car theft, petty larceny, breaking and entering—he's really quite proud of it. Do you mean to say——"

"Curly's clean," said Paxton, unsurely. "He's never been inside."

"He's been inside four times, and his photograph is on record from here to Hawaii." Greg sat back, very much at ease. "You know you should have talked to him more. Like we did."

"Even if that's true, he's not known in this country."

"I think you'll find," said Greg, "that Canadian liaison with the FBI is reasonably close." He sat up again suddenly, his head on one side. "You'll know in a few moments, anyway."

Paxton sprang to his feet. "What do you hear?" he asked tautly. And then he heard it himself: the engine noise again, loud and clear even through the curtains.

Paxton's gun was in his hand. He took two quick steps to

the window, and peered out through the centre gap. His hunched shoulders betrayed an extreme of tension.

Behind him, Greg's voice came mockingly: "Don't tell us, Paxton. Let us guess. I say it's *not* the finance company."

Paxton turned with a snarl. His face was glazed in the lamp-light, and the hand holding the revolver shook.

"All right, smart boy!" he said. "That's the end of the comic strip. Now *I'm* going to enjoy myself."

Greg eyed him steadily. "Is that the police?" He made as if to rise, but Paxton waved him back.

"Stay where you are!" he said. "You won't have so far to fall."

"You won't shoot me," said Greg. Beside him he felt Ellen trembling in sudden terror, and he put his hand over hers. "So far it's only life imprisonment. That would mean hanging."

"It won't be either," said Paxton. "They won't get me."

"What are you going to do?—swim for it?"

"I'll think of something," said Paxton.

Behind him, the window curtains suddenly lit up as bright as sunlight.

"Don't look now," said Greg. "But there's a searchlight just behind you."

"Don't, Greg," begged Ellen in a shaking voice. "He means it."

"You're damn right I mean it," said Paxton. "You've ridden me for the last time."

"What's the plan?" asked Greg. "You tell me yours and I'll tell you mine."

A thunderous voice from outside over a booming loud-speaker suddenly said:

"PAXTON!"

"That's you," said Greg, almost cheerfully. "They must have got Curly—and the ransom note."

"Well, they haven't got me," said Paxton. He crossed to the light switch, still keeping his gun trained on Greg, and put out the lights. Eerily lit from the glare through the curtains, the room subsided into shadowy twilight.

The giant voice called again: "PAXTON! COME ON OUT!"

Paxton's shadow moved against the curtain as he took up his position once more.

"What are you going to do?" asked Greg.

There was no answer from the dark, one-dimensional figure at the window.

"I'll tell you what you're *not* going to do," said Greg. "You're not going to swim for it."

"Yes, I am," said Paxton suddenly. He turned, and the dull light gleamed on the gun barrel. "I'll use you as cover till I get to the water. Then I'll plug you and take off. They can't watch the island all the way round."

"It's a plan, certainly," conceded Greg. His voice was oddly calm in the darkness. "But it won't work. They'll fish us both out of the water about twenty miles from here."

"What do you mean?"

The loudspeaker voice boomed again: "PAXTON! WALK OUT OR WE'LL COME AND GET YOU!"

"Let's keep your friends waiting," said Greg, "while I explain. . . . I was born in these parts. D'you know what this area is called? Suicide Bay! They've lost more people here from drowning than anywhere else in North America. It's the current, and the undertow. It's actually illegal to swim here." He laughed suddenly. "They could even arrest you for that, Paxton."

"Funny boy," said Paxton uncertainly. "I'll take a chance."

"All right then," said Greg. "Let's go."

"Don't, Greg," said Ellen, clinging to his arm. "He'll kill you."

"He'll kill himself too, darling," answered Greg. "I'd rather be shot than have my lungs swell up and burst with dirty river water."

"Is that right about the current?" asked Paxton after a pause.

"Believe it or not," said Greg, "the insurance rates for boats in this area are nearly double anywhere else."

There was a sound of a second engine behind them on the other side of the house. Paxton swore vividly.

"While we've been talking——"

"That was my plan," said Greg suddenly. "I told you I had one, didn't I? A weapon for every animal. Mine is the human voice." There was tension in his tone now: this was the curtain to the act, one way or the other: the next few moments might cost his own life, and perhaps Ellen's as well, or they

112

would emerge and breathe the free air again, and the ordeal would be past. "The game's over, Paxton. I talked Curly into giving himself up, and I've talked you past the escape point. It's too late for anything now."

"No, it's not, by God!"

"The place is surrounded."

"They haven't got me yet."

The thunderous voice again: "PAXTON! WE'VE GOT EIGHT MEN WITH GUNS! WE'VE GOT TEAR GAS! WE'VE GOT THREE BOATS AND PLENTY OF LIGHTS! I'LL GIVE YOU ONE MORE MINUTE TO WALK OUT OF THE FRONT DOOR WITH YOUR HANDS UP!"

"You see," said Greg, "they have a plan too."

Paxton seemed to reach his decision. "We're going to take off, like I said. You first. Maybe I won't plug you if you behave yourself. It'll be a bit of insurance. If I'm caught——"

"Have it your own way," answered Greg, "but there's no 'if'." He stood up unhurriedly, and walked forward. Paxton did not check him; the gun was now hanging loosely by his side. "*When* you're caught," Greg continued, "I could confirm that we weren't actually ill-treated. It might help a bit. But not too much, I hope. I'd hate to see a rat like you get less than twenty years."

"Why, you snotty little——"

Paxton's gun arm came up again, but Greg, standing in the shadows, was quicker. The heavy bronze ashtray in his hand flew through the air. It was aimed, not at Paxton, but at the foot-wide gap in the curtains behind him. It hit the big picture-window fair and square, and the whole glass shattered with a splintering crash. Involuntarily Paxton jumped and turned, and as he did so, Greg rushed him, low down, right shoulder forward. Though his weight was light, he had the advantage of a running start, and he caught Paxton in the small of the back, toppling him into the jagged window.

Paxton must have fallen on just the wrong piece of glass at just the wrong angle, for except for a jugular, bubbling gurgle he never made another sound.

The room was full of uniforms and people; the lights were on again; gruesome photographs were being taken. But for

Ellen and Greg, it might have been an empty arena. They were both unutterably tired; all they had left was swamped in the enormous relief of tenderness.

"I'm so dirty and untidy," she said, holding him close. "And my hair. . . . I'm hardly fit to kiss you."

"Just," said Greg, putting it to the test. Both sides seemed satisfied.

"For someone who hates violence," said Ellen presently, "you produced a really terrific flying tackle."

"Shades of high school!" answered Greg. "That was one of the many things the coach said I would never be any good at." He sighed, not too unhappily. "Yes, that deplorable rough-house stuff quite spoilt my record. I must do penance somehow. . . . And then, all the terrible lies I had to tell!"

"Lies?"

"Oh yes! They were part of the pressure, the steady needling. . . . I had to slander the poor old Thousand Islands —the swimming round here is as safe as your own bath-tub. And I had to slander Curly, too. I don't believe he ever *has* been in prison."

"There's a first time for everything," said Ellen unkindly. 'But about this habit of lying so convincingly——"

"I guess I've told enough to last a lifetime," said Greg mournfully.

"A married lifetime?"

"Well, that's a different proposition altogether," he said. "Let's find out as soon as possible."

The police photographer, a frustrated romantic, called out: "Hold it!"

Presently he decided that he needn't have said anything.

Up the Garden Path

I was dealing with my post, the post which had meant an hour's concentrated work every day of the year since the last big book was published. After the business letters came the ones from friends; after the friends came the strangers; after the strangers, the begging letters.

I was just finishing the strangers, the letters I liked best of all.

"Dear Mr James," I dictated, "Thank you very much for writing to me about my book. I am so glad that you enjoyed it. Your letter is about the two-thousandth I've received, but it was one of the nicest." (For some reason, this always seemed true.) "If you were in the Navy you'll understand what I was trying to say. Good luck, and thanks again. Yours sincerely."

My secretary did a squiggle on her pad, and waited.

"That's the last of the genuine ones," I said. "Now we have four oddments." Oddments was our euphemism for the begging letters.

"Only four!" she asked. "They're falling off."

"The ugly rush is over. . . . Dear Mr King," I dictated, "Thank you for your letter. While I have every sympathy with you in your trouble, I am afraid I cannot undertake the financial guarantee for which you ask. Yours sincerely."

Pause.

"Dear Mr George," I dictated, "Thank you for your letter. I am afraid that patents and inventions are a bit out of my line, and I am not prepared to back the project for harnessing domestic bath-water, which you described to me. Yours sincerely."

Pause.

"Dear Miss Crawford," I dictated, "Thank you for your letter. While I have every sympathy—no, I used that before —while I appreciate your dilemma, and am sorry to hear of it, I am afraid that I cannot help you. There are, as you know, established institutions which can give advice and assistance. Yours sincerely."

I became aware that my secretary had sighed.

"What's the matter?" I asked. "Am I being harsh?"

"Poor girl," she said, "It was such a sad letter."

"I thought it was the phoniest of the lot."

My secretary sighed again. Men, she seemed to be saying: the cause of all the trouble—and then they harden their hearts.

I said: "How much, then?"

"About twenty pounds."

Now it was my turn to sigh. "Twenty pounds? Good heavens! Suppose I gave twenty pounds to everyone who asked me for it! I'd be bankrupt in a week."

"You wouldn't," she answered. "And you don't give twenty pounds to everyone, anyway. I see to that myself."

Not for the first time I considered firing my secretary. Not for the first time I knew I would never do so. With all her blatant manipulation of me and my writing and my appointments and my life, she was far too good to lose.

"All right," I said. "Have it your own way. You write the letter, I'll sign the cheque."

She made another squiggle on her pad. I noticed that she allowed herself only a slight smile, nothing more. She waited for me to finish dictating.

"Dear Mr Chatterton," I began, reaching for the last letter, and then I paused. This was the letter I wasn't sure about. It read like a straight touch, and as such I was prepared to turn it down. But for some reason it had made me uncomfortable. It recalled too much of my own past. I looked through it again.

'Dear Sir,' it said, 'I am writing a book and starving at the same time. I know it is a good book, but unless I can get some money I don't think I shall be able to finish it. First they will take the typewriter away, and then they will take *me* away. If you read what I have written so far, and like it, will you help me? Yours truly, Alan Chatterton."

I held the letter in my hand, thinking back a long way. It was not the sort of letter I had ever written myself, but it did recall the wonderful, terrible life of twenty years before, when I was struggling with my own first book in the same way, and worrying about the rent, and wondering whether, in the race between selling the book and starving—a melodramatic but accurate word—I would be able to win.

Chatterton's letter recalled so many other things—the wretched room in Paddington that I knew as "home", the makeshifts of poverty, the meagre meals of tea and bread-and-jam, the doubts, the heartbreaks over publishers' rejections, the moment of triumph that paid for everything.

No one had helped me in the way that Chatterton was asking. But many friends had been kind—more than kind, they had been saviours. Perhaps Chatterton had no friends like that. Perhaps he *could* write. Perhaps help would not be wasted.

"Dear Mr Chatterton," I dictated—and the words came out easily, though they were the opposite words to the ones I had planned a moment ago: "Please call and see me, at any time convenient to yourself, and bring your manuscript with you, as you suggest."

The young man who was shown into my study a few days later (followed, since he was good-looking, by a lingering glance from my secretary) was exactly the sort of young man I had been expecting—remembering once again my own earlier efforts to scratch a living at writing.

Alan Chatterton was tall, thin and shabby: he looked hungry, and at the same time scornful of the fact, as if every true artist in the world were always hungry. . . . While he paused at the door, his quick arrogant glance took in everything about my room: its comfort, its elegance, its undoubted perfection as a place in which to think and work.

There was for a moment a suppressed smile on his face. I knew well enough what he was thinking during that moment. He was contemptuous of luxury, and derisive of worldly success. But he would have given his right arm to have had a room like this to write in. . . . I remembered, in the old days, examining in the same way the houses of my richer friends.

When we had shaken hands:

"It's really very good of you to see me," he said. His voice was easy and pleasant: it was obvious that he had, when he chose to use it, a ready charm.

"I was interested in your letter," I answered. I motioned towards a deep armchair. "Tell me something about yourself —and the book."

He told me, and it was for me a familiar enough story, though that did not make it any the less attractive as far as I was concerned. Alan Chatterton was twenty-two; he had no parents, and very little money; he had tried a lot of jobs, but the only thing he wanted to do was to write. That was what he was doing now—and it was a race, as he had said in his letter, between finishing his book and starving.

"And the book?" I prompted.

"It really is good!" There was assurance in his voice, but it was not an offensive assurance; the grey eyes that held mine were full of truth as well as confidence. "I've got the manuscript here"—he patted a worn brief-case—"that is, the first quarter of it, the part that's ready to be looked at. I hope you'll like it. I'm sure you will."

"How long before you finish it?"

"About six months."

"And during that time"—I hesitated, not sure how to word it—"during that time, you'll need help?"

Chatterton was not embarrassed. "I'm broke," he said candidly, "and I must finish the book. If you could lend me some money just to tide me over."

"The book might not be accepted."

"I'm sure it will be. And I'm sure it will hit the jackpot, too." He looked at me, and then round the room, with the same half-bitter, half-envious air. "Like the last one you wrote yourself. How many editions has that gone through now?"

"About half a million copies." I tried very hard not to sound self-satisfied. "And the same in America."

He laughed. "If I could just strike it lucky, like that."

I felt bound to correct him. "Luck doesn't really come into it," I said austerely. "I spent twenty years learning how to write. This is the result." I realized that this sounded pompous as well as austere, and my realization was for a moment reflected in Chatterton's eyes. But quickly he recovered.

"Sorry!" he said readily. He lost his arrogance and became, for a brief moment, much younger. "Of course I know you worked hard for it. It's just"—he grinned—"a million copies! That really is the jackpot! How long did it take you to write?"

"Two years," I said. "And twenty years of learning. I

used to be"—again I hesitated—"I used to be broke, like you."

He looked interested, and the look was flattering. "Did you really? I'd like to hear about that."

When Alan Chatterton had gone, some time later, I glanced through his manuscript. There was not a great deal of it—his estimate that this was one quarter of the total book seemed optimistic—but I certainly liked what there was. He could write, after all: some of the characterization was brilliant, and the plot, though not entirely original, was promising. I decided, long before the end, that I would help him out.

I could never make up my mind, either then or afterwards, how much that decision had been affected by Chatterton's obvious interest in my own writing career.

"Dear Mr Chatterton," I dictated, later that evening, "After reading your manuscript, I am prepared to make you a small allowance until the book is completed, on the understanding that. . . ."

By the time the letter was finished my secretary was, for once, looking really pleased with me.

"Such a nice young man," she said at the end. "He must have suffered too. . . . Did you notice his eyes?"

My offer to keep Alan Chatterton alive—for that was what it amounted to—until his novel was finished, was the beginning of a curious relationship. We did not see a great deal of each other since we were both busy on our respective books: but now and then he rang me up, and sometimes, though less often as time went on, he came round to see me.

The book, he always said, was going well. He didn't want to show me any more of it until the whole thing was complete. But progress, apparently, was satisfactory.

That was more than could be said for the other aspect of our relationship, the financial one. True to my undertaking, I arranged with my bank to pay Chatterton a small monthly sum. It would be enough, I thought, to keep him free of worry, not enough to make him extravagant. But presently he asked for more.

He did this so very hesitantly, and on so reasonable a note, that I could scarcely refuse. Indeed, he somehow contrived to make me feel that, if I did refuse, it would be unfair and even dishonest of me. Had I not promised to support him? ... The cost of living, he said, was proving higher than he had thought. There was stationery to be bought, and new typewriter-ribbons. His rent had been raised. His shoes needed mending. He would like to go to the dentist.

I knew from the past that all these things could be true and pressing: they were part of the cramping meanness of poverty, part of the worry that could destroy an artist. They could also inspire him—but clearly Chatterton wasn't that kind of artist.

"I'm at a rather tricky part of the book," he told me. "It's so difficult to concentrate when I'm worrying about money all the time. If you could just manage a few more pounds a month, it would make all the difference in the world."

On that first occasion I agreed to what he asked without much hesitation. Pity was involved, and the honouring of my promise: there was even a touch of vanity in the idea of having this young man so completely dependent on me, and being able to wave the wand on his behalf. But later on— for there were quite a number of these occasions—I began to have my doubts.

The next time he asked for money, it was for a holiday. London was terribly hot, his room airless and noisy. If he could just get away for a bit. ... A few pounds for a spell at the seaside would make all the difference. He had read in the paper that I myself had recently spent a month in the South of France.

The subtly implied criticism made me angry. "Of course I went to the South of France!" I said. "I needed a holiday too—I've been working like a black for over a year, and I've just finished my new book. I've earned a break if anyone has!"

"Good heavens!" he said, immediately contrite, "I didn't mean *that*! I meant that you, of all people, would be able to understand how I feel, staying on and on in London in this sort of weather, without a hope of getting away. I don't wonder you went off to Antibes. If I could just have a couple of weeks myself—at Ramsgate. ...'

It was difficult to judge if Chatterton were being clever on purpose, or by mistake. But whichever it was, it was certainly effective. ... I said I would think it over. Later my secretary remarked how ill and worried Chatterton was looking. He needed a holiday, she said, staring me dead in the eye: then he could get nice and sunburned, just as I had. . . . I sent Chatterton a cheque for fifty pounds next morning.

When Chatterton came back to London he called round to thank me for his holiday. It had been wonderful, he said: just what he had needed. Now he was rested and absolutely fit, and he could really go to work.

I heard nothing more for several weeks. Then presently he started dropping in again. His visits had always the same purpose.

First there was his rent, which had once more been raised by a landlord who seemed to pay little regard to rent restrictions. Then he wanted an overcoat to ward off the increasing cold of autumn.

Then he asked for something both ludicrous and irresistible—a new typewriter.

"You must have been working the old one very hard," I said on a somewhat caustic note.

He smiled engagingly. "It's absolutely on its last legs."

"How's the book, then? Nearly finished?"

"Well," he hesitated. "I wouldn't say that. But it's coming on."

"I'd like to see it."

"I'd rather you didn't." Then he noticed my expression. "I mean I do want you to see the finished product, and nothing less. To tell you the truth"—he smiled enchantingly again—"I'm a bit shy of showing *you* my stuff. Especially when it's not complete."

"How long do you think it will take?"

"A few more months. . . . You really have been terribly kind. . . . If I could have the new typewriter I could go much faster. . . . You know I'll pay you back. I'll put it in writing if you like."

"I don't want that. I just want to read the finished manuscript."

"It really won't be very long now."

But the book still wasn't finished at the end of that year. And by that time (I could not help calculating) I had already given Alan Chatterton something like a thousand pounds.

I did not see Chatterton again till well on into the new

year, though I had a monthly chit from my bank to confirm that he was drawing his allowance as usual. I hoped that the new typewriter (so much superior to my own battered relic) was proving its worth. Then, some time in May, he came to see me again.

When he walked into my room I took it for granted that he needed more money: indeed, I had been speculating, cynically, on what it would be labelled this time. It could hardly be a second overcoat; but Chatterton was almost due to take another holiday. . . . However, though he wore his usual expression—humble, hesitant, and yet somehow sure that he had a legitimate claim upon me—he did not mention money at all to begin with.

Instead, he talked about his book. It was 'going well', as always. Then he talked about the weather, and the crowds in London, and the current crime wave. Then he talked flatteringly about my own work. Then suddenly, while I was still digesting an undeniably acute compliment, he said:

"Look—I'm in the most terrible hole. I've got to get married."

"Married!" I exclaimed blankly, startled out of my complacence. "How on earth can you get married? You haven't a penny in the world!"

"I know that. But I've got to, all the same. I'm awfully sorry. That's the way it is."

"Tell me."

He told me, and it was so commonplace a story, so simple and yet so overwhelming, that I needn't enlarge upon it. It boiled down, in all its essentials, to what he had said. He had to get married. And before very long.

I called him all sorts of a fool, and he took it well. At the end he said:

"I'm terribly sorry. I thought I'd better tell you straight away. It's been hanging over me for so long. . . . Unless I get it settled, *I doubt if the book will ever be finished.*"

That brought me up short as perhaps it was intended to. It was one thing to call him a fool, quite another to abandon him to his foolishness as I had been planning to at that moment. I saw now that, if I did wash my hands of Chatterton at this crucial point, all the things I had invested in him—not only the money (though that was close on £1300), but all the past eighteen months, and my belief in him, and my genuine hopes of his talent—all would go for nothing.

I knew then that it would be too much to lose, too much to abandon. As usual, between dependence, flattery, and emotional blackmail, Chatterton had me in a cleft stick.

As if he read my thoughts:

"I'm terribly sorry to put it to you like this," he said contritely. "But I've got a plan." He fished in his inside pocket. "If you could help me through this, I'll give you a half-interest in the novel. I've got it all written out here—a sort of contract. I've been thinking it over. It's really the very least I can do."

For some reason I was oddly touched by his action and by the thought behind it. Chatterton was a fool, all right—but he was a good-hearted one all the same. He had got himself into a scrape, and he was seeking an honourable way out of it, not only with the girl but with myself as well. I took the paper from him. It was a short letter making over to me, unconditionally, a half-share in his book. It was already signed and dated.

I hesitated for some moments before accepting it. Chatterton and I had never put our affairs on a definite financial footing. I had simply taken it for granted that when his book was published, and if it proved to be the success we both hoped, Chatterton would pay back what I had given him. If I accepted his offer it would mean a different relationship altogether: perhaps not such a satisfactory one.

I didn't want a half-interest in his book. I just wanted him to finish it, and prove himself, and vindicate my judgment, and pay me back what he owed me. But perhaps it would be better to take him at his word, and accept the half-share. Better for him, certainly. The sooner he faced his responsibilities and set a margin to them, the sooner he would grow up.

"How much?" I asked.

He looked at me, fingering his chin. "We want to get a little flat," he said slowly, "and settle down properly. Big enough for me to work in too. . . . Say, five hundred pounds?"

I don't often go to dinner-and-dance clubs, and certainly not to places like the 'Two Hundred', whose opulence, chic, and clientele are all well above my settled station in life. In particular, I object to spending the proceeds of a week's hard work on a single meal, and being looked at sideways by a supercilious head waiter if I dare to glance twice at the bill.

But chance, and an invitation from one of my richer friends, took me to the 'Two Hundred' a few days later. Waiting for my host to shed his coat, I walked forward and looked over the balcony on to the dance floor below.

The first person I saw was Chatterton. He was at the head of a table for eight, and host to a party which included four personable blondes and a great many champagne bottles. He was lounging back in the cushioned alcove, giving orders to an attentive waiter. The way he gestured with his cigar was particularly elegant.

The head waiter was now by my side. I pointed downwards.

"Do you happen to know that gentleman's name?" I asked.

"Oh yes, sir," he answered readily. "That's Mr Chatterton." And as I continued to look blank: "The author, sir. . . . He's always a very good customer here."

I was still in a towering rage when Chatterton, at my urgent summons, arrived next morning: it was a rage which I had nursed throughout a long and wakeful night. There had been something about the sight of Chatterton taking his ease in an expensive night-club which had caught me on the raw, and I wasn't prepared to tolerate the situation any longer.

Twenty years before I had been struggling in the depths of poverty to finish my own first book. Because of that memory I had been helping Chatterton on his way. I had helped him for eighteen months, giving him every conceivable encouragement and keeping him alive to the tune of about £1800, including £500 in a lump sum so that he could get married and settle down.

Four days after that last payment I had found him giving a large party in the most opulent night-club in London—the sort of place that, even now, I could hardly afford myself. And the head waiter knew him there as a 'good customer'.

I tackled Chatterton immediately he came in.

"I was at the 'Two Hundred' last night," I said brusquely. "I saw *you* there. What about it?"

He had the grace to look startled. "Oh," he said awkwardly, and then: "That was my wedding party."

"It didn't look like it. . . . You know perfectly well I gave you that last £500 to get you out of trouble, and settled into a flat; not to throw away on night-clubs or anything else."

"It was just the once."

"It *wasn't* just the once!" I exclaimed. "The head waiter told me you were often there."

"Keeping a check on me?" he asked cheekily.

"Never you mind about that. I want an explanation."

"But it's all experience," Chatterton answered. There was now something in his manner I didn't like at all, something cocky and careless, as if he were cornered at last and knew there was no way out. "It won't go to waste. . . . That's the kind of book I'm writing."

"I'd like to see that book."

"It won't be long now."

"It's been too damned long already!" I stared at him, at his arrogant face, his shabby clothes, his careless take-it-or-leave-it air. Suddenly I was wildly angry. "I've given you over eighteen hundred pounds," I said bitterly, "to keep you alive, to help you finish your book. So far as I can see, there's no book, and there never will be. And you've chucked my money away buying yourself a good time with a lot of night-club loafers."

After a long pause he said: "Trust you to keep an exact account!"

"What do you mean?"

"You've made *thousands* from your last book," he said, with equal scorn. "You'll probably make thousands from the next one. Now you grudge me a miserable loan when I'm working on something really big." There was a bitter sneer on his face: the truth was flowing out at last. "Why should you worry, anyway? You're getting your cut, aren't you? I've given you half the book already. What more do you want? The whole thing?"

During the long moment we stared at each other all friendship and all respect ebbed away to nothing.

"I wanted you to be honest," I told him slowly. "I wanted you to try your very best—to be *really* writing, not pretending, not fooling about in night-clubs at my expense. The money I gave you was for the book that's inside you. Nothing less, and nothing else."

"But I've told you, I need that sort of material."

"I saw the material. Four examples of it, in fact—all

blondes. And I gave you that last loan because you came to me and said you were in a desperate jam. . . ." Suddenly I could hardly speak for the anger choking up inside me. I strode across to the bureau, took out the 'contract', the letter that gave me a half-interest in his book, and tore it across and across. "I've finished with you!" I shouted, "and with your rotten fake book as well—if there ever was such a thing. Now get out!"

"You'll be sorry," he said, now careless again. "Just you wait and see."

"I *am* sorry. . . . Eighteen months of trusting you—and nearly two thousand pounds down the drain."

"Money, money, money!" he answered, loathsomely mocking. "Anyone would think you'd been betting on me and lost. . . . I hope I never get like you."

"You won't," I told him. "Not in a hundred years. That I can guarantee. . . . Now go away from here, and never come back."

There was one other thing I did about Alan Chatterton before I put him out of my mind, and I did it to satisfy my curiosity. During the next week or so, I made a few discreet inquiries among my writing friends, and they added up to what I had suspected. Before I lost interest in this odd piece of research, I discovered at least two other men who had been approached in the same way as I had been.

Chatterton must have picked his prospects well. Both of them had been supporting him to the tune of many hundreds of pounds for the last two years.

But it was just possible that I, and these others, had destroyed both Chatterton and his book in the course of our good intentions. For the really sad part was that the small section of the manuscript he had shown me had been *really* good.

I was out of England on a lecture tour, when Chatterton's book was published. Indeed, the first I heard of it was in my club on the evening I returned to London. Stephenson, one of my writing friends who had also subscribed to Chatterton's upkeep in the past, waylaid me in the hall.

"Looks as though we picked a winner, after all," he said cheerfully.

"How do you mean?"

"Why, Alan Chatterton, of course!"

"What about him?"

He stared at me. "Haven't you heard about his book? I thought everyone in England had. It looks as if it's going to be a runaway best-seller. . . . Where have you been lately?"

"Lecture tour," I answered. "Then a long slow voyage home from Cape Town. I haven't seen an English newspaper for nearly four months."

"You haven't missed much," he said caustically, "but you *have* missed Chatterton's book. Everything seems to have happened to it. Book Society Choice—Book-of-the-Month in America—a couple of newspaper selections here—it's been a sensation. I believe it's sold over two hundred thousand copies already."

"Bless my soul!" I said. "I didn't believe there *was* a book. Is it any good?"

"It's sold a couple of hundred thousand," he answered, grinning. "And I've had a cheque from Chatterton for everything I've lent him. . . . And yes, it's a really good book, as well."

"I haven't had a chance to look at my mail yet," I said. "Perhaps there's a cheque for me as well."

"I'm sure there will be," said Stephenson heartily. "Say what you like about Chatterton—careless, and broke, and all that—but he was basically honest, wasn't he?"

It was rather like *Alice Through the Looking Glass*. There *was* a cheque for me when I got home—dated a month previously, made out for eighteen hundred and fifty pounds, and accompanied by a card with the single word : 'Thanks. A.C.' I began to feel rather a fool. And I felt even more of a fool when I got hold of the book next day, and started to read it.

It was all that Stephenson had said, and more. It deserved all its 'choices', all its two hundred thousand sale (which was likely to be doubled before very long), all the praise I had now begun to hear on every side. Chatterton had used a little of the manuscript he had shown me originally, but not much. From that slim beginning the novel branched out into a hugely-planned, brilliant picture of contemporary London, ranging from the House of Lords to the barrow-boys in the Edgware Road, through scores of characters and hundreds of scenes. It was Dickensian in its scope, phenomenal in its observation.

Chatterton must have worked at it consistently for months and even years on end. All the time that I had been lending him money and thinking it wasted, he had in fact been slaving away at his work without respite: observing, travelling, taking notes, getting it all down on paper, dreaming its future pattern with a single-minded devotion.

I saw, now, the necessity for his incursions into the night-club world. Indeed, that section, with its contrast between the surface glitter and the drab sometimes fraudulent machinery underneath, was among the best in the book. And that was saying a great deal. No wonder he had been angry. . . .

I felt stunned, and I felt all sorts of an idiot at the same time. The answer to my wretched doubts lay between my hands now—a monumental book which the world was acclaiming and which might well pass into the realm of permanent literature. But I was glad and humbly proud to have helped Chatterton to write it. The eighteen months of doubt, the £1850 which had seemed thrown away, were a very small price to pay for a piece of work of this quality.

I did not even mourn the fact that I had torn up a gift-contract for a half-share in it.

I acknowledged his cheque with a sentence—'Thanks and a thousand congratulations'—which came straight from the heart. I had hoped to meet Chatterton personally, but he was of course very busy with the trappings of success which so few novelists get and which all of them (whatever they say to the contrary) secretly desire—the autograph parties, the literary lunches, the broadcasts, television appearances, commissioning of articles and short stories, the public adulation. He was on the crest of the wave, with his book going from strength to strength, and he deserved every moment of it.

But later that year I ran across him again in a Piccadilly hotel. He was on his way to a party, he said. Judging by his tail-coat, it must have been a pretty smart one.

"And the book?" I asked, after we had chatted for a few minutes.

"Still going well," he answered. He was looking at me in a somewhat disconcerting way—half mocking, half challenging, as if daring me to pass judgment on him or his work. "Getting near the half-million mark, I believe. And we've just sold the film rights."

"I must congratulate you," I said sincerely. "And I shall always be very glad that I helped."

"Helped?" he repeated, on a surprised note.

"Well," I said, awkwardly, "I did, didn't I? For over eighteen months."

"Oh—*that*!" he said, as if we were speaking of something scarcely mentionable. "Yes, it did come in useful at the time, of course. But you never really believed in me, did you?"

The Man who wanted a Mark Nine

IT WAS nice to meet Walker again, although we had never been close friends. I had not seen him for several years—not since he got his appointment as First Secretary to the British Legation at Estakia. We met, as everyone does, in Piccadilly Circus.

"Walker!" I exclaimed. "What are you doing here?"

"Long leave," he said as we shook hands. "Just four and a half months."

We talked idly for a few minutes while I examined him with interest. We were of the same age and, I suppose, much alike in physical appearance: medium-grade civil servants, half-way up the ladder, already a trifle set in our ways. If I had slightly outstripped him from the career point of view it was doubtless a matter of luck.

"And how are you?" Walker asked presently. "I saw your name in the New Year's Honours. Congratulations."

"Thank you," I said. "A simple CBE. The effluxion of time, of course. . . . Are you going back to Estakia?"

"Oh yes," he answered. There was an enthusiasm in his long grey hatchet-face that I would hardly have mustered myself, if confronted with the same prospect. "And I'm taking something with me, too. A Centurion—Mark Nine."

Once again I looked at him with interest. I knew very little about cars, but I knew enough to rank Centurions with Rolls-Royces and Bentleys. I knew also Walker's salary as First Secretary. It hardly ran to a Centurion.

"Centurions must be very expensive," I prompted.

"Five thousand pounds even without purchase tax." He looked at me eagerly; a tall, angular forty-year-old man with the expression of a boy. "An aunt left me the money quite unexpectedly. Joan and I—we've never had any children. We both decided that we would spend it all on a car—a Mark Nine. I've had my eye on a Centurion for at least ten years."

Though it was none of my business how officers in Walker's

position spent their money, yet his idea seemed to me extravagant, and unbecoming. "It's a great deal of money, none the less," I said reprovingly. "Do you really think it's worth it?"

"Wait till you see the car!" answered Walker. "I ordered it a year ago. It's going to be ready for me today, the first day of my leave. I'm going along to collect it now. Come with me!"

I considered this proposal with some care: it seemed to me to call for a policy decision. The purchase of a £5000 car by a medium-grade civil servant in one's own Ministry was something that one should think twice about before becoming involved in it oneself. There was bound to be criticism, and the fact that I had gone to view the car in person might be construed as approval—even connivance.

But, on reflection, it seemed to me to be my duty to keep an eye on Walker at this stage, and I said that I would be delighted to go with him.

"They're practically hand-made," Walker said, awe in his voice. He was almost bounding along beside me in a way I found embarrassing. "That's why they cost so much. People say that driving a Centurion is a new experience altogether, like riding a racehorse after ambling along on a donkey."

"You make it sound positively poetic," I said. Passers-by were staring at us, and I laid a restraining hand on his arm. "Calm down," I said. "A few minutes more won't really matter, will it? Didn't you say you'd waited a year for the car already?"

He nodded. "Nearly fourteen months, in fact. That's the Centurion way of doing things. First you choose the style of bodywork you like. Then the upholstery. Then the colour-scheme. Then you have to say whether you want a radio and an internal heater and air-conditioner and a set of fitted suitcases and a cocktail cabinet. Then, when you've settled exactly the kind of car you want, you join the queue for your chassis."

"There is a great demand for these—these paragons?"

Walker nodded again. "I was lucky—being in Estakia. I came under the export quota. Otherwise I would have had much more than fourteen months to wait."

I returned to something that had been puzzling me. "Why

131

is it called a Mark Nine?" I asked. "Are there nine different models?"

"No, no!" He sounded shocked. "This is the ninth version of the Centurion they've made. They change their design every seven years or so. The Mark Nine is the latest." He pointed suddenly. "And there she is!"

I hardly had time to notice that he had said 'she,' as if speaking of a ship, before he seized my arm, and dragged me to the nearest shop window.

Perhaps 'shop' was the wrong word to use in the present connection. Beyond the vast plate-glass, and the sign 'Centurion Motors' picked out in black and gold, was a showroom covering at least a quarter of an acre, the parquet floor of which shone like a sunset. There were only two cars inside, banked by masses of potted hydrangeas. One of them was black, the other red and cream.

Under the nearest one, a painted signboard said simply: Centurion, Mark Nine, £7,918.

"That's with the purchase tax," said Walker, following my glance. "I come under the export quota—I get mine for nearly three thousand less."

"Which one is yours?" I asked coldly. It all seemed unnecessarily opulent.

"Neither of them," answered Walker uncertainly. "Mine was to be dark green. I expect it's still at the works."

A uniformed commissionaire, with an imposing double row of medals, held open the door for us. As we passed through, Walker said, not quite under his breath: "At last!"

Close to, the cars were almost overpowering: they seemed to be at least twenty feet long, curved and shaped like jet aircraft, polished like jewels. By my side, Walker, sighing like a lover, breathed: "They go over a hundred-and-twenty miles an hour. *And ninety-two in third. . . .*"

A man rose from a nearby desk, and walked towards us. I noticed that his desk bore a lettered nameplate, with 'Mr Broadwood' inscribed upon it. The man himself was of formidable height, gracefully built, aged about forty-five, and dressed in a black coat and striped trousers. His face as he neared us was supercilious and aloof.

"Good morning, gentlemen," he said. His voice was cultured, his tone severely reserved. "What can I do for you?" To my relief, Walker was not hesitant or put out,

132

either by his reception or his surroundings. He said, simply:

"Is my car ready?"

I could not help being proud of Walker at that moment. I wondered where he was drawing his assurance from, and then the answer came to me. He had lived so long with his dream of a Mark Nine, he had looked at so many catalogues and specifications, filled in so many forms, taken so many decisions on colour-schemes and uphostery and cocktail cabinets, that he felt he owned one already.

Mr Broadwood's manner had become hesitant.

"You have ordered a Mark Nine? May I have your name, sir?"

"Walker," said Walker. "George Walker, British Embassy, Estakia. It was to be ready when I arrived home on leave."

"Walker. I will inquire."

Broadwood retired to his desk in good order and became busy in a lowered voice on the telephone, while Walker and I stepped nearer to the cream-and-red Centurion.

"Gear-change on the steering column," he said. "That's a new departure for Centurions. Foot-operated horn. Three separate sets of headlamps. Defroster—it blows hot air on to the windscreen. Hydraulically operated windows. Cigar lighter."

"Cigarettes, surely," I objected.

"Cigars," said Walker firmly. "It's half an inch broader than the normal kind. See those front seats? You can adjust them for the height and the distance from the steering-wheel."

"Like a dentist's chair."

"I suppose so." But he wasn't really listening. He had opened the door of the car, and then sat down very slowly and gently in the driver's seat. There was a look on his face of dedicated joy.

We were interrupted by Mr Broadwood who approached us again across the parquet floor. He was frowning as he addressed himself to Walker. "I have confirmed your order, sir," he said. "You are certainly on our waiting list."

"Waiting list!" exclaimed Walker as if he could scarcely believe his ears. He got out of the car immediately and faced Mr Broadwood. "Waiting list? I've been on the waiting list for the past fourteen months! My car was to be ready for me now, at the beginning of my leave."

Mr Broadwood spread his hands, ready to deal with the onslaught according to the Centurion code. "You'll appreciate that it takes a very long time to build these cars. There have been many delays. Yours is nearly ready."

Walker swallowed. "How nearly?"

"A few weeks only," answered Mr Broadwood. "Perhaps two months."

"Two months. . . ." I had rarely heard such ruined disappointment as there was in Walker's voice: he might have been jilted by someone he had dearly loved for a score of years. "But I wanted it for my leave in England!"

"I'm very sorry, sir." Mr Broadwood was regaining his full confidence. "Where Mark Nines are concerned one has to be patient."

"I've been patient for over a year."

Mr Broadwood shrugged his shoulders. Mark Nines were part of a different world, he seemed to be saying. A year was nothing. These were cars that one *waited* for.

After a long pause, Walker asked: "But will it really be ready in two months? I have to be back in Estakia in July."

"That gives us nearly four months, doesn't it?"

"But I want to drive it about here."

Mr Broadwood smirked. "A great many people want to, sir."

I saw a good deal of Walker during the next four months. It happened that we were fellow-members of the same club, the Voyagers', which (possibly by reason of its somewhat romantic name) is a great favourite with the more sedentary type of civil servant. Walker spent the greater part of his time there since it was close to the Centurion showrooms; and the Centurion showrooms had now become the core of his existence.

Had I been ready and willing to spend five thousand pounds on a motor-car I'm damned if I would have put up with the kind of treatment to which Walker was now subjected. The latest news was always the same.

Mr Broadwood, it seemed, continued to have every hope; but Mr Broadwood, and Centurion Motors, seemed to be dogged by a succession of misfortunes which they passed on to Walker as a matter of course. There had been some confusion over the shade of the leatherwork of Walker's Mark

Nine: it did not match the outside paintwork, and so the latter had to be altered.

And so on. Whether or not he got his Mark Nine in time was clearly going to be a near thing; and when, four days before he was due to sail, he met me in the entrance hall of the Voyagers' Club and called out: "It's here!" I was, in spite of this public salutation, very much relieved at the news.

When he was a little nearer he said: "It's down at the showrooms now—Broadwood just telephoned. Would you like to come with me?"

We reached the Centurion showrooms. I could see a gleaming, dark-green model at which Walker pointed a shaking finger. "That's it!" he exclaimed. He rushed through the door, without waiting for the commissionaire as if he were going to take a flying leap into the car there and then.

I followed somewhat more sedately, though I must confess to feeling a certain excitement myself. Mr Broadwood rose from his desk and came forward. He was as suave, aloof, and controlled as ever, but there was today a a slight, concessionary smile on his lips.

"A happy occasion, gentlemen," he said. He gestured towards the Mark Nine, and then looked at Walker. "Worth waiting for, don't you think??"

Walker did not answer. I don't suppose he heard a word of what was said. He was staring at the huge green car in fascination, his eyes caressing its lines with slow reverence. Presently he walked forward, and opened the door.

"Rather a nice colour," I remarked conversationally to Broadwood.

He inclined his head.

A sudden exclamation from Walker made us both look at him. He was trembling and his face was the colour of paper. "The steering wheel," he stammered. His voice was almost a whisper, but the shocked horror of his tone came through clearly enough. "The steering wheel."

"What's the matter with it?"

"It's right-hand drive. Like an English car."

"But this is an English car," I said, puzzled. I thought the sudden sight of the Mark Nine had affected his wits.

"Estakia's the other way about!" If anything, the stricken

135

plete stop to British imports—even those entering under diplomatic permit. We have hopes of getting it relaxed, but it may take some time. I will let you know how things develop."

From the vantage point of the Foreign Office I had been keeping an eye on Estakia myself, and the omens, which included student riots and the traditional march on the British Embassy, were not favourable. But within six months Walker was able to write to me on a hopeful note:

"I have been busy entertaining the Estakia Director of Imports," he said. "He is a man called Borsthenian, who used to be the Embassy barber here. He still favours the tipping system! But I think I can arrange a permit for the Mark Nine. Please tell Broadwood."

I was on holiday when I received this letter. When I returned Broadwood himself was away in the north of England. For some weeks I put the matter on one side, only to be rung up, at Christmas time by Broadwood himself.

"I understand that your friend is coming home," he said coldly.

"Walker? Is he, indeed? I hadn't heard of it."

"We had a cable this morning. It is really very aggravating. Now he wants the car to be delivered in London."

"That should simplify matters, surely."

"In a sense, yes—though there may be a complication over purchase-tax. But your friend has undoubtedly given us a great deal of trouble." Apart from his frigid tone, I wished he would not call Walker 'my friend' as though I had a personal share in his shortcomings.

"We had arranged an export permit," went on Broadwood, "and reserved shipping space, and cleared the sterling-escudo transaction with the Bank of England. Then there was all that trouble in Estakia itself. Now the whole thing will have to be cancelled."

"I'm sorry," I said, equally coldly. "But I know that Mr Walker will be glad to get his car after all this delay." It was now two years since the scene in the showroom. "I hope that the steering-wheel will be on the right side this time—that is to say, the left."

Mr Broadwood hung up. . . .

Walker got in touch with me as soon as he arrived at

the Foreign Office. "Hello," I said. "Have a good trip?"

"Good enough." But there was in his voice, instead of the usual homecomer's satisfaction, a note of emergency that I did not like. "I didn't expect to be transferred so soon, though."

"Well you've got the car, anyway."

"No," he paused, his eyes staring at mine fixedly. "I'm not staying in England. I've been posted to Pirania."

"Ah," I said, noncommittally: the prospect sounded very dull. "Well South America will be a nice change for you. And there's no likelihood of trouble in Pirania—it's been determinedly pro-British ever since Queen Victoria's day."

"Yes," he agreed, "very much so." But now his eyes and his whole manner were truly frightening. "So much so that they copy the British in every single thing they do. *They even drive on the left-hand side.* They won't allow any other kind of car to come in." His voice was gradually rising to an uncontrolled crescendo. "There's a total ban, laid down by Presidential decree—a car with left-hand drive can't get past the customs." After a long pause he added, beseechingly: "*Please* come down to see Broadwood with me."

I remember that unpleasant interview. For the second time—so Broadwood phrased it—Walker had let Centurion Motors down. For the second time he was refusing to take delivery of a car for which he had given a specific order in writing. Really, gentlemen, really . . .

"I know it's far from satisfactory," said Walker miserably when he had endured ten minutes of Mr Broadwood's astonished sarcasm. "But I can't help it. That's what happens in the Foreign Service. One gets moved around."

"It appears," said Mr Broadwood grandly, "to conflict with the ownership of a Mark Nine."

"But it can't happen again," interrupted Walker. There was a suppliant eagerness in his voice that I found wretchedly embarrassing. "After Pirania I'm sure to be in England for some time. Either way, a right-hand-drive car will be all right."

"You wish to order *another* car?" said Mr Broadwood, as if he could hardly credit the idea.

"Yes—that is, if you'll agree—you'll have to take this one back, of course——" Walker was floundering pitifully. I longed to tell him to forget the whole damned thing, but I knew it would be no good—his life had been completely reshaped to include as its core a Mark Nine.

I tried to help. "Surely there is no difficulty," I said to Mr Broadwood. "You can take this car back—by your own admission there is a constant demand for Mark Nines—and simply order another one for Mr Walker."

Broadwood turned his cold eyes on to me. "Simply? No difficulty?" he repeated, distantly. "I can assure you, sir, I have had quite sufficient difficulty already, explaining these —*manœuvres* to my directors without embarking on them for a third time. Here at Centurion we are not used to this sort of thing not used to it at all."

Mr Broadwood affected to consider the matter. The frightful pantomime that now ensued was almost past endurance, but Walker followed it as if his sanity hung upon the outcome. Perhaps that was nearer to the truth than I then knew. Broadwood looked up at the ceiling, then at Walker for a long minute.

"It will not be easy. . . . But I will see what I can do."

"Thank you—oh, thank you very much!" said Walker. After a pause, he grinned nervously. "And what about delivery?"

"Eighteen months," answered Mr Broadwood frigidly.

"Oh. . . ." Walker's face fell. "Couldn't you make it a bit sooner? I've waited such a long time—three and a half years already."

"I *must* remind you," said Mr Broadwood, with loathsome emphasis, "that this will be the *third* Mark Nine we have built for you."

I had no further contact with Mr Broadwood after that. The relationship had become somewhat unpleasant and in any case there appeared to be very little that I could do to help. But Walker, who had settled down as our First Secretary at Pirania, kept me up-to-date with events and with his progress towards ownership of a Mark Nine. That progress was not swift.

Eighteen months, indeed, was clearly the minimum that Mr Broadwood was going to aim at as far as delivery was concerned; and there were further complications. Shortage of raw materials (so Walker wrote) had resulted in a change of chassis specification; this in turn meant an alteration in the interior fittings, and thereafter in the electrical lay-out.

All these variations in the contract had to be the subject of lengthy correspondence before they were agreed.

Before long Walker was compelled to forfeit his place in the queue so that two Mark Nines could be delivered to an Arabian oil potentate whom the British Government (and therefore Centurion Motors) wished to compliment.

Then, when all seemed ready, Centurion Motors put their prices up.

Walker told me of this in an agitated letter. 'They have raised the purchase price by *ten per cent*!' he wrote, in a crabbed, angular style like that of an old man. 'That may not sound much to you, but it is over *five hundred pounds* more than I bargained for, and, as you know, I was relying on my legacy to cover the *whole* cost of the car. I have written to Mr Broadwood, asking for a little more time and saying that I will do my *very best* to raise the additional money.' (I could imagine Mr Broadwood's reaction to this bourgeois plea.)

Later, he told me that the Foreign Office Accounts Department had refused to sanction an advance against his future salary; later still, that he had sold an insurance policy ('at a terrible loss'), and that the full purchasing price was now in Mr Broadwood's hands.

There was some element, not only in Walker's handwriting but in his choice of words also, which made me feel that the strain was really beginning to tell on him; and accordingly I made it my business to have a look at his papers. It was as I feared. He was not doing at all well at Pirania: the Ambassador's guarded reports on him indicated, between the lines, that Walker's grasp of his job was less than adequate. The word 'unusual' occurred not once but three times. In a long experience I have never known a man's career to recover from the use of this adjective.

There was, lastly, a note in his papers that he had taken thirty-six days' sickleave already during his tour of duty. He had resigned from the Voyagers' Club.

It was not an encouraging picture: clearly, the ownership of a Mark Nine was likely to cost Walker a great deal more even than the £5,600 which was now its purchase price. But finally, to my great relief, Walker wrote that all his worries were over: after two years of waiting, the car was at last on its way to him, and would be in Pirania within three weeks.

This was, he added, five and a half years since he first ordered the original model. . . .

When I first saw the newspaper headlines 'REVOLUTION IN PIRANIA—EXTREMISTS TAKE OVER' I paid little attention to them. It was not a part of the world that concerned my Department, and in any case a South American revolution was a commonplace event.

But in this case the word 'Pirania' attracted my attention, since Walker had so recently been in my thoughts; and when I had a moment to spare I walked across to the South American department to look at their telegrams. The final sentence read: 'The most extensive rioting took place in the dock area.'

It was not till some time afterwards that I heard what had happened to Walker's Mark Nine. But piece by piece I assembled the whole picture, partly from the Piranian newspapers, partly from our Ambassador, and the whole picture was truly memorable.

Walker, it seemed, after a frenzied week in which he had done not a stroke of work (save to ring up the shipping agents twice daily), had gone down to the docks to see the ship come in and his car unloaded. He had been warned not to do this, since the capital was now in the middle of its current revolution; but he had disregarded all advice.

By mid-morning, the ship, the *Piranian Star*, was sluggishly discharging its cargo: by noon, however, work had almost come to a stop again, as fresh shooting was heard from the direction of the town, followed by a pall of smoke from a burning building.

But one crane, doubtless manned by a determined—or deaf—individualist, was still working methodically; and by and by the Mark Nine came into view, hoisted from the forward hold by a cradle of four slings, one under each wheel. Walker gazed at it fondly. High in the air it rose, dark green, gleaming, resplendent, till it reached the top of its arc and was ready for lowering. Then firing broke out much nearer at hand, within the dock area itself, and the crane-engine clanked to a standstill.

The Mark Nine stayed where it was, twisting on its axis,

swinging gently thirty feet above the ground, catching the sunlight agreeably. The firing continued and soon a man climbed down from the crane-cabin, dodging behind the struts, and made off at a run. Then silence fell again on the deserted quay. Walker remained in isolation, looking upwards at his car.

The Mark Nine, and Walker, stayed where they were for a full three hours. Inland shooting was still to be heard: on the quay complete silence reigned. The car, now at rest, hung idly where it was, reflecting the lowering sun, the most splendid thing in view.

Walker, sitting on a bollard, bided his time patiently. Occasionally he looked up at his car. He had waited five and a half years. Half a day more would not matter.

The first bullet struck the Mark Nine at about four o'clock, hitting the windscreen and shattering it completely. It was quickly followed by others. One could not say for certain where the firing originated, but it seemed to come from the top floor of the Customs building. Walker counted three rifles and one light machine-gun; and he had no difficulty in determining what the men behind them were doing. Having nothing serious to aim at, they were shooting at the most attractive target in sight. There could be little doubt what that was.

Walker, crouched in anguish against the side of the nearest building, watched the slow, methodical destruction of the Mark Nine. Finally, when it was hardly possible to mark or hole the car further, the men in the Customs started firing accurately at the rope slings by which the Mark Nine hung from the crane.

The Mark Nine, released, plunged down like a stone. It hit the lip of the dock with a sickening crunch, concertinaed over half its length, and then toppled forwards into forty feet of water.

Then a man—this last item was from the local newspaper —a man who must have been Walker was seen to run forward and peer over the edge into the dock basin where the ripples were already subsiding. He was lightly hit by a bullet in the arm but to this he paid no attention. He appeared to be crying bitterly. Presently he dived into the dock, and, until he was hauled out, swam round and round in circles. . . .

143

Walker asked if he might see me on his way through London, and with little or no hesitation I agreed. He was still First Secretary, I saw from the Appointments List, and en route for Lichtonia, a very quiet post where we maintained only a token establishment. His sick leave had been spent in Cornwall.

I had been prepared for changes in him, but I was truly shocked at his appearance. The Walker of six years ago when he first went along to the Centurion showrooms had vanished completely: in his place was an old man—grey, hesitant, his face sunken, his eyes shadowed over. If I had not known that he was forty-seven I would have taken him for sixty—and a bad sixty at that.

"I see you've been posted to Lichtonia," I said. "A very pleasant spot."

"I'm looking forward to it," he said. His clasped hands were trembling, but I noticed that, when he raised his eyelids, his eyes were very much alive, almost alarmingly so. "It's near the Italian border, you know. They have some of the best roads in Europe."

"Indeed?"

"Yes. The Centurion should eat them up."

I started. "But surely——" I began, and then hesitated. With Walker fresh from his convalescence I did not want to reopen the tragic past. Perhaps, however, it would be better to feign normality since Walker himself had introduced the subject. "Are you really getting a Centurion?" I asked.

"Of course," he answered. His burning eyes held mine steadily. "The insurance companies are still fighting about the last one, but that doesn't concern me at all."

"Well, well," I said, somewhat at a loss. "Another Mark Nine?"

"Oh no!" he said. "They've stopped making Mark Nines."

"Dear me!" I said, inadequately. "I'm sorry to hear it."

"But there's a new model, a Mark Ten," he said. His voice was regaining its old enthusiasm. "I can't tell you what it's like—an absolute dream! Automatic transmission—*a hundred miles an hour in thirty-two seconds*. I went down to see Broadwood today. You remember Broadwood?"

"Yes, indeed."

"I ordered a Mark Ten from him." Walker's eyes, fastened on mine, were now positively hypnotic. "We signed the papers together. Eighteen months for delivery. But it'll be worth waiting for, don't you think?"

I Was There

SHE WAS a lovely boat, and a thousand times during that long trip across the Channel and up the French coast from Southampton to Flushing I found myself wishing she were mine. But country lawyers in a small way of business don't own sixty-ton diesel-powered yawls like the *Ariadne*: if they are lucky, they get the job of delivering them from their builders to other, more fortunate people. That was what I was doing that June evening, and not hurrying the job either; we had a fortnight to make the trip, ironing out the snarls on the way, and none of us wanted to cut that fortnight short.

'Us' was three people altogether: myself, on holiday from the dry-as-dust legal business of an English market town; George Wainwright, about whom I knew nothing save that he was on the fringe of London's theatrical world, and an excellent small-boat navigator; and Ginger, who tripled as steward, deck-hand, and running commentator. "Call me Ginger!" he had said in a cheerful Cockney voice as soon as we met on the dockside: "My mother was scared by a carrot!"

I had left it at 'Ginger'; he was the kind of man who didn't need a second name.

This was the sort of holiday I took every year, signing on with a yacht-delivery service and pulling strings to wangle the best boat and the best trip I could. It was the only way I could get to sea nowadays; the war had taken my own boat, and the post-war my bank balance. George Wainwright told me, airily, that he was 'resting between shows', though I fancy he was glad enough to pick up free quarters and twenty pounds for making what was virtually a pleasure cruise. He was a big man, sinewy and tough. I had the impression that he had done a lot of ocean-racing at one time in other people's boats, though I couldn't imagine him in any conceivable part in any West End play.

Ginger, the steward, didn't volunteer anything about himself. He never stopped talking, for all that.

The crew on these 'builder's delivery' jobs was usually a scratch lot, though it struck me that this time we were remarkably assorted. Middle-aged lawyer, forty-year-old actor, a red-headed Cockney who might have been fresh out of jail—the crew of the *Ariadne* seemed to have been picked at random from the Yellow Pages. But we had made her sail like a champion, all the same.

We had made her sail to such good purpose that now, with two days in hand, we were loafing along on the last hundred miles of the journey. Earlier, we had come smoking up the Channel before a Force 6 gale; *Ariadne*, handling beautifully, had logged a steady ten knots under her storm canvas. But then the wind had fallen light, and the leg from Dover to Calais had become a gentle drifting under hazy sunshine, while the decks and the sails dried out and we made what small repairs were necessary. Nothing had gone wrong that didn't always go wrong in a boat fresh from the builders—a leaking skylight, some chafed rigging, a cupboard door that wouldn't stay shut in a seaway. By and large, she went like a dream—as far as I was concerned, an envious dream of ownership that I would never live in reality.

George Wainwright and I had taken turn-about at the wheel, with Ginger filling in for an odd trick or two to give us an extra margin of sleep. We had lived on tea, corned beef, beans, and something which Ginger called 'cheesy-hammy-eggy', and which, for cold, hungry, and tired men, was a banquet in itself. Rum, twice a day, completed our paradise.

Now, towards the end of that paradise, we were punching eastwards against the ebb tide at six o'clock of a magic evening. *Ariadne*, under all plain sail, could not make much of the light air; we were barely holding our own, creeping up the flat coastline with the sun warm on our backs. I had the wheel, letting the spokes slide through my fingers with a sensual joy. Ginger, standing with his head poking out of the cabin top, was drying cups and saucers. George Wainwright, his elbows planted on the chart, stared landwards through his binoculars.

"We're not making any headway," he said presently. "Barely a knot, I should say."

"Suits me," said Ginger irrepressibly. He could never resist a comment on anything, from UN politics to juvenile delinquency. "I've got all year."

The water gurgled at the bow. The sail slatted, empty of wind.

"We might as well anchor," I said. "The tide will be against us for another four hours. What's the depth here?"

George Wainwright glanced at the chart. "About four fathoms. Sandy bottom. She'll hold all right."

"We'll anchor till the flood," I decided. "Give us a chance to catch up on our sleep." I eased *Ariadne* up into the wind, and our way fell off. Ginger went forward to see to the windlass. "How far are we off shore?" I asked George.

"About a mile," he answered. "The tide sets us inwards."

"And where, exactly?"

"Off Dunkirk."

Dunkirk. . . . As the anchor-chain rattled down through the leads, and *Ariadne* swung and settled to her cable, I was conscious of an odd foreboding. It was true that we were a mile off Dunkirk: I recognized, as if from a hundred photographs, the oily swell, the sloping beaches, the flat mainland enclosing a loose-knit grey town. Here were the waters, full of ghosts, full of sunken ships and dead men, which a decade earlier—no, it was now nearly *two* decades—had resounded to a murderous uproar. In my mind's eye I saw them all again; the straggling lines of men wading through the shallows, crying out for rescue or waiting in dull stupor to be picked up: the burning town behind, the Stukas overhead, and the small boats darting in and out—going in light, coming out laden to the gunwales—on an errand of mercy and salvage that went on hour after hour, day after day. That was what Dunkirk would always mean to me—a name at once grisly and proud, a symbol, a haunting from the past. I was curious to know what it meant to the other two, and I did not have to wait long to find out.

Ginger, having secured the anchor, came aft again. George Wainwright looked up from his chart, where *Ariadne's* observed position was now marked by a neatly pencilled cross. There was no need to wonder which of them would speak first. It would have been an easy bet to win.

"Good old Dunkirk!" said Ginger jauntily. He wiped his hands, greasy from the windlass, on a bunch of cotton-waste, and looked round him at *Ariadne's* benevolent anchorage. "Makes you think a bit, don't it?"

"How do you mean, Ginger?" asked George Wainwright.

"All this. . . ." Ginger waved his hand round vaguely. "It's nineteen years ago now, but by cripes it's like yesterday! . . . The bombers coming over as thick as bloody fleas, the lads waiting. . . . I'll never forget it, not as long as I live. By cripes, skipper!" he turned to me, his creased leathery face alight, "I could tell you a yarn that would curl your hair! A yarn——"

. . . a yarn which, as the sun sank to the westwards, and *Ariadne's* wavering shadow lengthened and faded on the tranquil waters off Dunkirk, recalled all the horrors, terrors, and triumphs of those mortal days. Ginger told it well; I knew that he must have had many audiences, many chances to polish and perfect.

The lads, he said (and we could all see them as lads, beefy Lancashire lads from the mills, grey-faced lads from the Yorkshire coal pits, likely lads from Bermondsey and Bow)— the lads were fed up. The officer had promised them they'd be taken off that night, and they'd been content with that, after a week's dodging the bombers on their way back to the coast, and they'd settled down on the beach to wait. But they hadn't been taken off, not that night, nor the next, nor the next. That was the army for you—waiting about, nobody knowing what was happening, all a lot of bull, put that bloody light out! . . . First they had waited on the beach; then at the water's edge; then chest-high in the water itself.

The straggling line inched its way outwards from the shallows to the deep water. "Link arms, there!" said the officer; so they linked arms, and with the other hand held their rifles safely above water. "Because you'll be using those rifles tomorrow," said the officer. "Keep them dry, keep them ready for instant action!" " 'Ark at 'im," said the lads. . .

They waited in the shallows and the deeps. It was cold at night; then it was hot; behind them the town was burning, and the perimeter force kept blazing away with everything they'd got, and the Stukas circled, and swooped, and roared away again, leaving behind them a salty human flotsam— men mixed with sand, men mixed with water, seaweed, other men, all draining slowly away as the tide ebbed. "Where's the bloody Air Force?" asked the lads, scanning the alien sky between waves of noise and pain. "Tucked up in bed with anyone they can get hold of" . . . "Heard from your missus lately? . . ."

149

It was cold at night, then it was burning hot. Men got hit, and dropped out; men got cramp, and floated away; men went mad, and tried to hide beneath the waves. There were other straggling lines within sight, like feelers weaving and groping towards home. Their own line grew thinner; sometimes part of it disappeared altogether, as if by weight of noise and pressure. "Close up!" said the officer. "And no smoking there! Might give away our position."

The officer was the last to go. He was one of the lads himself, only a bit lah-di-dah. . . . When it was their turn to be taken off, the boat from the destroyer, bobbing inshore after a stick of bombs had straddled the shallows, drew alongside the wavering line.

"Look lively!" said the sailor at the helm, as cool as fresh salad, and they looked lively—as lively as they could after three days of it. There was one lad going off his head with the noise and the sun, and he tried to clamber on board, suddenly screaming with mingled pain and joy, and the officer came up behind and gave him a heave into the boat, and then himself crumpled up like a sodden newspaper and disappeared without a trace.

They fished around for him, couldn't find him, suddenly abandoned the idea and drew swiftly away. Better to save twenty lives, they reassured themselves. . . . But it was funny how surprised he had looked after three such days, just before he faded out.

Dusk came down like a blessing. *Ariadne* rode to her anchor proudly; she was gleaming new, and the white of her doused sails seemed to hold the sunlight long after it had dipped below the horizon. I would have needed a lot of things—a lot of luck, a lot of horse-sense, a lot of drive I had never had—to possess a boat like this. But somehow, sitting relaxed in the cockpit, nursing a rum-and-water, I found it easy to imagine that it had all happened, and that she was mine.

The lights of Dunkirk were coming on one by one. George Wainwright took an anchor-bearing from them, satisfied himself that we were not dragging, and sat down by my side again. He raised his voice against the lap and gurgle of the tideway.

"That was a good yarn of yours, Ginger," he said. "I know exactly how you must have felt. . . . But it was just as bad for the little ships that had to come close inshore and take the troops off. If you want to hear a story. . . ."

. . . a story about a big man in a small boat (and, looking at George Wainwright's broad shoulders as he lounged at the after-end of the cockpit, we both knew that it was *his* story.) Hundreds of little ships played their part in the evacuation of Dunkirk; everything from old paddle-wheel ferries to ship's lifeboats, nursed across the Channel by a man and a boy. Their job was to run a shuttle service—to come close inshore, load up with troops, and bring them out to deeper water where the bigger boats and the destroyers were waiting.

Some of the little ships kept it up for three or four days. The two-and-a-half-ton sloop *Tantivvy* was one of these.

Tantivvy (said George Wainwright) was nothing to look at though she was the owner's pride and joy. She'd sailed across from Dover with the rest of the mob, following a call on the radio which asked for every small ship that could stay afloat to report for emergency duty. The motley fleet fanned out like a crazy Armada, then converged on Dunkirk. Dunkirk, with its pall of smoke, its mass of shipping, its hurricane of gunfire, was something you couldn't miss.

Tantivvy, drawing less than four feet, could get within half a mile of the shore; and there she anchored, and presently launched from her upper deck a small pram-dinghy propelled by a large man whose bulk left room for, at the very most, two other passengers. . . . All day, and most of the night, the dinghy plied to and fro, taking off two soldiers at at a time from the waiting hordes, loading them on to the deck of *Tantivvy*, and then going back for more.

There came a time, towards dawn, when *Tantivvy* had fifty passengers. They sprawled in the tiny cabin, grey-faced, dead to the world; they lay about on the upper deck, soiling it with their blood; they sat with their backs to the mast, staring at nothing, waiting for peace. After his twenty-fifth trip, the big man looked at them, and said: "Not many more, I'm afraid."

One of the soldiers, still awake and still able to talk, waited for a lull in the bombing, and called out: "Let's get going, for God's sake!"

"We might manage two more," said the big man, resting his swollen, aching arms on the oars.

"Don't be a bloody fool!" said the soldier in a cracked voice. "You'll lose the lot of us if you do. We're damn' near sinking already."

A bomb fell with a screaming crump! and a shower of dirty water, close beside them.

"Well . . ." said the big man. His face was deadly tired, his eyes puffy and discoloured.

He climbed on board, secured the dinghy to the stern post, and started up the tiny motor.

"Help me with the anchor," he said to the soldier.

The two of them shambled forwards, picking their way between half-dead men who, even when kicked out of the way, could not spare them a glance. They heaved on the anchor and finally brought it home. The big man stood upright, and then suddenly stiffened.

"You stupid bastard!" he said to the soldier.

"What?" said the soldier, in amazement.

There was an enormous explosion ashore, and the small boat, gathering way, rocked as the hot shock-wave reached them.

"*Don't you know better*," asked the big man, with murderous sarcasm, "*than to walk on a wooden deck in those blasted hobnailed boots?*"

There was a breeze coming up from the southward, sending the small ripples slap-slapping against *Ariadne*'s shapely hull. An hour before moonrise, it was now very dark; Dunkirk's glow was reflected in the sky overhead, but between the town and the boat there was a waste of inky black water, deserted, featureless. It was as if the soldiers had all been picked up, and we were free to go. . . .

In the glow from the binnacle Ginger's perky face was sombre. Perhaps, for him as well, the ghosts were still thick around us. If only for our comfort I knew that I had to tell them about the triumphant part, the end of the story. . . .

. . . the end of the story, which I could see now, as clearly as the others had seen theirs.

She was an old destroyer, a bit cranky in her ways (which were the ways of 1916, not 1940) and bringing her alongside at Dover, feverishly crammed with shipping, was not easy. Not if you'd been on the bridge for thirty-six hours, and made two trips to Dunkirk, and dodged the bombers all the way there and all the way back, and waited off-shore, sweating, while eight hundred and sixty-two men scrambled, clawed, and bullocked their way on board. Not if you had to go back, as soon as this lot was landed, and do the whole thing over and over again till there were no more soldiers showing above water.

The old destroyer slipped between two trawlers leaving for a routine minesweep, stopped in her tracks with a sudden boiling of foam aft, and edged sideways towards the quay. The lines went snaking ashore, the windlasses took in the slack; presently she was berthed, and the hum of the main engines ceased. The captain walked to the back of the bridge and looked aft along the length of his ship.

This was the dividend, this was what the excursion had been for. . . . There wasn't an inch of the deck that was not covered with men—men in khaki. On the trip home they had lain there as though stunned or dead; now they were stirring, moving towards the gangway and peering down at the Dover dockside as if they could scarcely believe their eyes. Their uniforms were filthy, their faces unshaven, their many bandages bloodstained; they looked like a wretched scarecrow army in some hollow Shakespearian comedy. About half of them had rifles. There was no other equipment.

The destroyer captain thought: if this is what's left of the British Army, then God help us. . . .

They began to disembark, shambling down the gang-plank like men sleepwalking in a dream of death. They collected in groups, and then in ragged lines, filling the whole quayside. There was a bunch of them directly below the bridge, standing as if in a shattered trance.

Then suddenly one of them, a small lance-corporal, looked up at the bridge, and then directly at the destroyer captain himself. For a moment they held each other's eyes as if they were seeking some rare, unheard-of element that could bridge the ground between a stunted Cockney soldier and a tall, beribboned Royal Navy captain; and then the small lance-corporal grinned, and looked round at his weary comrades, and shouted, on a cracked note of energy:

"Come on, lads! Three cheers for the bleedin' Nyvy!"

They could hardly be called three cheers; they were like the thin rise and fall of a groan, or a spectral sighing from an army of ghosts. But they did emanate from those bedraggled ranks, and they did reach the gaunt, teak-faced destroyer captain on the bridge.

The captain, when he went ashore, was the elder son of an earl; and, when afloat, an unbending disciplinarian who had been known to deal out exemplary punishment for a sloppy salute. It was a difficult moment, covered by no textbook, no family code, and indeed no war so far. But he also had something important to express, and he did the best he could. He leant over the wing of his bridge, stiff as a rod in spite of his weariness, and enunciated very clearly:

"My compliments to *you*, gentlemen—my *best* compliments."

They liked my story, I could tell that; it reminded them that the Dunkirk disaster could be read two ways. In the binnacle glow, Ginger's face grew cheerful again, and George Wainwright took a swig of his rum as if toasting Victory herself. The night breeze, from landwards, brought a warm homely smell of Flanders fields. At anchor off Dunkirk we had mourned long enough; for the tragedy had a happy ending after all.

"That's what we tend to forget," said George, echoing my thoughts. "We *did* take off more than three hundred thousand of them, and they *did* get back again, in the end."

Looking up after the long spell of talking, I became aware that the lights of Dunkirk were no longer on *Ariadne*'s starboard beam, but traversing slowly round astern of her. The Channel tide was flooding.

"We're swinging, skipper," said George Wainwright, noticing at the same moment. "The tide's with us now. The wind's got some weight in it, too."

I clicked the switch of the navigation lights, and the friendly red and green eyes brought *Ariadne* to life.

"Let's get under way," I said.

"Now you're talking!" said Ginger. "This place gives me the creeps."

We were all standing up, ready to go about our tasks—hoisting the foresail and the main, getting up the anchor, putting ourselves and *Ariadne* to work again.

"Of course Dunkirk is haunted," said George Wainwright suddenly. "But it gave us something to be proud of, all the same."

Some quality of wistfulness in his voice prompted me to ask a question which had been in my mind ever since the three of us started talking.

"Tell me something," I said. "*Were* you at Dunkirk?"

It was light enough to see him grin. "Not actually, old boy," he answered. Suddenly he *did* sound like an actor, rather a good one. "I was touring with ENSA at the time. *Private Lives*—eight shows a week. I wasn't actually *at* Dunkirk."

It seemed right that he did not sound sheepish. . . . I turned towards the slight figure clambering up to the fo'c'sle deck.

"Ginger? Were you?"

"Not me!" I might have been charging him with picking pockets. "1940, wasn't it?—I was in the glasshouse already! Asleep on sentry-go, the man said. What a —— liberty!"

I knew what was coming next.

"Were *you* there?" George Wainwright asked me.

I didn't want to embarrass either of them; in any case, I couldn't be sure that, even now, they were telling the truth. One of them was an actor, the other a liar; they lived, congenitally, in opposite corners of the same dream-world. And I myself led such a dull life nowadays. . . .

"Afraid not," I answered. "Bad heart, you know. . . . I was doing civil defence work in London all that summer. I wasn't at Dunkirk either."

But the moment of revelation did not make us ashamed among ourselves, nor were we truly liars, whether we were lying or not. For our last three answers had all been wrong. Every Englishman was at Dunkirk.

The Dinner Party

THERE ARE still some rich people in the world; and there were very many more in the enjoyable world of thirty years ago. I hope that no one will be led astray by the fiction that rich people lead dull, boring and frustrated lives; compelled to listen to unintelligible chamber music every other night, to sit through interminable operas which they do not understand, to bow unwillingly to Royalty, and to force down their gullets such dietary dross as *pâté de foie gras*, trout in aspic, and champagne.

Please be assured that many of them lead lives of particular pleasure, commanding the finest artists to play and sing exactly what they wish to hear, greeting Royalty on terms of pleasure and intimacy, and eating and drinking precisely what they want—often *pâté de foie gras*, trout in aspic, and champagne.

But rich people do have their problems. They are seldom problems of finance, since most rich people have sufficient sense to hire other people to take care of their worries—whether they are concerned with taxes, politics, the education of their children, the estrangement of their wives, or the greed of their servants.

But there are other, more genuine problems. They are the problems of behaviour.

Let me tell you one such a problem which beset my uncle Octavian a full thirty years ago.

A full thirty years ago, I myself was fifteen. That is not really important, though it was important to me at the time, on the threshold of the dazzling adult world. More important to this story, my uncle Octavian was then (in 1925) a rich man in the lavish pride of manhood.

He was (as any suitable contemporary will confirm) a charming and accomplished host whose villa on the Côte d'Azur was an accepted rendezvous of the great; and he was (as I will confirm) a hospitable, contented, and most amiable man—until January 3rd, 1925.

There was nothing special about that day in the life of my uncle Octavian, except that it was his fifty-fifth birthday. As usual on such a day he was giving a dinner party, a party for twelve people. All of them were old friends; two of them, indeed, were what were then called, unambiguously, 'old flames'. (My uncle, aged fifty-five, would scarcely have found it possible to give a birthday dinner party not attended by at least two such guests. He had long been addicted to what was then called, with equal unambiguity, a 'full life'.)

I myself, aged fifteen, was deeply privileged. I was staying with my uncle at his exquisite villa near Cap d'Antibes; and as a special concession on this happy day I was allowed to come down to dinner. It was exciting to me to be admitted to such company, which included besides the two 'old flames' and their respective husbands, a newspaper proprietor of exceptional intelligence and his fabulous American wife; a recent Prime Minister of France and a monumental Elder Statesman of post-war Germany; and a Habsburg Prince and Princess.

At that age, on holiday from school, you will guess that I was dazzled. Even today, thirty years later, one may fairly admit that the company was distinguished. But I should also stress, to give point to this story, that they were all old and intimate friends of my uncle Octavian.

Towards the end of a wonderful dinner, when dessert had been brought in and the servants had left, my uncle leant forward to admire a magnificent solitaire diamond ring on the princess's hand. She was a handsome woman of regal bearing. I remember the candlelight flashing on, and within, the canary-yellow stone as she turned her hand gracefully towards my uncle.

Across the table, the newspaper proprietor leant across and said: "May I also have a look, Thérèse?" She smiled and nodded. Then she took off the ring and held it out to him. "It was my grandmother's—the old empress," she said. "I have not worn it for many years. It is said to have once belonged to Genghis Khan."

There were exclamations of delight and admiration. The ring was passed from hand to hand. For a moment it rested on my own palm, gleaming splendidly with that wonderful interior yellow glow that such jewels can command. Then I passed it on to my next-door neighbour. As I turned away again, I thought I saw her pass it on. At least I was almost sure I saw her.

It was some twenty minutes later when the princess stood up, giving the signal for the ladies to withdraw. She looked round us with a pleasant smile. Then she said: "Before we leave you, may I have my ring back?"

I remember my uncle Octavian murmuring: "Ah yes—that wonderful ring!" I remember the newspaper proprietor saying: "By jove! mustn't forget that!" and one of the women laughing.

Then there was a pause while each of us looked expectantly at his neighbour. Then there was silence.

The princess was still smiling, though less easily. She was unused to asking for things twice. "If you please," she said, with a touch of hauteur. "Then we can leave the gentlemen to their port."

When no one answered her and the silence continued, I still thought that it could only be a practical joke, and that one of us—probably the prince himself—would produce the ring with a laugh and a flourish, perhaps chiding her for her carelessness. But when nothing happened at all I knew that the rest of that night would be dreadful.

I am sure that you can guess the sort of scene that followed. There was the embarrassment, immediate and shattering, of the guests—all of them old and valued friends. There was the freezing politeness of the prince, the near-tears of the princess. There were the demands to be searched, the overturning of chairs, the minute scrutiny of the carpet, and then of the whole room. There was the fact that presently no one would meet anyone else's eye.

All these things happened, but they did not bring the princess's ring back again. It had vanished—an irreplaceable heirloom, worth possibly two hundred thousand pounds—in a roomful of twelve people, all known to each other.

No servants had entered the room. No one had left it for a moment. The thief (for now it could only be theft) was one of us, one of my uncle Octavian's cherished friends.

I remember it was the French cabinet minister who was most insistent on being searched; indeed, in his excitement he had already started turning out his pockets before my uncle held up his hand and stopped him.

Uncle Octavian's face was pale and tremendously tense

as if he had been dealt a mortal blow. "There will be no searching," he commanded. "Not in my house. You are all my friends. The ring can only be lost. If it is not found"—he bowed towards the princess—"I will naturally make amends myself."

The dreadful and fruitless search began again.

The ring was never found though the guests stayed nearly till dawn—unwilling to be the first to leave, wishing to comfort my uncle (who though deadly calm was deeply stricken) and still hoping that, from the shambles of the dining-room, the ring would somehow appear.

It never did appear either then or later. My uncle Octavian, to the last, remained true to his rigid code, and adamant that no one was to be searched.

I myself went back to England, and school a few days later. I was very glad to escape. The sight of my uncle's face, and the knowledge of his overturned world, were more than I could bear. All that he was left with, among the ruins of his way of life, was a question mark; which of his intimate friends was the thief?

I do not know how, or on what scale, my uncle Octavian "made amends". I know that he never returned to his lovely house near Cap d'Antibes, and that he remained a recluse for the rest of his days. I know that, to our family's surprise, he was a comparatively poor man when he died. He died, in fact, a few weeks ago, and that is why I feel I can tell the story.

It would be wrong to say that he died a broken man, but he did die a profoundly sad one, with the special sadness of a hospitable host who never gave a single lunch or dinner party for the last thirty years of his life.

Licensed to Kill

WHEN MY brand-new, enchanting, and unpredictable wife announced that we were going to fly six thousand miles, from London to South Africa, in order to spend our deferred honeymoon with her father, even I, the world's most placid chartered accountant, tried to put my foot down.

It was after dinner; she was looking entirely ravishing in the sort of housecoat that no modern house should lack; the traffic outside was a low murmur; the fire burned brightly; the poodle was asleep. Against these heavy odds I strove to put the realistic point of view.

"It's too far to go," I said, just to start with.

"It's twenty hours," said Helene. (I don't know any other woman in the world who can make a sentence such as "It's twenty hours" sound like "I love you *now*".) "It's just a little hop," she continued on the same note of insidious witchcraft. "People spend twenty hours just going to *Scotland*."

"Let's do that," I said.

"I want some sunshine." She raised a slim arm and a beautifuly formed hand to tick off her list of requirements. "I want some sun. I want to see my father. I want *you* to see South Africa. I want a nice honeymoon."

I took the last point. "We can have a nice honeymoon," I said, "and scarcely take a step."

Helene looked at me, a melting look, no good at all for resistant husbands. "Yes, indeed," she said. "But this will be something special. South Africa is the most beautiful country in the world. You *must* see it. Dad has a house right on the sea between Cape Town and Port Elizabeth. There's a wonderful place—a sort of island peninsula, called the Robberg—where we'll go and fish. We can lie in the sun, swim, picnic, look for wild orchids, shoot guinea-fowl, and catch sharks weighing *hundreds* of pounds."

I considered all these things. Guinea-fowl are something I can take or leave alone (except at the dinner table); sharks

160

I have been brought up to avoid. But the rest sounded magical. Weakening, I went through a modest catalogue of objections.

"I can't get away."

"You've more than two months' leave due to you."

"It's too expensive."

"We can use the wedding cheques."

"There won't be room in the house."

"There's a whole wing of it, just waiting for us."

And finally, in a judicious, chartered accountant voice: "It's very unusual," I said, "to spend a honeymoon with one's father-in-law."

"He's a poppet," said Helene. "I adore him, and so will you. Next to you he's the nicest man in the world. He'll just love having us."

"But it's a *honeymoon*."

"That's all right," said Helene. "He's terribly deaf."

"Better for us if he were terribly short-sighted."

"Now that," said Helene, "is one of the most unkind remarks I've ever heard."

Naturally we caught the Johannesburg plane forty-eight hours later.

Helene had been right as usual: South Africa (politics apart) *is* the most beautiful country in the world, and the corner where my father-in-law lived was a jewel of sunshine, noble scenery and soft-lapped luxury. It was called Plettenberg Bay; in the nineteenth century it had been a famous whaling station, named for the Dutch governor of the province who undoubtedly showed wonderful taste in choosing this base for his operations.

The small village lay in the arm of a bay on the Indian Ocean, well-protected, benevolent in all its aspects. It had a long sandy beach, a gentle warmth, and a back-drop of mountains with the unpronounceable name of Tzitzikhama which supplied, every morning, noon, and night, a contagious hazy magnificence. After grumbling about everything, from the price of the airline tickets (three hundred and seventy-four pounds each) to the quality of the souvenir leopard-skin slippers which we bought at Nairobi on the way south, I still had to admit that it was a dream.

My father-in-law (whom I had never met) was not a

dream; he was something else again. His name was James
Forsyth; he was old (eighty), highly individual, and a man
of extreme local influence. He was rich, as all father-in-laws
should be. In his day he had been a famous athlete; indeed,
he was the oldest living South African rugby football international. He was tough, magnificent, endearing, and totally
formidable. He was also selectively stone-deaf.

After he had embraced Helene he turned to me. His handshake was sinewy and enveloping. As I clasped his hand I
hoped that when I was eighty years of age I could still give
as good an account of myself. In a deep rumbling voice he
said:

"Welcome to my house. . . ." And then, pointing towards
Helene, with whom he clearly had a special tender relationship, he said with Old Testament authority: "Make her
very happy."

Our first dinner was well up to what I came to know as
South African standards: a fish broth, a fresh-caught yellow-
tail, a mountainous steak, a cheese soufflé, and coffee as
thick and strong as manila rope. My father-in-law, casting
envious glances every few minutes, ate two soft-boiled eggs
and drank a glass of buttermilk. After that Helene went
off to unpack while I sat outside on the wide stone *stoep*, and
gazed with deep contentment at the Indian Ocean a few
score yards off, and watched the stars come out, and talked
with old James Forsyth.

London, and foggy drizzle, and dreary politics, seemed
much more than six thousand miles away.

I thought my father-in-law delightful if somewhat disconcerting. He was indeed deaf: one had to shout; but
occasionally, it seemed, his hearing came on again and he
picked up a near-whisper not necessarily intended for his
ears. Mostly on this night I was content to listen, while he
rumbled on in a deep bass voice. It was small talk from a
large man: village politics, local stock losses, the fishing
prospects, the weather. Life for him and for everyone else in
Plettenberg Bay was clearly tranquil, blessed alike by nature
and by man.

Only as we said good night did something alien and dis-
quieting intrude upon this paradise.

"Well, now!" said old James Forsyth. He levered up his

immense frame from the armchair, and consulted a gold pocket watch that must have weighed half a pound. "That's my bedtime." He gave me a sudden startling, conspiratorial wink. "You'll be sitting up late, I suppose."

It was odd to blush and to have such an appreciative witness of it.

"Well, no," I answered, "I think it's about my bedtime, too."

"She's a good girl," said James Forsyth. "The best that I have. . . ." He walked towards the doorway calling as he did so: "Timothy!"

Timothy appeared on the instant, a small spare smiling negro in immaculate white from pointed shoes to cotton gloves. I already knew, from Helene, that he had been everything from kitchen-boy to children's nurse, from chauffeur to major-domo, in this not inconsiderable household during the past thirty-five years.

"Master," said Timothy.

"Have you locked up?" asked James Forsyth gruffly.

"Yes, master. All safe."

"Garage too?"

"Yes, master."

"All the boys in?"

"Yes, master."

"Put the bar on the kitchen door. And then help me with my boots."

It sounded strange, and I remarked on the fact.

"Do you really have to lock everything?" I asked.

He cupped his hand to his ear. "Hey? What's that?"

"Do you have to lock all the doors?" I shouted. "In a village like this?"

"I haven't locked my front door since 1906," said James Forsyth, "but I'm doing it now. . . . We've been having a lot of robberies in the village. Nasty ones. Beating people up. It's the first time it's ever happened in Plettenberg Bay."

"Who's responsible?"

"Natives, for certain. *Skollies*." He used the Afrikaans word for shiftless young troublemakers. "Who else would do it . . .? We had an old chap hit over the head only last night. He's in Port Elizabeth hospital now with a cracked skull. And if he dies," said James Forsyth heavily, "it's more than robbery. It's murder."

Robbery and murder seemed very far away next morning, one of the fairest days I had ever seen in my life.

The day started early, as most days do in the enticing air of South Africa. It was easy to face life at six o'clock in the morning, when six o'clock meant pure sunshine, a calm dancing sea below one's window, and smoke rising in true vertical ascent from a hundred village chimneys. When I left Helene still asleep, and put on a dressing-gown and padded out on to the *stoep*, there was my father-in-law already sitting deep in an armchair, staring towards the mountains and sipping coffee from a patterned mug which undoubtedly held a full pint.

He gestured towards the coffee pot, not speaking either then or for the next half-hour. The beautiful morning was enough for both of us. When the coffee was finished and the sun well up above the horizon he said simply:

"Fine day. . . . That chap I was talking about died in hospital—I heard it over the radio. . . . The car's all ready. . . . You should go and see Robberg."

We went and saw Robberg, Helene and I, a couple of hours later, and it was an entrancing journey. Just as she had described it in London, Robberg was a slim peninsula, almost an island, jutting out into the sea for three or four miles. The rock formation, washed by the sea at its base, rose steeply to a sandy plateau; the wild orchids which Helene had promised me were there in astonishing abundance, as well as flowering gorse, and calla lilies, and delicate freesias seeming to burgeon from the bare rock. Stooping down, one found the bare rock to be ancient seabed, with perhaps the world's oldest seashells embedded in its grip. All around us was the wash of the ocean, and deep peace, and the burnt smell of Africa, and hundreds of *dassies*—the timid rock-rabbit of this part of the world—scuttling and peeping and freezing into immobility at the sight of us.

"Isn't it lovely?" asked Helene, her arm in mine.

"Ravishing," I said. "Like you."

"We must fish," she said, inattentively. "Tomorrow or the next day. . . . Only please don't fall in or get washed off the rocks."

"I can swim."

"You can't swim in that." She pointed downwards, where the grey-green sea dissolved into white foam as it met the rocks. "There are sharks down there, my friend—little sharks, big sharks, all sorts of sharks. There's one enormous one called Cinderella—honestly, she looks just like a submarine. Must be over two thousand pounds. She swims by every day at the top of the tide. All the gillies are scared to death of her."

"We'll catch her tomorrow."

"My hero. . . . Now let's go back and I'll show you round the village."

The walk round the village was highly instructive to someone like myself who had never seen this part of the world before. Plettenberg Bay provided a classic cross-section of South Africa, with its leisured beauty, its slow pace, and its feudal fabric intact.

It held, in all, about two thousand souls, stacked in tiers on an immemorial pattern which, without deep inquiry, seemed to suit this part of the world very well indeed. At the top was a handful of white aristocracy—traders, hotel personnel, doctors, bank managers, post office officials, and the visitors who made Plettenberg Bay their annual mecca. Below them came the body of the population—the mixed-blood, Cape coloured villagers who did the work, caught the fish, built the houses, and loafed in the sun. Below them again (and no one was more sensitive on this point than the two 'black' races) came the pure negroes—servants in the big houses, messengers in the hotel, garbage removers, marginal scavengers.

There was one hotel, two banks, four general stores, two garages, one church. There were scores of sweet people who treated me with the grave, traditional courtesy of every South African *dorp*, and welcomed Helene as if she were a small beloved child who had escaped some grave danger. They seemed glad that she was married, sceptical of all life that lay outside their small known world. Mrs Boersma, who owned and ran the smallest general store, put it thus:

"Ach, my baby!" she said, enfolding Helene in a huge embrace. "Did the English let you back again after all?"

Helene laughed, returning the embrace, including me in the warm welcome.

"I've been away four years," she said, her eyes bright. "But look what I caught while I was away!"

Mrs Boersma inspected me; her glance was sharp in a brown motherly face. Then:

"Feed him up well, child!" she commanded. "You must never lose a good man."

It felt fine to belong to this family.

And then, on the way back to the house for lunch, I had one of the biggest surprises of my life. We had left the car for a minor repair, and were strolling, unselfconsciously hand-in-hand, down the main street. At a crossroads we passed a small shabby garage, and Helene looked at it inquisitively.

"This is new," she remarked, "though it doesn't look it. I didn't know we had a second garage."

There was a man leaning against one of the petrol pumps, staring somewhat vacantly downhill towards the sea. I glanced at the slack figure, and then looked again with a shock of astonishment. It was someone I recognized very easily indeed because he had twice saved my life in Holland during the war.

We knew him then, and I knew him now, as Murderer Martin.

War is only licensed killing—a merry game for louts and lunatics, an ordeal for all others. But if war does come you have to be good at it, you have to be perfect. . . . Though it was long ago now, I still found it terrifying to remember the things we learned and the things we did in that noble pursuit of victory.

Myself, I got to be a captain in the Royal Marine Commandos, a tough and seasoned outfit which saw action at a score of tricky points, from the Salerno beaches to Walcheren on the Dutch coast. George Martin I first remembered as a raw recruit, small and sallow, who joined us some time in 1943. He did not stay raw for very long.

At that time my own Commando was trying to find out what sort of defence system had been set up on the opposite side of the Maas River preparatory to making a permanent landing in force. 'Finding out' meant frequent night raids in small boats, and raids meant everything: surprise, treachery, murder by stealth, stabbing from behind, garrotting, the dragging away of half-dead prisoners—in fact, a swinish carelessness about life. We were very proud of our prowess.

George Martin proved an apt pupil in this kind of warfare; that was when he first got his nickname of 'Murderer', and it stuck to him ever since. After a few weeks of tuition (which was my special assignment) he suddenly seemed to become first-class at everything connected with individual killing, from the judo-chop across the throat to the hole in the back of the head; he also brought to the job an overtone of sadistic joy which was funny at the time, though disgusting thereafter. On one occasion, when we were making the Rhine crossings, I watched him fire seven slow shots into the stomach of a prostrate German who had, a mite too slowly, put up his hands in surrender.

Murderer Martin. . . . He had, beyond question, saved my life, once by quick shooting, once by close and gory work with a saw-edged bayonet. Now in that sunny South African street I walked towards him, holding out my hand with all the cheerful friendliness I felt, and said:

"Hallo, Murderer!"

I suppose Murderer Martin must have been as surprised as I was, for he seemed to jump a foot in the air as I greeted him. His hands flashed out of his pockets in a way which recalled the distant past very vividly and unpleasantly, and then he took a second look at me, and expelled a long breath and said with a grin:

"Good Lord—it's the skipper!"

"Hallo, Murderer!" I said again.

He stared back at me, and said: "Haven't heard that name for a long while."

By this time it seemed that Helene had been sufficiently mystified, so I introduced them and explained what it was all about. While they were chatting, I examined Murderer more closely. He had altered a lot in the past twelve years, which I suppose was true of all of us; but his alteration was rather odd. Just like the garage, he was shabby and seedy, a soldier defeated by peacetime; but there was a sort of tension underneath his manner, as if he were not really reconciled to defeat, and would not acknowledge it.

He reminded me of a dog lying underneath a sofa, forlorn, dejected, yet cranky—waiting for passing ankles.

When I asked him what he had been doing since we last met:

"This and that," he answered off-handedly. "Couldn't

settle down, really. . . ." He gestured round the run-down, littered garage. "Had this place for two or three years now."

"How's business?"

"So-so."

A woman came out of one of the outbuildings, a dispirited-looking girl in a faded print dress. Murderer introduced her as his wife, and then we all stood waiting as if we had lost contact.

"Murderer saved my life a couple of times," I volunteered suddenly.

Helene's face broke into a wonderful smile. "Then I like him very much indeed!"

Murderer Martin grinned briefly. "Long time ago."

The girl was watching us without much interest or any sort of effort; the sunshine on her thin yellow hair was too searching, the day too bright for the bedraggled dress.

"Well," I said to Murderer, "I'm here for two or three weeks. We'll have a good talk a bit later on."

"OK, skipper."

Helene and I bade them goodbye and continued on our way down the hill.

"Rather sad," said Helene presently.

"Yes. . . . I'm glad I've got you."

We heard a bit more about Murderer Martin a little later on when the local police sergeant, Van Willigen, called on my father-in-law for his customary weekly visit.

"Coming in to pay his respects," explained old James Forsyth. "Does it every Saturday. Picks up a damn' big whisky-and-soda at the same time. . . . Good chap—bit slow. Dutchman, of course." To my father-in-law, reared in an earlier Cape Colony tradition, all Afrikaners were Dutchmen.

I liked the look of Van Willigen, a huge man bursting out of his khaki uniform, cast in the authentic Afrikaner police mould—blond, blue-eyed, slow-moving, *not* slow-thinking. He sat on the edge of his chair, sipping away at his 'damn big whisky-and-soda' (my father-in-law had given me an outsize wink as he poured it), and brought us up to date on the local news.

About the robberies he had nothing fresh to report.

"It's got us a bit worried, sir," he told James Forsyth,

"particularly now that there's a murder involved. . . . We reckon the gang must have got away with over a thousand pounds during the last two months."

"*Skollies*, eh?"

Van Willigen nodded. "Must be. We've rounded up a dozen or more, but there's always others drifting in. Man, sometimes I'd like to get into them with a *sjambok*!"

"Can't do that," said my father-in-law.

"I know, sir."

"We *used* to, of course. . . . No *skollies* in the old days."

Van Willigen grinned, shifting his bulk. "Here's to the old days, sir."

Then I mentioned Murderer Martin. "I discovered a friend of mine today," I told Van Willigen. "Mr Martin. Runs that garage."

Van Willigen regarded me more closely. "Is he really a friend of yours?"

'I knew him during the war. We were in the same Marine commando. I haven't seen him for about twelve years."

The police sergeant pursed his lips. "We've had some trouble with Martin."

"Trouble?"

"Yes. He was getting a bit rough with his niggers—knocking them about for no reason. They were pretty good boys."

"What's that?" demanded my father-in-law.

"Martin, sir," said Van Willigen, raising his voice. "You remember we had to take him to court."

James Forsyth nodded. "Bad business, that. Got to keep them working, of course. But Martin went too far."

"I wonder how he's making out with that garage," said Van Willigen ruminatively. "Not much cash coming in that I can see. But he was driving a new car last week." He grinned, swallowing the last of his whisky, and stood up. "Must be more money in the garage business than you'd think. Who'd choose to be a policeman, eh?"

It was as if each day in Plettenberg Bay were pure magic; but the next one seemed to Helene and myself the purest of all. We spent it, and the night as well, fishing, sunning ourselves, cooking rough meals, and sleeping in the fishing hut at Robberg Point, the southernmost tip of the peninsula.

It was a matchless twenty-four hours, perhaps the best in our joint lives so far.

We had to work for it, of course. . . . From the mainland to the Point was four arduous miles, clambering over rocks, traversing sand slides, crossing mile after mile of springy turf, loose shingle, and clinging hot sand. It was more than a journey, it was a *trek*.

Timothy had seen to that. He had packed for us as if for a navy on the march: rods, reels, spare line and hooks, bait, beer, food, fresh water, and kerosene for the stove. We took with us two local gillies—White (the blackest coloured man I had ever seen) and Eddie. But we all had heavy loads, and we were glad to get to the Point at last, after three hours' slogging.

But from then on it was pure bliss. Helene, looking wonderfully workmanlike in khaki drill shorts and shirt, caught eight brutal-looking fish, called mussel-crackers, in the space of two hours. The two gillies hauled in dozens of small mackerel which we used as live bait. Even I caught a thirty-pound shark with help from the bystanders.

I was standing, rod in hand, looking out to sea and thinking how nice it was to be married when Eddie's strident voice at my elbow roared out:

"Strike, master!"

I struck, and was rewarded by a monstrous answering tug that nearly tumbled me off the rocks. Eddie clasped his hands round my waist; White clambered down with a twenty-foot gaff; Helene shouted encouragement from above. I played that shark for more than half an hour till my wrenched arms and shoulders were aching. But I—or let's say we—landed him in the end.

Later, at the end of that blissful evening, we sat on the rocks outside the fishing hut, talking and smoking till the dew drove us indoors. The sound of the surf pounding on the rocks below was the last sound I heard before, sore all over and dog-tired, I fell asleep.

But just before that, Helene's voice came from the narrow wooden bunk across the hut.

"Darling, why did you call that man 'Murderer'?"

"That was his nickname in the Commando."

After a long pause: "Did he do terrible things?"

"We all had to."

"But you've got rid of them now, haven't you?"

"How do you mean?"

"There's no hangover, no sort of delayed nightmare?"

"No, no hangover."

Before she went to sleep she murmured: "I wonder if that's true for everyone."

Had we but known it, that wonderful day was the last day of peace we were to have in Plettenberg Bay. We fished again next morning without much success except with the sharks; towards noon we packed up and made the long *trek* back to the mainland. But then came the first of many surprises, many horrors. Our car was stopped on the outskirts of the village, flagged down to a halt at a road-block manned by two policemen.

One of them was Van Willigen. He gave a brief salute as he recognized us, and then glanced closely at White and Eddie in the back seat.

"How was the fishing, eh? Were they running?"

We told him, beaming, and showed him the eight mussel-crackers.

"Lucky for you you've all got an alibi," he said not quite jokingly. "We had a killing here last night."

Helene clutched my hand, and I found myself turning cold in the warm midday sun.

"A killing?" I repeated. "What happened?"

"Another murder, that's what happened."

Police-Sergeant Van Willigen seemed tense and pre-occupied, as well he might be; he was obviously anxious for us not to loiter at the road-block but to leave him and his field of operations clear. Courtesy, however, made him answer our shocked questions.

"Same as last time," he told us grimly. "A robbery at Kloof's store. The till emptied and the little tin-pot safe ripped open. Must be eighty or ninety pounds gone, so the daughter says. Poor old Kloof—he was going to retire this year."

"Dead?"

"Dead on arrival."

We bade Van Willigen good-bye and drove on into the village. It was in a ferment—police everywhere, groups of people at street corners, serious faces, angry looks. For the first time coloured people and negroes turned aside when we walked by, as if fearing a blow or a threat. . . . Up at Mrs Boersma's store the old lady was full of sorrow.

"Poor old Kloof," she said, echoing Van Willigen's phrase. "He was over seventy, and a good friend. Who would do that to an old man?"

Helene touched Mrs Boersma on the shoulder. "You must be very careful," she said, anxiously. "This is the sort of place——" She broke off.

"They wouldn't rob me!" declared Mrs Boersma stoutly. Generations of Afrikaner pride and obstinacy were in her voice. "They know better than to try, those *skollies*!"

It seemed obvious, on the evidence, that hers was exactly the sort of place that they *would* try to rob, whoever 'they' were, but I let it go.

"Well, do take care," repeated Helene. "Don't open your door at night, or anything like that."

Mrs Boersma said, with a wonderful twinkle: "I haven't opened my door at night for forty years," and we all laughed.

"But what happened to Mr Kloof?" I asked. "Was he hit with something? Shot?"

"Strangled, they say. What a world, eh?"

"How horrible!" said Helene. "In Plettenberg Bay of all places."

That was just what old James Forsyth said, a little later on when we drove through the uneasy streets back to his house.

"Never heard of such a thing," he boomed. "I was looking up the records this morning. We haven't had a violent death in Plettenberg Bay for more than twenty years—and *then* it was just a drunken fight among the fishermen. Now we've had two in less than a week."

"Do you still think it's a native gang?" I asked.

"Yes," said my father-in-law promptly. "And if I had my way, I'd round 'em up, throw every one of them into jail, and keep them there till this business is sorted out."

"I imagine the police have something like that laid on."

"Damn' Dutchmen," grumbled my father-in-law. "They couldn't catch a cold in a snowstorm."

I didn't agree, but it wasn't the moment to advance a counter-argument. It would only have made James Forsyth very, very deaf.

"Oh dear!" sighed Helene. "And we'd had such a beautiful day."

"We'll have lots more, darling."

"I wonder."

Because I didn't agree with my father-in-law's caustic comments about the South African police, who had struck me (in the person of Van Willigen) as patently tough and probably competent, I walked up the hill that evening to call at the police-post. The brooding atmosphere which now infected the whole village had begun to settle on the household, and I wanted to find out what was going on. James Forsyth, by reason of his patriarchal position in the village, was entitled to be kept informed. Personally, I myself was inquisitive, and uneasy as well.

Passing Murderer Martin's garage I noticed Mrs Martin serving petrol at one of the pumps. I waved a greeting and then called out:

"Is your husband in?"

"He's asleep," she answered sulkily without looking up.

I shrugged, and passed on. It was only six o'clock, but if he was asleep, he was asleep.

At the police-post, Van Willigen greeted me genially. He was much more relaxed than he had been at the road-block earlier that day; clearly he had done plenty of spade-work, made his dispositions, and eased off at the end of the day.

"I've got twenty-five men on the job," he said, explaining what he had put in hand. "That's three officers, and twenty-two native constables. Some of them are in plain clothes. There's a man watching every shop in the village and most of the big houses as well." He grinned. "For instance," he said, glancing at his watch, "it took you eleven minutes to get up here."

I laughed. "I'm out of condition." But I was impressed. "Are you really watching everybody as closely as that?"

"Not every *body*," corrected Van Willigen, "but certainly every worthwhile building. We'll be looking for people breaking in, of course. But people slipping out are likely to be almost as interesting."

"Do you still suspect a native gang?"

"Maybe. . . . They could always be somebody's servants, or boys from the hotel. But—well, maybe. . . ."

"Strangling's a pretty horrible business."

173

Van Willigen looked at me under lowered lids, his jaw very prominent. "What gave you the idea it was strangling?"

"I thought it was. . . . That's the rumour going round. . . . I believe Mrs Boersma told us."

"Ma Boersma was wrong," said Van Willigen somewhat grimly. "It wasn't strangling, though it looked like it at the beginning. It was something I've never seen before. Old Kloof was knocked out by a wrestling trick—an illegal one, of course. His throat was smashed."

"Smashed?" I felt rather sick. "How do you mean?"

Van Willigen touched his own strong neck, just underneath his chin. "Here. . . . It was all smashed in. A blow with a piece of wood. Or even a fist. . . . We just got the doctor's report. . . . The larynx, they call it."

The larynx. . . . Somewhere deep inside my skull a bell was ringing loud and clear and insistent. I tried not to hear that bell, but it continued to ring as I sat opposite the sergeant in the bare, white-washed police-post, and talked about methods of murder.

I was thinking back through the years, thinking about a certain way of killing an enemy, a vilely treacherous way suitable to a dark night and a free hand. For me, it was a part of the war roughly labelled 'Disposal of Sentries'.

It entailed grasping the hair from behind, wrenching back the head, and delivering a chopping blow across the throat which splintered the larynx and choked the victim. Instant disablement was automatic; and it was usually enough, we had found, to kill older people.

I knew all this so well because it was one of the ways I had taught my own commandos to kill.

For the next four days nothing worse happened in Plettenberg Bay than surprise police raids, a strict evening curfew, an invasion by the Press, and a spate of rumours. We had to live with our record which was suddenly notorious; any village which has six robberies in a month and two murders in a week cannot expect to jog along in tranquil seclusion. Thus the discomforting limelight bore down upon Plettenberg Bay for the first time within living memory. But that, for four days, was the limit of the community's ordeal.

It was not the limit of my own. I had two other things to live with: memory and conscience. Memory led me to

174

suspect Murderer Martin, almost beyond doubt, of yet another murder, because old Kloof had been killed commando-fashion, Martin had been an expert commando, and the coincidence was too rich a mixture to be disregarded.

Conscience worked two ways in this private wrestling match of mine. If Martin had killed, he had killed in a way I had taught him; he was therefore *my* murderer. And if I knew this for certain, or even suspected it strongly, then I had a clear duty to hand him over to justice.

I should have told Helene, of course, quite apart from the police. She would have helped, she would have split the burden, she would have set me right. . . . But for four days I did nothing because I couldn't face any of it, and I wanted above all to be wrong in my suspicions.

I wanted the past wiped out, I wanted Murderer Martin (who had twice saved my life) to be an honest citizen who had forgotten all the killing I had ever taught him. I wanted both of us to be innocent bystanders. More than anything, I wanted to be a chartered accountant on a happy honeymoon in South Africa.

I was wrong, of course. Cowards are always wrong. I knew this all the time, and the fifth day blew it all apart anyway. For on the fifth day, or rather the fifth night, we had another murder in Plettenberg Bay, and I knew for certain that Martin was the executioner.

This time it was a senseless murder, the wayward killing of a coloured fisherman who couldn't have had a penny in his pocket. He died in precisely the same way as old Kloof had died. His body was discovered at dawn down on the beach on the first night that police patrols were relaxed and people were free to move about again.

Of course the police patrols shouldn't have been relaxed, except that Van Willigen was short of men, and was also being pressed by public opinion to free the village of its curfew. But by ill-chance it was done that way, in the same fashion as my own silence, my cowardice, had developed from various haphazard pressures. The result was a tattered, worthless body down on the beach, not fifty yards from James Forsyth's house, and a return of extreme local tension.

As soon as I heard about the third killing, the whole thing

175

suddenly became crystal clear, and frightening in its clarity. As if Martin were my own manipulated puppet, I knew that he had done it, and I knew why. It was not just for the fun of killing, though that was something which the war and I myself had implanted in him, long ago. It was his only way of demonstrating his strength and cunning in a hostile world, a world which for the past twelve years must have seemed determined to prove him futile.

Only the war had brought Murderer Martin to full flower. Shoddy peace had withered him. Now the delayed shock of that licensed murder had caught up with him, and he was going back to war again. It was just as Helene had said in the Robberg fishing hut a few days earlier: Martin was a casualty of a hideous battle long ago, and he had *not* got rid of the past.

It meant that he was mad anyway, but that did not lift any of the burdens, least of all from myself.

Behind doors which were now barred as early as five o'clock in the evening, our household discussed the situation. Or rather, I threw in an occasional monosyllable, while my father-in-law, an old and angry man, laid down the law about murder, crime, and the decay of discipline, and Helene watched us, and especially me, with clear anxiety. She sensed in me, and in my silence, a deep disquiet which sprang from something much more fundamental than a spoiled honeymoon. In an aside, while her father was contrasting the good old days with the bad new ones, she tried to reach me:

"Darling?"

"Yes?"

"What are you thinking about?"

"Nothing much. . . . All this, I suppose."

"It's terribly depressing, I know. But don't let it spoil things."

"They *are* spoilt."

"I know. . . . But we're not really involved."

"Everyone's involved!" declared my father-in-law, choosing this moment to be able to hear the softest whisper. "It's a challenge to the whole community, nothing less!"

There was a knock on the door, and Timothy appeared.

"Master," he said, bowing. "Policeman."

It was Van Willigen, paying his weekly visit. As we shook

hands I marvelled at how much had happened since the last one. My father-in-law poured the sergeant his customary stiff whisky-and-soda, but there was nothing ironic in his manner tonight. I think we all felt that Van Willigen was probably earning it.

"Still nothing new, sir," said the policeman in answer to James Forsyth's inquiry. "That murder yesterday was a crazy job, right enough. . . . We're working on the theory that it's probably a madman."

James Forsyth frowned. "Madman or not, he's got to be caught."

"We're busy on it, sir."

Watching his stern expression, I wondered how many other people, in authority or not, were breathing down his neck at this moment. We knew from the radio that the reign of terror in Plettenberg Bay had already been raised in Parliament.

For the first time that evening I spoke a sentence longer than a couple of words. I found it extraordinarily difficult.

"If it *is* the work of a madman," I said to Van Willigen, "then it might happen again, any time. It might happen tonight."

"I can guarantee it won't happen tonight," answered Van Willigen grimly. "We've really got this village laced up. . . . But I can't keep it like that for ever. Sooner or later things have got to return to normal, which means that our friend, whoever he is, is free to go to work again."

Our friend, he had said. . . . In my jittery state the words were like a cold shaft in my throat. I glanced at Van Willigen swiftly; though there was nothing in his expression to indicate any special significance, yet it was easy to imagine that his words had been used to test me, to probe beneath my skin.

Now everyone seemed to be staring at me—Helene, my father-in-law, and Van Willigen—and the latter was speaking again.

"That's why it's so important," he said slowly, "that we have a hundred-per-cent backing from the public. This thing is too big for the police alone. If *anyone* knows *anything*, or suspects anything, or sees anything that's out of line—" I was sweating under his gaze, and the seemingly insistent eyes of the other two—"then they must come up the hill and report it to us."

I went up the hill early next morning. But it was not to see the police that I went. Because he had been my friend, and my own creation, and because he had saved my life, I had to see this man who was on my conscience.

I wasn't going to warn him (so I swore to myself). I just wanted to talk to him, look at him, find out what had happened to him.

Bright and early, while Helene still slept, I went up the hill to see Murderer Martin.

Martin's garage, under the strong morning sunlight, wore the same derelict air as I remembered from my first visit. The old-fashioned crank-handle pumps stood like rusty sentinels, guarding nothing of value. There were a couple of derelict cars, a towing-jeep with a flat tyre, and a fly-blown window display of fan-belts, batteries, and gaskets. A coloured boy was sweeping the oil-stained yard in front of it, moving indolently, whistling on a single, sad note of mourning.

The main door was open; perhaps it was never closed. As I stepped up to it, Mrs Martin appeared.

"Good morning," I said. Same dress, I thought; same hair, same pathetic air of defeat. What a wonderful life for a hero's bride. . . .

"Is your husband in?"

"He's asleep," she answered in the grudging tones she had used before.

"I'd like to see him."

"Come back a bit later on."

I raised my voice. "I have to see him now."

She faced me. "He's asleep. . . . What's it all about?"

Martin's voice called from the back of the premises. "Who is it?"

"Nobody."

On a sudden impulse I stepped forward, and using an authentic parade-ground snarl, roared out: "MARTIN!"

He snapped back: "Sir!" and came trotting out almost before the echo had died.

He stopped in his tracks, blinking against the fierce sun, as soon as he saw me. Perhaps we were both startled, he by this crude interjection from the past, myself by the appalling present. His appearance was a shock in itself. He looked wild—unshaven for several days, dirty, his clothes stained and rumpled. But underneath this, as he drew near, I sensed an electric tension. Fancifully, it seemed that if I had reached out my hand and touched him I would have died of the contact.

When he was two paces off he grinned jauntily, and said: "Hallo, skipper!"

"I thought we'd have that talk," I said.

"Talk?" He looked at his wife jerking back his head, and she shuffled into the building again. "What talk?"

"About the old days."

"Oh, them. . . ." He reached into the pocket of his khaki shirt, drew out a cigarette, and lit it in a series of jerky movements. The tremendous tension was still there, waiting for a spark. "Not much to say about them, is there?"

"Perhaps not. . . . How are things going now?"

He looked at me with a very level glance and said, with an air of interior satisfaction which appalled me: "I reckon I'm doing pretty well."

A braver man than I, or a different man, would have glanced round the wretched garage at that point, but I couldn't bring myself to do so. Instead, I said:

"That's fine. . . . I like Plettenberg Bay a lot. . . . Though it's certainly in a bit of an uproar at the moment."

"Yes. Comic, isn't it?"

"*Comic?*"

"All those coppers running about, not getting any-where."

"Murder isn't funny."

"Oh, sure. . . . How did they die, anyway?"

"Someone gave them the gate."

He stiffened, and I could have swallowed my tongue as I saw it. Accidentally I had used a commando phrase, a phrase both he and I knew well from the old days. 'Giving the gate' was the expression we had all used for that murderous chop across the throat. Sweating in the sunlight, I wondered if it was really by accident that I had said it. Perhaps it was a Freudian slip, the slip one wishes to make. . . . His glance locked with mine; his eyes were already veiled, and darkly secretive. We both knew what had happened.

He said in the most off-hand voice I had ever heard: "What a thing to do," and then, turning away from me: "Well, I've got some work. . . . So long, skipper."

A moment later I was alone outside the garage.

"You've got to tell them!" said Helene vehemently. "You've got to tell them now!" I had never known her so emphatic nor her eyes so intent. "Don't you see that, apart from everything else you're in the most terrible danger yourself?"

I was sitting on her bed back in my father-in-law's house, a few minutes after the meeting with Murderer Martin. She was looking most beautiful; in other circumstances, there would have been room for nothing else in my mind. The house had its customary early-morning peace; above our heads we could hear the slow majestic steps of James Forsyth, pacing to and fro across the *stoep*. But as I described to her that meeting with Martin her excitement and foreboding had outstripped my own. She insisted that I go to the police—then and there.

"But it's only guess work," I said, lamely.

She shook her head; her hair as she leant forward matched the wild unrest in her eyes. "You know it's more than that," she answered. "You know it's a certainty. . . . If you don't go I shall go myself."

"He saved my life."

"He's not going to save it now. . . . Don't you understand," she said fiercely, "that whether he's mad or sane you're the one person in Plettenberg Bay whom he *must* kill."

"Somehow I still feel it's all my fault."

She laid a hand on my arm. "Darling, if there *is* any fault, this is the only way you can retrieve it."

I knew, of course, that this was true; I knew that, as often happened, Helene had sliced away the unessentials and got to the heart of the matter. I had to tell the police for the same reason that I had had to tell Helene; because, after the involved unstable encounter with Murderer Martin, I myself had to get back to firmer ground or perish.

I remembered that Freudian slip, the way I had betrayed my suspicions to a man I believed to be a murderer. There was a gross infection here, and it had already touched me. There was, after all, only one way to be cleansed.

I kissed Helene, got up off the bed, and stood looking down at her.

"All right," I said. "I'll go now."

"Go straight there," she commanded. "Don't go any-where else. And take care of yourself. I love you."

The police did not love me; indeed, in the person of Van Willigen, they seemed to love me less than anyone else in the world. As I told my story the police sergeant's face grew increasingly bleak; at the end he was looking at me as if I myself were the murderer who had set his village in an uproar. Obviously as a pure-bred Afrikaner, he had never wasted any love upon Englishmen, and this was clearly the moment which justified that reservation.

"Why didn't you come to us first?" he demanded as soon as I had finished. "I told you the other night that we needed all the help we could get. Remember?"

"I know that," I said haltingly. "But I was only guessing after all. I felt that if I could talk to Martin I'd be able to judge whether I was right."

His pencil tapped on the desk. His blue eyes were very direct and prominent. "You said he was a friend of yours, from the old days."

"Yes."

"Sure you didn't tip him off on purpose, eh?"

"No. It was all a mistake."

"You're damned right it was a mistake." Van Willigen rose, towering above me, and reached behind him for his belt and holster. The revolver butt caught the sun as he strapped it round his waist. "You'd better come along on this trip," he said with heavy irony. "In case of any more mistakes."

The garage was the same as when I had left it an hour earlier; shabby, run-down, deserted. What a place to come home to, year after year. . . . Mrs Martin answered Van Willigen's knock.

"Mrs Martin?"

"Yes. What is it now?"

"I'd like to see your husband."

"You've just missed him," said Mrs Martin. It was possible to imagine a gleam of triumph in the dull eyes. "He had to go out. . . . Emergency, he said. . . . He won't be back for some time."

"What sort of an emergency?" asked Van Willigen dis-believingly for the fifth or sixth time. "What would take your husband out in such a big hurry? He must have given you *some* idea."

181

Mrs Martin faced him across the table in the dusty garage office; after an hour's close questioning she still held her ground in pathetic, mutinous loyalty to her husband. Van Willigen had tried it all ways—bullying, wheedling, reasoning, appealing to her common sense, appealing to her love for a man thought to be in trouble. It had had no effect whatsoever. Either she knew nothing at all or Murderer Martin had briefed her well.

For the fifth or sixth time she repeated: "He doesn't tell me everything. . . . Why should he? It's business. . . . He said it was an emergency."

"But he didn't take the breakdown car?"

"No. . . . I told you. . . . He took his own car."

"What sort of an emergency was it, then?"

She stroked the side of her face nervously. "I don't know."

"Was there a telephone call? You know we can trace it."

"Then you don't need me, do you?" she countered, desperately pert.

Van Willigen brushed it off. "Which way did he go?"

"I wasn't watching."

"Don't you care where he goes, then?"

"Of course I care!"

"What good would he be in an emergency?"

I had had an idea that she might be near the breaking-point, but when it came, it was still a shock. She looked at Van Willigen with hatred in her eyes, and suddenly shouted:

"Why don't you leave him alone? He's worth a hundred of you!"

"Maybe," agreed Van Willigen, instantly placid. "I just want to talk to him, that's all." There was a kind of signing-off note in his voice, as if he had found out what he wanted, and I was not surprised when he stood up. "You won't help us, then? Is that it?"

"I tell you, I don't know where he's gone," said Mrs Martin.

"*We'll* tell *you*," said Van Willigen cruelly, "just as soon as we find out."

He walked back with me, the big blond policeman, striding down the main street of Plettenberg Bay like an authentic Great Trek hero. As he walked, he spoke his thoughts.

"She knows," he said grimly. "She knows the lot. . . . Notice how she said, 'He's worth a hundred of you'? That's *his* idea, he must have said it to her. And he would only have said it to her if he was talking about the murders, and boasting that he could get away with them."

I was doubtful. "She might have meant," I said, "that though he was poor and the garage was a failure, he was still a good man, as far as she was concerned."

The police sergeant shook his head. "It was more than that. . . . It was his idea, his very own words—him against the police. I can just hear him saying it." He came to a stop at the crossroads, where our paths divided. Hands tucked into his belt, he narrowed his eyes, staring down at the sea. "The pig!" he said suddenly, with extraordinary venom. "The damned, useless, white pig!"

There was a world of bottomless hatred in the word 'white'. To Van Willigen, as to every other South African policeman, Martin's crime was the ultimate crime. White men weren't ever meant to break the law; white men traditionally stayed in line. The only true enemy was the black man; the white transgressor let the side down, ruined the whole pattern unforgivably.

I felt him looking at me, staring at me. "Your *friend*," he said, with the same venomous emphasis, "may be anywhere by now. He's got the whole of South Africa. . . . Any ideas on that?"

"He may turn up," I said feebly.

"*You* know how his mind works," said Van Willigen as if he had not heard me. "If you do get any ideas, come and see me. And this time, come and see me *first*."

After thinking about it for a full day I knew exactly what I had to do. I had to help to the limit of my ability. I had to appoint myself the senior executioner. But there was a fundamental domestic shock awaiting me. Helene, having at first insisted that I go to the police, was now wildly opposed to my joining forces with them in the field.

"Haven't you done enough harm already?" she asked bitterly.

I thought that was unfair and I said so.

"Unfair?" she mimicked. It was our first serious quarrel, and we were both tremendously aware of the fact, and of the crazy occasion that had sparked it. "Unfair? What do you think this is—a game of hide-and-seek? There's a murderer on the loose—mostly because of you—and now you want to play boy scouts with him. . . . What possible help could you be to the police, anyway?"

"I know how Murderer's mind works." I was growing angry, but I was also deadly serious about the whole thing. "That's where I can help them."

"You just want to *hunt* him! You're going to enjoy it!"

"I won't enjoy it. . . . You said it was all my fault and I wouldn't argue the point. But it's been my fault from a long time ago."

"Oh, for heaven's sake!" she burst out. "Don't be so romantic!"

"Perhaps it would be better if it was I that caught him."

"How 'better'?"

"Better than someone else."

"But he's mad!"

"Yes, that's what I mean."

I couldn't really explain it either to myself or to her, and Helene was still blazingly angry when I left. But it was true that I didn't want Murderer Martin to fall into alien hands. Not to begin with, anyway. He was still my own creation.

Up at the police-post Van Willigen studied the wall-map of the district, his broad back towards me. Martin had now dropped out of sight for twenty-four hours, and the hunt was on.

Over his shoulder, Van Willigen said gruffly: "Let's hear what you think."

I swallowed before speaking. I was aware of tension between us; obviously he blamed me for making a mess of things, and perhaps he suspected me of treachery as well. There were very many reasons why I must do the best I could.

"I've been thinking about it," I said slowly. "Thinking about what he'll do. . . . You see not only did I teach him how to kill. I taught him how not to be caught when this sort of thing happens. We had a drill for chaps who were on the run."

Van Willigen was facing me now. "What sort of drill?"

"It varied. . . . But basically it came down to one rule: not to hide, but to melt. That means doing only normal things; finding some simple background and sinking into it. For example, you must never hide in a haystack—you must stand beside it, and try to look like a farm-hand. You don't crouch under a bed—you get into it."

Van Willigen grinned suddenly. "And try to look like a husband, eh?"

"Just that. . . . Don't run—walk. Don't be alone—mix with the crowd. All that sort of thing."

"Well?"

"Martin will remember all that. He's obviously got a good memory. . . . But he'll also remember that I'll be helping you and that these were the things I taught him. He'll have to decide whether to follow the rules or to bluff."

"Well?" said Van Willigen again. He was frowning.

"According to the rules, our rules, he should make for the nearest big town—that's Cape Town or Port Elizabeth—and get lost in the crowd. The worst thing for him to do from the commando point of view would be to try and hide out on his own somewhere round here."

"So we have to guess?"

"So we have to guess. . . . And my guess is that, in order to bluff *me*, he'll make for the most obvious, most dangerous place he can think of. He'll put himself into a trap, a place where a trained man *wouldn't* go."

"Where's that, then?"

I pointed to the map behind him. "That," I said, "is the Robberg."

"The Robberg," repeated Van Willigen as I stopped speaking. He gave a brief glance at the wall-map and then sat down at his desk. From there he looked up at me, his eyes direct under frowning brows. "The Robberg, eh? Now how could he hope to get away from there? You say yourself that it's a trap."

I nodded. "That's the whole idea. It's such a trap that no one will think of looking for him there."

"So? He's still in a trap."

"It's a trap we won't be watching. He could lie up there for a year if need be till the hunt dies down and people forget the sort of man they're looking for."

"I won't forget," said Van Willigen curtly.

"You can't cover the whole of Africa. Martin can stay there as long as he likes, and *then* slip through to the mainland and do his disappearing act."

"He'll be seen. Or he'll starve."

"He needn't be seen." Convinced of my theory, desperately anxious to play my part, I pressed on with it. "Think of all those caves. We could search for six months and never find the right one. Martin can fish at night. He can trap rabbits and *dassies*. He can steal food from the fishing hut—people always leave their spare tinned stuff behind, but nobody ever makes a list of it. There's plenty of water, plenty of firewood. Even if people do notice him moving about in the distance they'll just think he's somebody on a fishing trip."

It was a long speech, and it took Van Willigen a long time to digest it in all its aspects. From me he turned to look out of the window; the view was all sunlight and warmth, with a vignette of sparkling blue sea at the upper edge. The contrast with the grim subject of murder and manhunt was startling.

"It's possible," said Van Willigen after a very long silence. "But I just don't believe in it."

There was another long silence. I was half relieved, half disappointed. Whether the police bought my theory or not, at least I had discharged my duty in putting it forward. But I wanted to be right, and apparently I wasn't going to get a chance to prove it. No one could have sounded more unimpressed than Van Willigen.

"I don't believe in it," he repeated. "Martin wouldn't be such a fool as to bottle himself up on the Robberg. He hasn't made any mistakes so far, and he's not likely to start now."

"It's worth keeping a look-out, surely?"

Van Willigen nodded. 'We'll do that. We're doing it in all sorts of other places. But the idea of a full-scale search of the whole peninsula isn't possible. Man, I'd need to take every policeman between here and Jo'burg to do it properly! Headquarters would have the skin off my back."

"Well," I said, preparing to leave, "that's where I think he is."

"We'll warn people to keep their eyes open when they're on the Robberg. But that's as far as I can go."

His voice was not cordial. Perhaps I was over-sensitive, but it was easy to imagine that he was glad I had come up with such a silly idea.

If the atmosphere at the police-post had been unenthusiastic, at my father-in-law's house it was positively sulphurous. Helene had lost none of her anger with the fact that I had tried to get involved, directly, in the hunt for Murderer

186

Martin; and clearly she had been working on old James Forsyth. Never had he been so gruff and formidable, never so deaf. Dinner that evening passed in defeating silence, like some rotten film on television when the sound fails. Occasionally, through the service-hatch leading to the kitchen, I caught sight of a pair of sad eyes in a creased black face. Timothy, it seemed, shared my view that this was no sort of a honeymoon.

I took up this precise point with Helene later that night when we were alone. It got me nowhere.

"*I'm* on my honeymoon," said Helene with chilly emphasis. "You're on something different. A manhunt or something. If that's what you want, go ahead with it. But you can't expect me to be very enthusiastic."

"But, darling, I'm *here*."

"What's the good of that if you're liable to go trotting up to the police-post every time the bell strikes?" She looked at me with cold curiosity. "What did Sergeant Van Willigen have to say, anyway?"

"We talked about what Martin was likely to do, and where he would hide. That sort of thing."

"And?"

"That's all."

"Are you going to go on helping them?"

"I hope so. I want to."

She shrugged. "Please yourself."

"But I'm here now," I repeated.

"Sweet of you to bother.'

She would not relax or melt at all on that night, nor for the next forty-eight hours. On a somewhat different plane the police preserved their own bleak detachment. But then, thank heavens, the tide turned and started to flow my way again.

In the early afternoon, two days later, Eddie and White, our two gillies, were fishing for live bait near the Platbank, at the narrow neck of the Robberg between the peninsula and the mainland. They were casting into deep water; behind them the cliffs rose sheer and craggy, defying a thousand years of the sea's attack. Eddie kept losing his tackle (so he told the story later); regularly he would cast into the angle of the bay, where he knew for certain there was no underwater ledge running out, get caught up in some obstruction, and have to lose everything—bait, hooks, wire traces, and endless fathoms of expensive nylon line.

It didn't make sense to Eddie, nor to White; they both knew the bottom should have been clear. While Eddie sat back, rather sulkily making up new tackle for the fourth or fifth time, White cast in at about the same spot. He struck almost immediately and this time his line came in freely.

But it was not a fish, nor weed, nor anything they expected to see. It was the linen cover off the back of a car seat.

They thought nothing much of it since people sometimes tipped rubbish off the top of the cliff and it might have gone unrecorded. But they chanced to talk about it in the village that evening, and Van Willigen heard the story.

Early next morning the police manhandled a derrick and some steel grappling hooks down to the rocks near the Platbank, and after two casts they got fast into something. There was a big crowd watching; scores of fisherfolk, and people from the village, and policemen, and reporters, and holidaymakers from the hotel. I stood by Van Willigen as the heavy cranks were turned and the chain began to come home. When something broke the surface, and we saw it was the battered front end of a motor-car there was a gasp, and then a watchful, fearful silence.

We were all thinking the same grim thought: when the car was free of the water, would we see a body as well? And if a body, what sort of a body, if the crabs and the sharks and the rock-lobsters had had their way with it?

Green sea-water sluiced and poured from the car windows, opaque with weed and sand. When it was clear, and the car hung dripping and shining in the sunlight, it was seen to be empty. The coachwork was badly smashed and a wheel was missing. But there was no one inside.

"Is it his?" I asked Van Willigen.

"Yes." He glanced far up, over my head. "Must have been driven or pushed over the cliffs. We'll find the tracks up there."

"Does the road go so far?"

"Not the road. It's a path way on to the Robberg. A small car like this could just about squeeze by."

"Looks as though he's here, then." I tried to make it sound noncommittal.

"Yes," said Van Willigen. He smiled at me, a friendly smile, acknowledging a different footing. "I'll have to take a lot back," he said ruefully. "How about joining the police?"

In a sense Van Willigen had meant it when he asked me "How about joining the police?" It was not that he really needed my help—he had thirty extra men drafted into Plettenberg Bay by midday; but the fact that I seemed to have guessed right about Murderer Martin made me valuable, if not as a policeman, then as something between a mascot and a consulting psychiatrist. At all events, he asked me to join the hunt without hesitation and without guile. We moved into the area in force that same afternoon.

When he had said at our earlier meeting that to search the Robberg yard by yard would take every policeman 'between here and Jo'burg', he had been right; it would indeed have needed an army, moving like ants, a foot at a time, probing every kind of inaccessible eirie. Even so, one lazy or careless man, bypassing one single cave or rock shelter, could have ruined the whole enterprise.

What Van Willigen had in mind was a compromise; a squad of more than seventy men beating their way slowly down the length of the peninsula. They couldn't look everywhere, but at least they could limit the areas where Murderer Martin might be holed up.

We advanced slowly from the neck of the peninsula (where Van Willigen remained to direct operations by walkie-talkie), down south towards the fishing hut and the place where rock finally gave way to sea. It was a hot day, as usual, but a rarely beautiful one none the less. There was the endearing smell of Robberg: a million aromatic succulents crushed by passing feet; tiny honey-birds no bigger than bees in flight; armies of *dassies* taking chattering refuge as we advanced.

I was stationed halfway up the eastern slope; below me was Eddie, and three other men who covered the area between myself and the sea. Presently, when we were half-way towards the southern tip of Robberg, Eddie let out a startled shout:

"Master! Down there!"

He was pointing towards the water and for a moment I thought he must have spotted Martin. But then I saw what he was pointing at. It was a colossal shark—clearly, the shark called Cinderella that Helene had told me about when we first arrived. It was swimming slowly along with the out-going tide a few feet from the edge of the rocks.

I had never seen a bigger fish, nor a more evil sight. It must have been thirty feet long, and enormously broad; it was olive-green in colour, and the lazy sweep of its tail set the water boiling in its wake. From where I was stationed, far above it, it seemed as big as a submarine. Once it rolled over gently, and I had a glimpse of a white belly and a huge pointed snout. I could see the smaller fish fleeing away in panic as it advanced.

We all stood transfixed until it was lost to sight.

Eddie shook his head comically. "Cinderella, master!" he called out. "No swimming today."

I let out the breath which unconsciously I had been holding. No swimming, indeed. . . .

We were nearing the middle of the Robberg. Occasionally I and the others had poked our way into caves; there were scores of them, the haunt of bats and owls and *dassies*, and now perhaps the haunt of Murderer Martin. I was wondering all the time what he would do next. He would know that he had fooled us for three days; now he would see the line of beaters, and guess that the car had been found, or that I had taken a hand to outwit him.

If he had found a good cave already he could lie hidden and let us walk over him. Or he could try a second trick.

We did not wait long to find out.

Glancing down the hillside towards the sea, I noticed that the beater below Eddie was lagging behind. Counting, I saw that he was the fourth man between Eddie and the sea. I found myself thinking idly that he must have been sent along as a reinforcement. Earlier I had only noted *three* others besides Eddie in our section; a policeman, another gillie, and a visitor from the hotel who had volunteered to help.

The fourth man's pace was getting slower, and I waved to him to hurry up and straighten the line. He waved back, and seemed to quicken his pace. Then a shoulder of rock hid him, and when next I looked down he was no longer in sight.

I stopped, feeling my stomach drop a yard. I called out urgently: "Eddie! Where's the man below you?"

He looked surprised, and pointed seawards. "All there, master."

"How many?"

"Three, master."

"I thought I saw four a moment ago."

His hand went to his mouth, the Cape Coloured gesture of dismay. "Ai!" he said. "There *were* four."

I turned, and raced up the hillside towards the link-man with the walkie-talkie. Even as I climbed with a pounding heart I could not help feeling a grim admiration for Murderer Martin. He had slipped through the cordon, using the classic 'escapee' trick: melt into your background, do what everyone else is doing, and then take your first chance of disappearing.

Murderer had joined the line of beaters just long enough to establish himself as a natural part of the landscape. Then he had melted entirely.

Gasping, I reached the hill-top and snatched the walkie-talkie mouthpiece. Van Willigen answered me.

"He's got through!" I shouted. "I'm almost sure he has. He's behind the line of search."

Van Willigen swore vividly. "I'm nearly alone back here."

"Spread your men out. I'll bring mine back."

"But what happened?"

"Tell you when I get back. Over and out."

We retraced our steps as quickly as possible. When we reached the neck of the Robberg there was the comforting sight of a dozen men spread across it in a tight controlled line. They were all in visual touch with each other.

Van Willigen explained: "Some more boys arrived, just when you signed off. He can't have got past. How did it happen, eh?"

I explained, as best I could, the stratagem I thought Martin had used. Van Willigen listened with a caustic expression.

"But didn't you *notice*, man?" he asked exasperated, as I finished.

"No. . . . Don't you see?—he was moving the same way as us from the first moment anyone saw him. Then, when he was part of the picture, he slipped out of it."

"He can't have got past here," said Van Willigen again,

looking around him. "There wasn't time. You must have walked over him again."

"Easy to do, with all those caves."

"Well, we won't take another chance. . . . We'll seal off this area"—he gestured—"so that nobody can leave the Robberg. I don't mind if we have to wait a year, like you said." His voice was grim and purposeful. "If we make this exit watertight he can't get off the Robberg. This is the only way by land and he can't swim because of the sharks. All we have to do is wait."

It was about seven o'clock in the evening, at the beginning of a magical dusk, when I left the Robberg. There seemed no point in my staying on. With all his men drawn back from the peninsula, and concentrated on the narrow approach, Van Willigen had a sentry to every yard of ground, and there was nothing that I could do which would not be much better done by a tough native policeman with a torch and a hard-wood truncheon. Besides, I wanted to go home again whatever sort of welcome (or lack of it) might be waiting.

On the way back, I found myself thinking of that last remark of Van Willigen's: "He can't swim because of the sharks." It was worrying me for some reason that I couldn't pin down. It rang a bell not a new bell, but an old important bell from the past which, try as I would, never sounded clearly enough for me to recognize it.

It was tied up with danger, escape, the solution of problems. . . . It did not seem to spring from watching the monster Cinderella swim by, though it might be linked with that terrifying sight. Finally, when I was near the house, I gave up the puzzle. I had a foreboding that I was going to be faced with another one—Helene.

Women are enigmatic, incomprehensible, adorable; and never had I received more entrancing proof of this than when, on opening the front door of my father-in-law's house, Helene called out to me and then ran into my arms as if I had come back in triumph from the North Pole. When I had left that morning, saying vaguely that I was going to see the police, she had not even bothered to raise her head.

She was raising it now. It was *very* nice to be kissing her again.

"Oh, darling!" she said presently. "I thought you were dead."

"Dead?"

"Yes, dead, darn it! . . .' She kissed me again; it was difficult to feel that one would ever die. "We heard about the car being found. I knew you'd go and look for that awful man. What happened?"

I sketched briefly the day's events, culminating in the abortive 'drive' down the length of the Robberg, and my certainty that Murderer Martin, though slipping through one cordon, was still firmly contained by another.

"So you were right all the time about what he'd do."

"It looks like it."

"How clever you are."

"Hungry, too."

"And loving?"

"And loving."

"We'll take care of everything."

She led me through into the sitting-room where I was confronted by the formidable figure of James Forsyth sitting in his armchair and glowering at me like some ancient, sculptured representation of Ill Will.

"So you're back," he barked out dauntingly. "About time, too!"

"Dad," said Helene firmly, her arm linked in mine, "don't be beastly to my husband."

His hand went up to his ear. "Hey? What d'you say?"

"You heard."

He started to speak, and then gave it up. I could hardly blame him. When Helene's back was turned he favoured me with a resigned, somehow congratulatory wink. It made me wonder what Helene's mother had been like. I had a fair idea of the answer.

Dinner was a cheerful meal. I should, I suppose, have been thinking about Martin cornered in terror and despair on the lonely slopes of the Robberg, cowering in a cave with only the bats and the *dassies* for company; but such thoughts were drowned out by the warmth and joy of coming home again. We drank champagne: my father-in-law told stories of early pioneering days in the Transvaal so exaggerated and improbable that I knew they must be true; Helene caught my eye continually, signalling her love. From the kitchen hatchway Timothy beamed at us all impartially.

Helene had gone to our room, and I was preparing to say

193

good night to James Forsyth, when he spoke the sentences which changed, or spoilt, or solved everything.

We were talking of Cinderella, the enormous shark.

"I'm glad you've seen her," said James Forsyth. "I never have, though I saw the one they caught at Durban a few years back. Over two thousand pounds. . . . Nothing much you could do about that if you fell off the rocks at the wrong moment. . . . Unless you had that chemical stuff handy."

That chemical stuff. *Shark repellent.* The bell rang clearly for the first and the last time, and I knew how Murderer Martin was going to escape.

The motto of the Royal Marines is *Per Mare Per Terram*, which in any language, classical or bad, means 'Go Anywhere'. It had led in wartime to some strange habits and some odd items of equipment; and none more strange or odd than the packets of shark repellent carried by Murderer Martin when we crossed the Rhine in 1944.

They had been a present from an American aircrew member who, with equal inconsequence, had coveted Martin's home-made ice-pick stiletto. Martin was very pleased with his new equipment. "Safety first, that's me!" he used to say cockily, showing the small 'dye-marker' packets to his friends. He seemed to have made up his mind that if he was likely to get his feet wet he had better be ready for every conceivable hazard of the deep.

Proudly he had tucked them into his pack together with the appropriate instructions on how to use them when forced down in shark-infested waters. There were certain ribald comments of an obvious kind, and a persistent rumour that Martin, for a bet, had tasted some of the mixture and promptly grown fins on his shoulder-blades. Then we forgot the whole matter.

War-time souvenirs are odd things. I know a man who still keeps on his mantelpiece the detonator of the land-mine which blew his foot off at Tobruk. I myself have an Iron Cross, Third Class, which I undoubtedly won in action.

I knew now, for certain, what souvenir Murderer Martin had brought to South Africa.

"Darling, I just *know*," I said. "It's the only thing that makes sense. He'll swim ashore, in spite of the sharks, and slip through the whole cordon. There's no one guarding the beaches at all."

"I suppose so," said Helene despondently. "But do you really have to go?"

"I must."

"Why not leave it to the police?"

"I want to do it myself."

"When we got engaged," she said, "you told me you were a chartered accountant."

"I will be one," I assured her. "Tomorrow."

It was our old argument which had sprung, I knew, from Helene's idea that I was running foolishly and needlessly into danger; but now it was on a different plane. Helene, besides looking heartbreakingly lovely, was tender and compassionate as well; she would not deny me, for all the reasons which bind women to men. . . . Once more, I could not have told why I wanted to deal with this thing myself, except for the one basic factor: I had started it, and I had to finish it.

"Take the big car," she said, deciding suddenly. "And be very careful."

"I promise."

"Dad has a gun. Do you want it?"

"Yes, I think I do."

Five minutes later, with James Forsyth's battered old Luger in my side-pocket, and Helene's perfume lingering on my lips, I drove out along the coast road towards the Robberg for my rendezvous with Murderer Martin.

I switched off the car's lights when I was still a mile from the Robberg, and while the sand-dunes still stood between me and the peninsula. Thus sheltered and camouflaged, I coasted slowly along the farm track leading down to the beaches. I had chosen the eastern side as the only place possible for Murderer Martin to make his landing. On the other flank of the 'neck' linking Robberg to the mainland there was no beach at all, simply a savage coastline against which the waves thundered eternally. No swimmer in the world could have made it.

I brought the car to a standstill and started to walk across the dunes to the lower beach. Within a few moments I had reached the edge of the sea.

To my left were the lights of Plettenberg Bay dominated by the clusters that lit up the approach to the hotel. Before me was the restless sea, still in darkness until the moon rose; it washed and sucked at my feet, sending a million small waves slurring across the sand as the tide advanced. To my right, high above me, was the enormous bulk of the Robberg.

Here all was activity. Van Willigen had brought up some portable floodlights; I could hear the steady beat of the generator, and see men moving to and fro in silhouette, and follow the beam of the lights as they stood sentinel over the whole approach to the peninsula. Here and there were the pricking points of camp-fires. A dog barked from time to time—a tracker dog, probably; and there was a constant thin screaming of sea-birds, disturbed by this great invasion.

A few score yards beyond the neck of the Robberg, the camp-fires and the floodlights petered out, and there was simply the whole dark lonely mass, the infected part which hid the quarry.

I sat down under the lee of a rock, just above the straggling line of weed and driftwood which marked the last high tide. Occasionally I raised the binoculars I had brought, and scanned the water at the Robberg's edge; but it was still too dark to see more than a few yards from the shore. It was very cold waiting but I would have been shivering anyway.

The next sound I heard was Helene's voice out of the darkness, saying: "I love you."

If one has to be startled out of one's wits this was the nicest way for it to happen. I scolded her for leaving the house when she had promised not to, then kissed her for coming. Husbands must hold a fair balance.

"But could you actually see me?" I asked.

"The car gave me an approximate line," she told me, "and you were silhouetted against the surf. It's getting a little lighter."

It was indeed true; to seaward the sky was paling, reflecting the moonrise.

"You're trembling," said Helene presently.

"It's a bit cold down here."

"I've brought some coffee. And a flask."

The coffee laced with brandy helped to relieve a vigil which managed to become tense and tedious by turns. We did not dare to smoke since the light might have been seen by watchful eyes, and this part of the beach must seem to be deserted. We talked in whispers, but the atmosphere remained oppressive. Two hundred feet above us, all was light and noise and bustle; the steady beat of the generator serving the floodlights seemed a guarantee of civilization and security. But down here was a lonely outpost, as lonely as Murderer Martin's; we had the sea for company, and the protesting gulls, and beyond that a brooding silence.

Every few minutes, as the moonlight strengthened and I could see further down the Robberg, I raised the glasses and studied the coastline. Now the whole peninsula was bathed in a cold light, and I could examine the wet rocks from which (if my wild guess came true) Martin must make his plunge.

I found myself dwelling on the terrors of that journey, and what fantastic nerve it would take to lower oneself into the black waters full of darting shapes, trusting to a few packets of chemical at least twelve years old, and then to swim and swim, with the cruel enemy behind and underneath and in front. He would have to throw some of the repellent ahead of him, and then swim towards it, trusting to cross the gap. . . . I shivered again, and Helene, nestling against my shoulder, looked up.

"Cold?"

"No, just thinking." There did not seem any need to explain.

"When he comes ashore," she said, "you'll be terribly careful, won't you? He'll be desperate—he might do any-thing."

"I'll have to keep a safe distance away, and so will you. He can't have a gun in working order—or if he has, he'll have wrapped it in something for the swim, and he won't be able to free it quickly."

"Don't take any chances, all the same."

It was midnight, then one o'clock. Above us on the Rob-berg neck the camp-fires were dying out one by one, but the floodlights still burned brilliantly, stabbing a pathway into the darkness, and figures still moved here and there in a watchful cordon.

I trained my glasses as usual down the edge of the Robberg, studying the rocks glistening in the moonlight, and the gulfs of shadow in between. About a mile away a new shadow seemed to move and then melt into a larger one. I watched the spot for a full minute, my eyes smarting and watering. Then the large shadow thickened on the side nearest the water, and up the track of the moon a man's figure, dwarfed by the great rocks, stood poised at the very edge of the sea. Then it slipped downwards and disappeared.

"That was him!" I whispered tensely. I felt the skin of my scalp pricking. "He's started!"

I swept the surface of the sea with the glasses, but there was nothing to be seen save foam-crests and the lift and fall of the waves. I moved my line of vision slowly to the left, away from the Robberg, knowing that Martin would swim away from the lights and towards the covering darkness in the middle of the beach. A wave lifted, and seemed to carry with it a darker patch of shadow. Something solid. Not the sea.

It happened a second time, only a little clearer, a little nearer. Swiftly I dropped to the ground, seeking a lower eye-level. At the next lift of the wave there was a man's head outlined against the horizon.

He swam slowly towards us, labouring, sometimes pausing for rest or (I supposed) to spread more of the shark repellent. I wondered how close some of the gliding forms had dared to come and if they had actually touched him. . . . Soon we could both see him with naked eye, and make out the whiter blur which was his face, and distinguish the small line of foam that marked his advance. He was going to land almost opposite to us.

"Keep behind me," I breathed to Helene. "Don't get between him and me."

Murderer Martin was within the line of breaking surf now, struggling towards the beach. Presently, with strange relief, I saw that he had reached shallow water, and was safe from all enemies except myself. Then he heaved himself upright and waded the last few yards. We could hear the hoarse sobs of his breathing. He must have been nearly spent.

He splashed and stumbled up the final slope and came to a stop, a wild dripping figure in the moonlight, staring about him like a jungle animal on the alert.

I stepped from the shadow of the rock, gun in hand, and said, as I had said once before:

"Hallo, Murderer."

Martin must have been tremendously startled and sickened by the shock of discovery; on top of the ordeal he had just survived and the strain of being on the run for three days, my sudden appearance out of the darkness must have been stupefying. He stared at me as if he could not believe his eyes; his exhausted, labouring breath checked for a moment, and then came in great gulps as if he were fighting for his life.

In the cold moonlight he himself looked frightening; his torn and bedraggled clothes ran with water, his wild mane of hair topped a stubble of beard like an ugly spattering of paint. His body seemed to shrink inwards as he whispered:

"By God! It's the skipper."

I was sorry for him and for this crushing end to his hopes; I could not help being sorry. I had to recall the brutal robberies, the three murders before I lost the feeling that I was flogging a prostrate man. . . . But it was made easier for me when his first move was to straighten up, gently and imperceptibly, and edge nearer to me.

"Stay where you are!" I called out. "This gun's loaded!"

"Windy, aren't you?" he sneered. But he had stopped, and stood a dozen feet away, still hard-breathing, staring at me with glittering, mad eyes. "I nearly killed you this afternoon," he said. "You walked back within a foot of me. . . . Wish I had. . . . That search-party was all yours, wasn't it?"

I nodded, never taking my eyes off him for a second. "I guessed you'd make for the Robberg," I said. "And I guessed the shark repellent, also."

"Good old skipper," he muttered bitterly. "Never misses a trick. . . . The war was all yours, too."

"What do you mean?"

"You taught me what to do."

There was a small noise behind me. I did not look round. Helene came forward from the shadow of the rock until she stood by my side.

"He didn't teach you this," she said.

Martin shifted his eyes to look at her. After a moment he said: "Husband-and-wife team, eh?"

There was no sneer in his voice, but an undercurrent of sadness, of mourning for what he had never had and would never now possess. Once more I had to steel myself to hate and fear what he had done.

Perhaps he was aware of this dividing thought.

"How about it, skipper?" he asked on a wheedling note. "Give me a break. . . . This is all your fault, you know, really it is. You taught me, you made me. I could never get rid of it. . . . And I didn't have a chance, not after the war." His insane eyes peered at my face as if searching for what would move me. "You don't know what it's like to try job after job, and make a muck of the lot, and have everybody laughing and looking down at you. . . ." His breath came faster. "I was only *living* properly while the war was on. Peace was rotten. . . . It's been a dead loss, right up till now."

"But that's twelve years ago."

"All the same, I only just came alive again."

"By murdering?"

"Getting a bit of my own back."

I heard Helene draw in her breath. It was as she had said: this was a case of delayed shock, and here was the horrible end-result of it.

"Give me a chance, skipper," he urged again. I felt a tension rising in him, like a spring coiling, and I took a half-step back, and a fresh grip of the gun. "Just let me go. . . . Just turn your back. . . . You'll never hear of me again."

"I can't, Murderer."

"What's it matter to you?"

"I've got to take you in."

"Give me a drink, then. I'm done." He made as if to move nearer.

"No!" I shouted suddenly. "Keep away!"

He was watching me with tremendous, evil concentration, and I stared back, my nerves triggered, alert for any vile trick. I knew that if he got the shadow of a chance he would jump at me, or perhaps grab Helene, use her as a shield, start to strangle her, anything.

He put both hands up to his face, rubbing the sea-water out of his eyes and smoothing back his bedraggled hair. He looked from me to Helene and back again, as if searching for a chink in our defence, but we were both out of range. His teeth began to chatter suddenly.

"I saved your life," he muttered. "How about it?"

"No."

"Let me run for it."

"No."

"Give me a drink, then, for God's sake."

I hesitated. "All right. . . . Then we'll get moving." With the gun still trained on him, I reached in my side-pocket drawing out the flask. "I'm going to throw it on the ground in front of you. Don't come forward."

The flask landed with a thud at his feet and he bent down to pick it up.

He very nearly brought the trick off. As I watched him grasping the flask, his whole body suddenly jack-knifed upwards, and he flung the heavy flask and a great scoop of sand full at my face. Though I had been keyed to the alert, it was still a mortal shock. As Helene screamed a warning, I jumped backwards, out of range but temporarily unsighted.

If he had made a quick break for it then, he might have got away. But the murderous instinct was too strong. Instead of darting away into darkness, he made as if to spring at me, his arms outstretched, his fingers curled like claws. It gave me time to recover. I roared out: "Stop!" and he saw the gun pointed again and came up short, a few feet from me.

"All right, Murderer," I said, hard-breathing. "That's the end of the party."

The moon was full on his face now, and it gleamed wet and dead-white like a landed fish.

"Good try," he said. He laughed shakily. "Trust you to spot it. . . . I'm going to run for it, skipper."

"If you do, I'll shoot."

"Better be shot than hung."

He was turning away from me. "Don't be a fool!" I said. "Give yourself up. Take your chance."

"I'm going to run for it."

His back was towards me now, his body bent forward and poised for flight. Over his shoulder he called out: "Shoot straight, skipper!" and broke into a quick, loping trot.

I hesitated for two or three long paces, aware of bereavement and of an enormous guilt within myself. I heard Helene whisper: "Oh, God!" in pity and horror. But then I shot straight. It was the least I could do for the man who had twice saved my life.

Postscript

The Ship that Died of Shame had its origin in a post-war encounter in a small naval 'get-together' club in London. The principal function of this shoddy establishment was to serve as a meeting place for ex-naval types who needed an excuse for getting boozy, who couldn't find jobs, and who hoped meanwhile to sell each other life-insurance. Among these forlorn step-children of war I met a man who had served in the same corvette with me in 1940 or 1941. He offered me a job, smuggling brandy and watches across from France in a converted gun-boat. I decided to become a civil servant instead. But the memory of that curious post-war crossroads remained, and I wrote the story in Johannesburg about six years later. My friend subsequently went to jail.

Printing history: Published in *Lilliput* magazine, *Saturday Evening Post*, *Sunday Chronicle*, and in Holland, Australia, South Africa, New Zealand, Denmark, Norway, and Sweden: broadcast by the BBC and in Australia; filmed by Ealing Studios.

Copyright Nicholas Monsarrat 1952

Oh to be in England! originated in a conversation with a perfectly horrible English celebrity on board the *Queen Mary*. I always hoped that the income-tax people would catch up with him in the end, but I had to invent this method of doing it.

Printing history: Published in *Evening Standard*.

Copyright Nicholas Monsarrat 1957

The Reconciliation, published also as *Dear Decoy* and *Their Secret Life*, is an attempt to illustrate the fact that you never really want something unless somebody else wants it at the same time. This applies particularly to women and, I suppose, to men. It can be seen in action at auction sales, at box offices selling tickets for a hit play, and during the social début season in London and New York.

Printing history: Published by *Saturday Evening Post* and *Argosy* magazine, and in France, Sweden, Norway, Denmark, Australia, and Germany.

The List is based, loosely, on the extraordinary diversity of the native mind in Basutoland, where many younger 'natives' make highly efficient office-workers and administrators, while their tribal chiefs are still periodically hauled into court, and subsequently to the gallows, for ritual murder. It has also been published under the title, *Master of Evil*.

Printing history: Published in *Weekend* magazine.

The Thousand Islands Snatch is set in a part of Canada where I spend most of each summer, on the St Lawrence River near Montreal. Sometimes enormous American yachts put in at our yacht club; often there are pretty girls on board. I have never wanted to kidnap one of them, save in a very limited sense, but I have no doubt that other people could be less scrupulous. The story was written specifically for the *Saturday Evening Post*, who just as specifically turned it down.

Printing history: Published in *John Bull*, and in Australia, Norway, Denmark, and Finland.

Up the Garden Path is based on personal experience, though of a less happy kind. A few years ago I did lend some money to a 'struggling writer' who wanted to finish a book. The book was published and succeeded moderately well, but I never collected. It turned out (*a*) that it was written in collaboration with someone else, who got half the royalties, (*b*) the rest of the royalties were swallowed up by some earlier undisclosed debts, (*c*) two other friends of mine had been hooked in the same way, and (*d*) it wasn't really a loan but a contribution to the living literature of our time.

This has not been my only exercise in Good Samaritanism, but so far (except for the Johannesburg stockbroker who pledged, in the name of friendship, an entirely worthless security in exchange for a loan of £2,300) it has been the least edifying.

Printing history: Published in *Daily Sketch.*
Copyright Nicholas Monsarrat 1953

The Man who wanted a Mark Nine is based on grisly personal experience in the rules-and-regulations jungle of post-war England, and has some faint connection with my decision to emigrate to Canada.

Printing history: Published in *Esquire, Everybody's Weekly,* and in Australia.
Copyright Nicholas Monsarrat 1954

I Was There. About the time of Dunkirk I was being taught to salute at the Naval Training Establishment at *King Alfred,* near Hove. So I wasn't there either. But the last five words of this story are profoundly true.

Printing history: Published in *Atlantic Monthly, Everybody's Weekly,* and in Scandinavia.
© Nicholas Monsarrat 1958

The Dinner Party is based on an anecdote current in my wife's family, who all assured me it was true. I believed them. That was in 1955.

Printing history: Published in *Evening Standard.*
Copyright Nicholas Monsarrat 1955

Licensed to Kill. During the war I spent a few weeks attached to some Royal Marine Commandos, and took part in a couple of raids across the Maas and into German-held territory. I often wondered, afterwards, what became of some of these young men who, at the age of nineteen or twenty had learned nothing but four or five atrocious methods of killing by stealth. About ten years later I was in South Africa and noticed what a wonderful hiding-place, as well as an incomparable beauty spot, the 'Robberg' was. The two halves of the story, which has also been published separately, thus came together.

Printing history: Published in *Saturday Evening Post, Evening Standard, Realités,* and in Australia and South Africa (including an Afrikaans translation). It was very nearly filmed, but I noticed just in time that the contract reserved the right to turn it into a 'musical drama'. I didn't want the money as much as that.
© Nicholas Monsarrat 1958

Nicholas Monsarrat

'One of those novelists - they are growing fewer - who have not forgotten that the primary aim of the novel is to tell a story, to tell it interestingly and to tell it convincingly.'

RICHER THAN ALL HIS TRIBE   35p

Monsarrat returns to the African island of Pharamaul for his gripping successor to THE TRIBE THAT LOST ITS HEAD.

'Not so much a novel, more a slab of dynamite'
– SUNDAY MIRROR

Other Nicholas Monsarrat titles available in Pan.

THE TRIBE THAT LOST ITS HEAD	40p
THE WHITE RAJAH	35p
SOMETHING TO HIDE	25p
THE STORY OF ESTHER COSTELLO	30p
THE WHIPPING BOY	30p
THE NYLON PIRATES	35p
THE PILLOW FIGHT	35p
LIFE IS A FOUR-LETTER WORD Vol I (illus)	50p
LIFE IS A FOUR-LETTER WORD Vol II (illus)	50p

C. S. Forester

'Excels in story telling' –
THE DAILY TELEGRAPH

Here are novels to banish boredom and grip the imagination. . . .

WAR

'Full of his concern for complex, vigorous action' –
THE TIMES

CRIME

THE HORNBLOWER SERIES

'One of the best loved and most human characters in modern fiction' –
THE SCOTSMAN

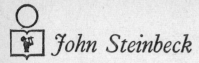

John Steinbeck

One of the greatest American writers of this century, winner of the 1962 Nobel Prize for Literature.

Uninhibited in his choice of material, insatiably curious about the human race, Steinbeck is also a natural storyteller.

'That tremendous genius, John Steinbeck' –
H. G. WELLS

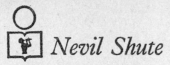

Nevil Shute